Make me Yours Evermore

Pierced Hearts, Book Three

by

Cari Silverwood

Taking what you want may come at a terrifying price

Copyright 2013 Cari Silverwood

Published by Cari Silverwood

Editor: Nerine Dorman

Secondary editor: Lina Sacher

Cover Artist: Thomas Dorman aka Dr. Benway on Deviantart and Facebook

Acknowledgement

Once more I owe a debt to those who have helped me figure out where I went wrong with my writing of this book. Whenever I did wander off the beaten path, I had my wonderfully insane crit partner Sorcha Black there to smack me over the head with something and bring me to my senses. Thank you. The MRI came out normal.

I also need to thank my sensational beta readers Bianca Sarble (a fellow Aussie author), Mj, Heidi Gillespie, and Lina Sacher.

Disclaimer

This book contains descriptions of many BDSM and sexual practices but this is a work of fiction and as such should not be used in any way as a guide. The author will not be responsible for any loss, harm, injury or death resulting from use of the information contained within.

Pierced Hearts Series

Take me, Break me

Bind and Keep me

Make me Yours Evermore

Coming in 2014 - Book 4 and 5 in the Pierced Hearts series

This book is set in Australia and contains some Aussie phrases, such as 4WD being used instead of SUV. To find out the meaning of most of them, there is a glossary at the end of the book.

Chapter 1

Kat

Dark. Then light filtered in. The fluttering wash of light, dark, light, dark occupied me as we bumped over something. My shoulder would feel numb and I'd shift but my hands were tied. Not much I could do.

Bondage wasn't my thing.

That thought popped up and stayed a while before it drifted away like so many others. My heart beat erratically. My thoughts followed like sheep. I struggled and caught that thought again. Bondage wasn't my thing. Then what was I doing tied up? My wrists were trapped before me. My ankles were caught. My mouth had something in it. My eyes were blind and I couldn't lift my eyelids – trapped also. A blindfold?

Chris. Panic slithered in and with it came clarity. *Fuck him.* He'd done this. I needed to get loose. I bit down on the gag as I writhed, but solid walls encased me and the gag stayed where it was. I lay on my side. My elbow thumped painfully into something above me. My bare toes did too at my front. My breathing rasped wetly, bubbling past the thing in my mouth. Just lifting my ribs became a hundred, thousand times more important than *anything*.

I dragged in air as something rocked whatever coffin it was I occupied. Distant voices. Man? Or more? Men? There seemed two different voices.

My teeth sank into rubber. My tongue tip slipped over the wet roundness.

Ball gag.

The bastard. He kidnapped me. He put it there between my lips. I remembered him, remembered his words.

"I'm going to get into your head right there. Where you can never ever get me out."

"You're going to be blind for a few days. When I take this off, you'll be somewhere far from civilization. There will be no one who can help you. There will only be me."

I knew where I was. There'd been an engine noise before, long ago. A car. He had me in a car. I slumped. Drowsiness returned and snuggled into my mind. I was hot and tired and breathing meant more to me than getting loose. *Breathe. One last kick. Maybe that other man will hear me. Maybe he'll let me go.*

I kicked and nearly broke my toe on timber. But metal creaked and the car rocked again. I listened, ears straining. Waves? Seagulls screeching? Brighter light flared through the tape across my eyes. Someone had turned up the volume on the sound. There were distant voices. Waves. Yes. Was I still on the island?

"Put that down, man. Get out of the car and walk away."

"The fuck I will. You've got a woman tied up in here! What the fuck…is this a scene thing? One of your kinky pretend things?"

"Andreas. You need to leave. Now."

"Okay. Okay. Sorry. The shit you get up to. Give me a call when you and her have finished fucking your brains out. Or whatever you intend to do."

Going? He was going? Despite the sogginess permeating my brain, I knew that was bad. I needed to make noise. I tried to speak but only gurgles emerged. I coughed and found liquid clogging my throat where words should have been.

"She's choking!"

"Fuck. The dose might have been a bit high. Listen. Ignore anything she says."

Fingers fumbled at my mouth. The thing was pulled from me, leaving my lips feeling bereft without the pressure. I breathed. Deep, cool air. Coughed again. The fog closed in.

Storms ahead. Words of no sense popped up when I needed sense. What was that other word?

"You okay?" Thick fingers brushed my cheek. Gentle.

No. I'm not. I'm not. I'm... "Kidnapped," I croaked.

"What? What did you say?"

"Andreas. Ignore. You don't butt in on a scene."

I swallowed then choked on that word again. "Kidnapped. Please. Need help." I was blind and my tongue was made of sludge but somewhere in front of me was a man who could save me.

"Chris. What is this? What shit is this? Dose? Even I know you don't use drugs with BDSM."

Someone sighed – long and deep. Chris spoke. "Right. Let me explain, Andreas. There are good reasons."

"Jesus. Reasons?" His voice rose high at the end. A long pause.

"I *can* explain."

"She's... How can you possibly explain this? You're more than a brother to me, you know that. But this...this had better be good. Like, I mean, better than anything you've ever explained...ever."

Chris chuckled. That alone made the hairs on my neck rise. So wrong.

"I need to make sure she doesn't call out. Smaller gag. Okay?"

"You want to put a gag back on her?"

Hope kindled. The man sounded doubtful. He'd get the cops now.

"Yes. She can breathe through it."

Though my tongue seemed disconnected from me, though my temples ached with each thump of my blood, I strained to hear. Andreas's reply was a long time coming.

"Mate, I can't see how you're going to get out of this one."

"Wait."

No way. I opened my mouth and sucked in air so I could yell only to have another ball pushed into my mouth. I squirmed and tried to shake my head but a hand held my face. My struggles grew weaker. Too much effort. Too much trouble to fight the cold fog that ate my thoughts, leeched at my muscles.

"Good girl," I heard whispered from inches away. "Stay there quiet while we talk."

The whispers repeated. *Good girl.*

Good? Not me. Not me… Never me. FieryKat. I will fuck you up, boys. Somehow. Just give me time. I will…

Inside me, the black fog spread and swallowed me down.

Chapter 2

Andreas

For once, the view out the windscreen of Chris's four-wheel drive was dirty. I frowned. In a long wooden box behind these front seats, a woman was…tied up, gagged, and blindfolded. And drugged. While I struggled to cope with that concept, my mind ran off on a tangent.

Dusty windscreen. Chris always had a reason.

Ah. You couldn't see in, could you? Not easily. He'd probably chucked a bucket of dirt over it.

The man, my *friend*, sighed and ran a hand through his sun-bleached blond hair. "Do you want me to explain or would you rather I answer your questions? Andreas?"

I shook my head while I stared past his ear. Then I met his eyes. We'd always been honest with each other. "Does it matter? This is insane."

Through the dusty glass, I could see other people lounging against their cars. As the bow of the ferry carved the waves, sea water sprayed high into the air. A brisk wind rattled the door and went whistling away. Sunlight glinted warmly off metal. Even with the door shut, we had to raise our voices to be heard over the ferry's engine noise. All…yeah, fucking normal stuff.

I swallowed. Chris just sat there, giving me time. Least he hadn't pulled out a knife. But was this the same man I knew?

As if to remind me, a dull knocking came from the box. There were air holes and a metal mesh, but if I heard that gurgly breathing again I was freeing her ASAP.

"Fuck it. What are you doing? Go on. Explain." I glanced at my watch. "This is surreal. You've got ten minutes before we reach the harbor."

"Truthfully, I'd rather you just leave."

"And forget I saw this?" I thumbed toward the box. "I can't. Couldn't. It's too late for that." In a moment of clarity, I was glad I'd decided to get into Chris's four-wheel drive. Whoever it was back there, she needed me.

Again with the sigh. But otherwise Chris regarded me levelly with his sharp blue eyes. Not hostile. We were too close for anything nasty to happen between us.

But I had to do something. "Not tempted to throw me over the side for the sharks?"

"Huh." Chris glanced down at my arm and the scars throbbed as if the damn thing knew it was getting attention. He shook his head then settled his shoulders back into his door. "No. If you have to go to the cops afterward, I can accept that. Life goes on."

Christ. The man was always so confident. Not a façade either. Just him. Then his jaw moved as if he were chewing.

Maybe this did bother him? Relief flooded me. I didn't want to see him as Ice Man. No one normal could brush off abducting someone as casually as if they'd found a new paint color they liked.

"Tell me then. Why?"

"If she gets loose." He jerked his head toward the back of the car, "A friend is likely to go to jail for ten or more years. What he did was something I would have done, you too maybe. He doesn't deserve it."

I blinked, thinking as well as I could. "What did he do?"

"I can't tell you that."

"You can't?" And that made it so much easier for me to judge this. "Then why her? What did she do? Did she make this up? This thing your friend did?"

"No. She snooped where she shouldn't have."

"Uh." I sat back. "So you've done this to her...something thoroughly illegal and dangerous that might get *you* in jail for fifty years, let alone ten, because she was nosy?"

Chris rubbed his fingers along the steering wheel. An extra hefty gust of wind shook the vehicle. "Partly that, yes. More that a friend needed help."

She, obviously, wasn't his friend.

"So...what are you planning to do with her? You're not, god forbid, killing her?" I knew the answer would be no, but I had to ask.

"You think I would do that?"

I shook my head. Fuck, I hoped not.

"Of course I wouldn't."

"And so instead, like a Good Samaritan," I waved my hand in a vague circle, "you're planning to set her up for life with a huge lump of money and a mansion in France?"

He laughed. "Comedian." Chris glanced back toward the box that held the woman. He leaned over, reached between the seats, and lifted the side of the box, keeping his body mostly in the way in case anyone passing by looked in.

Through the gap between my seat and Chris's body, I studied the woman. Her face slumped in either sleep or unconsciousness. Wrist cuffs locked her hands down onto a metal ring on the box beside her neck. She was breathing fine. The ball of the gag even had a large hole through the middle.

Youngish. Cherry red hair. So bright it must be fake. The edge of a tatt showed on her shoulder.

I wondered what she would look like without the black ball of the gag. My gaze slipped downward to where her breasts were jammed together by the position. The bunched-up pale blue T-shirt had a few specks of blood and grime on it. The neckline showed the top of her red bra. Pretty. Vulnerable. Pity and an urge to help her vied with a deep curiosity as to what she'd look like naked. That my head even went there bothered me. I pulled my gaze away.

Shit. This was like perving on a victim in an ambulance.

"She's good. Breathing's settled." He lowered the side of the box. Despite his nonchalance, I couldn't help but notice the absolute fascination he had for her, the last second of hesitation as he closed the side. Like he couldn't tear his eyes away. "Beautiful, isn't she?"

How did you answer that? I shrugged. "I'm not going there. You still haven't said what you're doing with her."

A line formed between his eyes. At last I'd stirred him. "I'm not going into details."

Then he waited again. Shit.

"You expect me to leave her with you based on that?"

"Yes. I never wanted you to get in the car. The less you know the better for you, me and her."

His chest rose and fell in a regular rhythm – too regular, forced perhaps. Or was I reading in things that weren't there? I needed a fucking lie detector. Wait, no. He wouldn't lie to me. Would he?

"Well. Too late, I did get in. I emailed you. Tried to phone…" We always hung out together when I visited the island. "When I saw your car, what else do you think I was going to do? Assume you had a woman tied up in the back and leave you be? I thought we'd go to the pub and have a beer somewhere. Have fun. Go fishing, swimming. Fuck some girls. You know…" I faked a laugh. "Shit, now…" I shook my head vigorously. "What are you doing with her? You have to tell me."

"I don't want to pull you into this."

"You *have*. You're my best mate. You saved my goddamned worthless life once or twice. I don't want to dob you in to the cops. Tell me something. I'm not going to walk away. She was having trouble breathing and you never saw it. You want murder on your conscience? Why? What are you doing with her?" I glanced out at the approaching line of the mainland harbor. "Five minutes left."

Chris rubbed his finger along his nose for a second. "Okay. Do what you want to. "I'm…" He took a deep breath. "I'm keeping her."

"What?" Oh shit. I remember a drunken night when we'd all spilled our guts.

What are five things you'd most like to do that are illegal. Then we'd shared. A bunch of teenagers at university having a stupid drunken party. The usual. Until I checked what Chris had written as number one on his list. *Kidnap a girl and keep her.* At the top of mine, I'd written, *keep a girl as my slave.*

Funny. But ever since then we'd been one. I'd never forgotten the list. We hadn't always lived in the same place but when we were together we partied and hung out and had great times. Until now.

"The list," I murmured, so softly he couldn't possibly hear.

But his eyes narrowed. "I'm driving to the Daintree area. A business friend has loaned me a house there. Somewhere quiet, away from anyone who might see or hear anything. I'm going to make her mine. Going to train her to obey me."

Shit. My blood thundered. My cock stood up all on its ownsome. This was so wrong that my head was spinning. "You can't do that."

"I can. I am. It's that or let her go to do so much damage to my friend's life, and now, to mine. She brought this on herself. Now are you going to open that door and walk away?"

What was I going to do? He was blaming her for this? I wrenched my logical brain into gear. "That's a six-, seven-hour drive. What if she dies? You can't watch her breathing. You're driving straight through?" I deadpanned those words but I was fucking tumbling through rapids in my head.

He nodded, pursed his mouth.

I couldn't leave her with him, but I didn't want to be with him either. With her...them. I wiped my mouth. "I'm not leaving her alone with you. I'm not having her death on my conscience. I'm coming with you until we sort everything out."

"You think I'm going to change my mind? I'm going to let her go? She'd go straight to the police and then everyone is up shit creek without a paddle. If you want that just go to the cops yourself, Andreas."

"I'm coming with you. This way we can figure out some alternative. And I can make sure she's not going to choke to death." I *had* to convince him to release her. I held up my hands. "I'm between jobs. No one's going to miss me."

"I wasn't going to leave her unsupervised, Andreas." Chris had a knack for knowing when to stop talking. The ferry was angling toward the jetty, engines throbbing loudly. "But okay."

"Good." I settled back into the seat. Once we were on the road, I'd prop open the flap to the box so I could keep an eye on the woman.

I attempted to calm my racing heart but some delayed logic snuck in. The box she was in was no spur of the moment thing. How long had he been planning this?

We were close mates but I knew how kinky Chris was and all about his love of BDSM. He'd let me watch him flog a girl once. Even though I could see she wanted it, that scene had fucked me up for days. While I'd watched I'd been a confused mix of aroused and horrified. I'd also seen the steel mask of concentration on his face. Chris was a sadist through and through.

I'd trust him with my damn *life*, but with this woman? What he might do to her scared me. There was no way I was leaving him alone with her.

Chapter 3

Chris

We left town with no fuss, the tires purring over the Bruce Highway on our way north. As soon as we were past the outer suburbs, I pointed over my shoulder at the box. Andreas propped open the front. Whenever I glanced sideways, I caught him looking back as if studying her. I wasn't sure what he made of all this, apart from that obvious disapproval and his desire to keep her safe.

In a way, I was glad he was here to watch her. It was safer for her. I just prayed this wouldn't backfire on Andreas. And I prayed like hell I could get rid of him fast once we got there. I needed to be alone with her. To sit and figure out what I wanted to *do* to her.

My fingers were hurting I'd clenched the wheel so tightly. Relax. I'd waited so long, thought about this scenario, off and on, much of my adult life, but…I could wait a bit longer.

No matter how well you know someone, as soon as you break the law, everything goes into a cyclonic blender. What would come out when he'd had time to digest all of this?

I hadn't seen him for a few months. He'd been out on the oil rig in the Bass Strait same as my brother. Soon we might be going separate ways. His wavy black hair ruffled in the breeze when he wound down the window for a while. From beneath the short ochre sleeve of his T-shirt, the scars from the shark attack ran like pale confetti down the muscles of his left forearm. Remnants of a time when he'd needed me. I liked that. My good friends defined my world.

Andreas was a solid man with a solid conscience. That might prove a problem for him.

Me? I'd stick with my decisions, no matter how wrong they might be in a moral world. But I wasn't in a moral world, hadn't been since I was twenty-two and uncle had introduced me to shaky accounting.

I tensed my forearms, using the steering wheel to control my frustration. Of all the people to arrive and fuck this up...to maybe, fuck this up.

But...I made a hard and cutting decision then and there. If Andreas decided to hand me to the police I'd go without protest. I wasn't jeopardizing things with him. No matter how deep into the dark this kink of mine took me. I could be Mister Evil to her, no worries, because it got me off. Not to him.

"You can take off her gag now," I said over the engine noise.

He nodded and did so. For a few seconds he held the gag before him like it was some creature he'd caught and he was afraid to let it go in case it bit then he wiped it with his T-shirt and placed it back in the box with her.

"I swear I can hear the thoughts running around in your head. If we get stopped or have to slow down near people, drop the flap back down. If the cops stop us for any reason and they find her, pretend you didn't know she was there."

He grunted.

Andreas wasn't normally the quiet sort but he didn't say another word until we were near the Mount Spec turn-off.

"I want to stop here. You have to free her, Chris."

Oh shit.

My stomach was so knotted up I'd probably need a valium myself before the day was out. I could have let this go. I could've not told Klaus my idea to take Kat out of the equation. But I had.

I hated that Andreas was here with me. This was my messed-up self. Not his doing. If I could've pushed him out the moving car without hurting him, I would have.

For most of my adult years I'd had a distant, back-of-the-cupboard, *dangerous* yearning to go further than BDSM allowed. Kat... Fuck, her prima donna personality and her pseudo-submissive, emotionally distant behavior had triggered every snarling instinct in me to wrestle her down and impose on her a set of laws that would make her behave. Those little shorts she wore, and the curvaceous body underneath, drove me crazy. I'd been allowed to strip them off her a few times when she agreed to scenes, but that had never been enough.

Being able to mark her with red, to make her scream, to run my hands over her hips and ass and, a few times, to get her off with a vibe or my fingers, if anything that had fed my craving.

Some Doms would have nothing to do with her, but me...I only dreamed of what might be possible.

But I never had, truly, been able to make her behave, because I couldn't. Hard limits, safe and sane, consensual kink – all those drew lines I couldn't cross.

"I'm not stopping unless you want to get out and take this to the cops. If you're doing that, I may as well drive us there. If we stop to chat like schoolgirls on a picnic, the drug will be wearing off. I may have to give her more and that adds to the danger."

The long, dead-straight road unrolling ahead, for the next kilometer, allowed me to drift my thoughts into remembering how Kat had looked back there. Controlled, for once, waiting for me to decide what to do with her. Her eyes half-closed. It was a miracle I'd wanted so badly for so long.

"Fuckit." Andreas had shut his eyes. Air hissed in through his teeth. "Fuckit. Fuckit. Fuckit. You're going to hell, you know."

I shrugged. "Maybe. You don't need to be here. I promise I'll take care of her. I can let you out somewhere and you can catch a bus back. Then you can forget this."

"What'd you drug her with?"

Ignoring me, hey? "You're a stubborn bastard when you want to be." I sneaked a look at his earnest face before concentrating on the road again. "Valium. I researched it, Andreas. Doses, effects. It was the safest one and the easiest to get hold of."

"It's hours yet to the Daintree. When does it wear off? What if she starts screaming?"

I kept my voice level. "If I have no choice, I'll give her more." I hoped he wouldn't ask how. The answer would freak him out. "It might take four to six hours to wear off. It might take less. It varies from person to person."

"Uh-huh."

Andreas seemed to relax at that – as if knowing I'd planned this well had reassured him. I turned the thought over. His response almost said he didn't want her to escape. Which was curious. I inhaled and the mind-cracking tension ebbed from my muscles.

"You know this is wrong, don't you?"

"Yes." A semi-trailer going the other way rocked our vehicle in its wake and I adjusted my hands on the wheel.

"So you're not going to shoot anyone if things go ass over turkey?"

"No." I checked him out. Meditative. "You're still wondering if you should hand me over to law enforcement?"

"No. Hell, no."

The road thrummed under the wheels. "Yes, I know it's wrong. Do I care if society condemns me for doing this? Only if I get caught. Will I hurt anyone over this? No, especially not you. I never thought I'd do this. If the opportunity hadn't arrived, I'd have kept going the way I was."

"The way you was?" he murmured. "Just BDSM with chicks who said yes, hey?"

"Yep."

"I keep thinking I've fallen into the wrong wardrobe and come out in Narnia or something. Jabberwocky land. Oz, maybe."

I pulled a contemplative face and nodded. "Oz is close."

He bit out a laugh. "You know she's listening? Doped out, but she is. I can see from the way she holds her head. Does that worry you?"

"Let her." Kat mightn't remember much of this. I wasn't sure of the long-term effects. But if she did... If she did, she'd remember her helplessness; remember us casually talking while she was back there unable to do a thing. I liked that. It gave my balls a warm feeling. I wished I could see her expression.

Yet this wasn't purely sexual. Even after all these years of being a kinkster, I wasn't sure what it was that grabbed me about dominating a woman sometimes. It just was *me*.

Not all sexual, but a part of it. I wanted to see her lips wrapped around my cock even if she didn't want them there. I took a deep shaky breath.

"The Daintree?" Andreas said it quietly, like it was somewhere interesting and this was a normal holiday chat.

"Yes."

"I always wanted to go there."

"Me too." I turned up the air-con. I didn't want Kat getting heat stroke. Despite the autumn weather, the box might become a sauna if the tropical sun heated the car.

"We'll have to stop to get petrol along the way. And I'll find somewhere isolated, off the road, where we can let her out to go to the toilet. But I'll have to watch her. To make sure she doesn't get away." I eyed him briefly then went back to looking at the road, then back to him again for a moment.

He swallowed and kept his gaze focused ahead. "Okay. When we get there, you and me, we have to talk."

"Sure."

I was beginning to wonder what Andreas was thinking about all this. Like any man, he'd have his little fetishes. We all had something dirty we'd like to do, even if we suppressed the ideas. But give us half a chance and a willing...or unwilling victim...most of us would do some damn kinky things to a woman. For some that meant coming on their faces or tearing off their panties and gagging them with them. For others it was ass sex, or milder things. Few men had the guts to let loose the dark beast inside them.

Me, I had a million ideas. Most I'd done at some time, to someone.

Part of Kat's appeal was the challenge. She'd never submitted to anyone properly. Not that I'd ever seen. Bitch Queen was her true name. She'd never even let me fuck her. I wanted to bring her low, so low she would kiss the dirt for me.

She was going to find out how hard-ass I could truly be when there was nothing stopping me.

Part of it, and just musing on this made that red scintillating *need* slither through me, part was I just wanted to hurt her and see her take it because she had no choice. Fucked up? Yeah. But it was a beautiful sort of fucked up. I wondered why I always imagined it as a red need? The link to blood probably. Red had a certain distinction to it.

Pain – red.

Fear – black.

Graphic novels followed that sort of color scheme.

Which made sadism a mix of both? There'd be no green though, definitely. Or blue. Screams, in a comic, should be orange. Crap. I was going a bit crazy with this.

Maybe I shouldn't be imagining what I was planning to do while I was driving?

In those few crystal clear times between us, I was sure I'd seen in Kat a yearning, like she wanted something she couldn't quite reach. The dominant and submissive relationship, even the malformed one we had shared, let me see things she wanted to hide from everyone. It was a matter of listening hard enough, and paying attention.

In a perverse way, I was sure she wanted someone to make her do what she didn't want. That was common in submissives, and the

Dom's role is to show them how to let go of control. The difference was that Kat never did let go. She clung to the edge with both hands.

Well, I'd pried away those fingers, and now she was going to learn to fly.

Chapter 4

Kat

It wasn't until I was on my feet and standing in the prickling grass that I could think. Everything swirled; my legs shook; my stomach rebelled. I opened my eyes. Nothing. And tried to open them again. Then remembered, again. Blindfold.

"You're somewhere hidden, Kat," Chris said, his tone managing to be both dry and thickly evil at the same time. "No one can see us."

Oh, you bastard. I blanked out his words while I fought nausea again. Tired, so tired.

Someone took my elbow and I jerked my head up, swaying as I attempted to focus on blackness. Blindfold. Stoopid.

"Go to the toilet." They didn't let go of me.

"Here?" Such croaky words. I'd spoken! No gag. Surprise, surprise. When had they removed it? I imagined my questions lined up like crows on a power line in my head. My lips seemed worn out and slick from constant dribbling. I licked them.

They...or *he*, had me, somewhere outside. Where was the car? Birds chirped nearby. Grass stalks scratched the soles of my feet. Could I kick him? Could I run?

There wasn't a chance in hell I could escape. Not right now. I tried to concentrate and still the slosh of thoughts and sensations filling my head. If I could just think...properly. The blackness before my eyes surged with color splotches, with random sparks of panic, of fear, of what the fuck is happening.

Focus! Think, think, think.

I leaned sideways, off balance, and everything turned to mud.

I bit back a moan.

"Kat. Last chance." Chris again. "If you need to go, go. Counting to ten. One, two…"

I did need to go. Someone had given me sips of water earlier, in the car. But they'd be watching. My shorts and underwear were gone. My hands were free but my arms were so heavy I couldn't lift them. Trembling, borrowing strength from the unknown hand, I lowered myself. The only thing that freed me to do this was the knowledge that watching women pee wasn't one of Chris's kinks. Halfway done, at the tightening of his hand on my arm, I remembered that humiliation was, sometimes.

I'd bet he was getting off on this.

When I was hefted up and loaded back into the box, the world in my head was too busy spinning to and fro for me to do more than weakly tug against their grip. Two sets of hands. The man who handled my upper torso clipped my wrists down. Metal clicked and I blindly turned my head seeking whoever was there. Fingers locked my chin within a rough hand. I gasped.

"You have no idea how much this pleases me. Seeing you at my mercy like this."

Though I tried to summon spit even that was beyond me.

Let him think I'm cowed.

Genius. I mocked myself. Couldn't squash a bug.

After a moment he let me be and lowered my head.

Bastard.

The engine started and the car rocked. The tires cracked over gravel, then came a jolt, then we hummed over smooth road.

I was supposed to be on holiday right now. Instead I was here, a prisoner, being taken somewhere far away from home for Chris and his friend to do god knew what to me.

Tears leaked into the blindfold.

Chapter 5

Chris

Our trip continued with little drama. Kat behaved so well I was almost dreading her misbehavior. The woman was akin to an unexploded bomb. Continuing to drug her to the eyeballs with valium wasn't an option. What would she do when she 'woke up?' The anticipation might not kill me, but it was giving me a severe case of blue balls. I sincerely prayed it would be good.

Nearly five hundred kilometers after leaving Magnetic Island, we reached the Daintree River, crossed it by ferry then went on to Cow Bay. North of here, very few roads penetrated the deep tropical rainforest, and wandering too far afield might land you in trouble with crocs or shotgun-wielding entrepreneurial growers of weed. I slowed and pulled over to the side of the road at the outskirts of the tiny town.

Andreas roused. "Why are we stopping?"

"This is where I get the keys to the house I'm borrowing. A man called Scrim should be meeting us here. Keep an eye on her." Not that I needed to tell him that. We'd lowered the flap on the box.

"Fuck. This is crazy," he whispered.

As if anyone would hear us.

Years after my uncle had introduced me to doing the accounts for a friend of his, that had led to me helping Vetrov, a man I'd never met, with *his* dirty laundry. Crime paid me well. I kept my distance, though. My only contact with Vetrov was David, one of his employees, and emails. I did the money for him and never asked questions unless they involved numbers.

But some things I learned along the way, like a sponge mopping up blood. On the rare occasions we went for a drink together, David had dropped info. After a few drinking sessions, I'd wanted brain bleach. Some of his stories had made me wonder if there was something wrong with me, because they'd sent me into a sexual haze. Things I'd long imagined had been made real. A few times, in the beginning, I'd wanted to back out, to maybe even go to the cops, but I hadn't. I was young, my family was involved, and I was just a small player on the periphery. I let it go. But the lodge, that info I'd tucked away for a time like this.

I creaked open the door and jumped out. My boots crunched over loose rocks on the bitumen.

From beneath a huge spreading fig tree a man emerged, a duffel bag slung across his shoulders. I assessed him. Compact. Efficient. A man who'd reached his thirties and learned how to handle himself physically. All these came to mind. Already, I didn't like him. Scrim was one of the boss's lesser henchmen. I'd met a few over the years but they'd never seen me as more than the accountant.

Today was different. Surely he'd been told very little? I just needed to get the keys to the lodge off him and go.

Late afternoon. The heavy shadows beneath the trees were gathering coolness.

He nodded and shifted the bag off his shoulders, letting it hang from his big fist. His smile creased around his mouth but did nothing to soften the squareness of his face. The skin under the grey to black bristles on his chin and scalp showed lines – old cuts and a gouge that dug deep above his right eye then swerved down to his cheekbone.

"How's it going? I'm Scrim. Chris, yeah?"

"Yes."

His free hand came up and we shook.

"You've got the keys to the lodge? David told you I was coming?"

"Yup. I'll show you the way. Do you want me in the front? Otherwise I can direct you from the back seat." He gestured toward the Toyota.

I nodded, as if agreeing. He wanted to come with us? "I thought I'd just be getting keys from you."

"No. I guess you could say I'm the caretaker. I just got off the plane at the Cow Bay airstrip. You want to use the lodge? I'm there too. It's part of the deal."

Fuck.

"Don't worry. There's two houses." He nodded toward the vehicle. "You'll have your privacy. There's a Range Rover in the garage at the Lodge. I'll keep out of your hair." He winked. "No matter what you get up to."

What had David told him? Not everything, surely? I didn't want a stranger watching and listening to what I was going to do to Kat, no matter how involved Scrim might be. The Lodge wasn't just a vacation house for the man who'd employed me on the side for the past five years. Scrim must know that too. But that didn't mean I wanted him anywhere near me or Kat. Or Andreas.

His gaze hadn't left my face and the crinkling around his eyes said he guessed something of my dilemma. He leaned in and said quieter than before. "Don't worry, mate. I've got orders not to interfere."

He knew. Knew a lot. Bugger David. Maybe I should have simply put out an ad for the world to see.

Anger simmered to the surface. "No. You won't."

We locked eyes for a moment before he shrugged.

"The front seat," I added.

Sometimes I cut loose from my controlled surface persona. It was best to be clear where we stood. A long way away from each other, I hoped. If not, I might have to have a word with Scrim. When he tossed the duffel bag in through the rear doors, metal clinked. Andreas slipped into the back to sit behind the box and he took Andreas's place in the front.

I assumed Andreas would be having kittens inside his head. He must be scared shitless Scrim would discover Kat was in the box. I managed to signal calmness to him and his subtle eyebrow gestures stopped. Hilarious, if it wasn't so serious. I'd have to concoct a good story for him.

There was only one possibility so far that fitted what I knew we would find at the lodge. I'd tell him Scrim was just a kinkster and the lodge a place he and his friends used.

As I slammed shut the rear doors, I eyed the bag where it nestled beside Andreas's backpack. Did he have a weapon in there? One of Vetrov's underlings would likely be armed, somewhere, somehow.

The shit was getting a little deeper.

On the winding route to the lodge, Scrim did little more than point or say when I needed to turn. If he understood what was in the box, and he must, he didn't show it. Only once did he show some emotion. As we passed a battered, red Rav 4 going the other way, he cursed and stared out the window.

"Fucking weed merchants. I told them not to grow anything near us."

I raised an eyebrow then went back to steering round the potholes. The summer rains here must have washed out the road.

"Drugs," he muttered. "Can't stand the little shits who get into that."

With what I knew of him and his boss – my boss – drugs were almost a picnic in the park. Everyone has their foibles.

The turn onto an even narrower paved road carried us deeper into the green world of the Daintree. Down here we seemed far from civilization – precisely the best place to do what I intended to do to Kat.

And for that day when she finally admitted in her mind that she was mine, I had brought with me the right gear to symbolize her submission.

Chapter 6

Andreas

I kept my forearm laid across the box to steady myself as the 4WD weaved along the last of the road. When I'd first done this, I'd been overcome by a strange feeling, as if by doing this I was protecting her. The more I learned, the more I dreaded what Chris intended to do. Yet there was no man I called a closer friend. Maybe in a few days, I'd be renouncing that. I fucking hoped not. It would tear me apart.

The jolts of the moving vehicle and the monotonous surge of the engine would soothe me then I'd snap back. There was a woman inside the box beneath my hand. I had to get her away from here…without hurting Chris. If I talked to him enough, maybe he'd see sense. If not, did I have the guts to help her escape?

I drummed my fingers on the box.

We rounded a corner. Beyond the veil of the tree ferns, the sleek green umbrella trees, and the vine-wrapped tree trunks, the lodge appeared. The engine idled as Scrim and I pushed open a pair of steel and corrugated iron gates. After Scrim directed Chris to the most distant of two houses on stilts, I traipsed along behind the vehicle.

The greenness hit me and I halted.

Despite the odd circumstances I had to stand there a moment to inhale…to just *be*.

The cool air was heavy with moisture. I'd probably grow mold if I sat still too long. Palm trees swayed and fluttered their fronds overhead. Ten or twenty of them had been planted inside the compound, or maybe they'd grown here by themselves? Somewhere over the high stone walls, birds whooped and clicked to each other and a distant murmur spoke of waves rolling in across a beach.

"Andreas!" Chris called.

I jerked and looked around. He'd parked underneath the two-story house and had the rear doors of the 4WD open. One end of the box had been slid up to the edge. Scrim was walking away, to the right, toward the first house.

This was it. Letting her out. Seeing what she would do, what he would do. What I would do.

"Coming." I stepped in closer, surprised to find myself seized by a mixture of excitement and fear. I didn't know her at all. She was an enigma. A woman in a box, like an out-of-season Christmas present about to be unwrapped. I shook myself. Weirdo.

Then it hit me. Shit. Obvious disastrous problem. "Him." I jerked my thumb in Scrim's direction, hoping the man didn't turn around and think I was acting strangely. "What if he sees her?"

"Scrim thinks she's here of her own volition."

When had they discussed this? Before he got in the car? I held up a hand. "Wait. Wait. You told him there's a woman in this box and he rode here without saying a *word*?"

"I had to tell him. He's kinky too. This place gets used for lots of role play." Chris turned and undid the first latch. "Just don't go chatting to him. He's a little odd but he's going to stay out of our hair. If we're careful and keep him away, it'll be fine."

"Uh." I curled up my fists but nodded like I knew what he meant. I knew shit. How strange did you have to be to come here to re-enact kink like this, and yet for Chris to declare him odd? How could Chris be so cool about this when what we were doing was so fucking illegal? I shook my head. "Yeah. Look, no problem. I won't talk to him anyway. Why the hell would I?"

"Good."

The chance that I'd spill something that gave away the truth was probably astronomically huge. Already I felt nervous with this guy living here, while Chris did god knew what with Kat.

She looked an absolute mess. After we carefully extracted her from the box, hard to do when she wasn't helping us much, we tried to get her to stand. The blindfold wouldn't throw off her balance. She wobbled and fell back against the 4WD – sitting on the lip of the door opening. Her lips were slack and her sweat-matted scarlet hair swung across her face. The T-shirt and the little black panties Chris had put back on her did little to conceal her femininity. I'd seen her half naked at the last stop, and knew it was sick to look at her in this sexual way, yet for a few seconds, I did exactly that.

"You okay?" I tucked some of her wayward hair behind her ear.

"Hold her there." Chris shut one wing of the rear doors while I supported her with an arm across her back. Then he leaned over in front of her. "She doesn't seem to be faking it. Kat? Kat? You'd better not be planning to kick me in the groin."

Nothing. She'd barely moved. Through the T-shirt I stroked her back. "Hey. Are you okay? Feeling sick?" I ducked my head to look at her face. "I think she's still out of it. Are you sure you gave her the right dose? Didn't you say it should've worn off?"

"Yes." The frown said he was concerned too.

"What if she was taking some other drug? Half the country is on something. If she is, it might have an extra effect."

He straightened and thought for a moment. "You could be right. It should still wear off with time. But we need to keep an eye on her. Let's get her upstairs and get the tape off her eyes."

"Uh." I checked out how it wound over the back of her hair in a thick swathe. "How do we do that without ripping off skin or hair? Fuck, Chris, this is going to hurt."

"I needed to make sure she was subdued."

I bit back the urge to call him an asshole. How much did he care for this woman? Not much, it seemed.

26

"Scrim said there's a bath here, upstairs. It'll come off if we soak it."

I eyed the stairs at the back of the garage, then her. "I'll carry her. She'll never make it up there on her own legs." Crouching, I took her in my arms.

She was as floppy as a rag doll that had OD'd on valium. My wonky left arm almost crumpled under her weight but I caught myself.

"You sure you can do this?" Chris stepped in.

"Yes," I snarled. "I can. My arm got chewed a bit, it hasn't fallen off." Fucking hell. The man had kidnapped her, drugged her, and now had the audacity to act concerned. I throttled back, swallowed. "Sorry. Yes, I've got her."

His eyebrows twitched. "Good."

Carrying her up the stairs then into the bathroom was hard enough. Figuring out how to get her into the spa-sized bath so her hair could soak was even harder. By herself she'd likely drown every fifteen seconds even if we sat nearby.

Which was how I'd ended up in the bath with her, with both of us in our underwear. Her red bra scooped low, showing off the upper curves of her breasts. I had her stretched out between my thighs with her head close to water level, so her hair would soak.

Letting Chris do this though, fuck it, not happening. We'd eye-dueled and I'd won. Though I was becoming ever more aware that Chris wanted to strangle me.

"Okay." He massaged between his eyes. "I need to go talk to Scrim. You have to be aware she's possibly faking it."

"What? You're joking." I looked down at her where her hair floated around her head in a red halo. Only two seconds before I'd had to grab her so she didn't slip deeper.

"Maybe. Just…take care. Of you as well as her. I'll be back."

"What are you talking to him about?"

"You. Partly. You weren't supposed to be here. He may not have said anything, but you're a glitch from his point of view. This place isn't exactly a public amenity. I need to tell him you're trustworthy. And figure out why there's no electricity." He looked up at the non-functioning bathroom light.

We had zero power. Luckily, there was a skylight, but the day was fading.

"I'll be back soon. Then, we are going to talk." He pointed at a bottle on the shoulder height shelf to my right. "Massage some conditioner into her hair. It might help dissolve the sticky stuff."

I nodded and watched him walk out the door. I'd wanted to talk since soon after I'd slipped into his car on the ferry. Now though, I wondered what I was going to say to him.

For a few minutes, I concentrated on working some conditioner into her hair and beneath the tape as much as possible, then I drew her up a little higher onto my thigh.

And I watched.

The water might be cold but she was warm against my skin. I couldn't help admiring her curves as I smoothed away the grime of all that had happened to her over the last day. A few times she stirred and pushed at my hand but I persisted. Her skin was pale, accentuating the red of her bra and black of her panties – color coded scraps of cloth that screamed sexual territory. All the best bits were underneath those. Her lips were plump with the promise of kisses. Long legs, female contours…

Damn.

I had a hard-on that wasn't going away while I had her nestled into me like a little defenseless creature.

At last the tape loosened and I gently pulled the bits away from each strand of her hair, revealing her face. What color were her eyes? I turned her face upward and stroked her cheek until she opened them.

Gray. A pretty and liquid light gray.

"Hi," I said softly.

She only groaned quietly and blinked.

When she turned her cheek away and nestled back into me, curving her back and drawing up her legs so the water swirled, I had to clamp down on a surge of emotion. Her eyelids drifted down again. She clung to my leg with both arms – determined yet weak. Her hair swept in lazy arcs against the masculine heaviness of my thigh.

Beauty personified.

I ached deep inside. What did Chris want to do to her?

The draw to protect her was so strong. I didn't care what she might or might not have done. So cute all snuggled around me. I'd never had a woman do this. Ever. Not in such a vulnerable way.

"Hey, baby girl." I stroked her cheek again. "I'm going to get you out of this."

She stirred but her eyes stayed shut. "Not a baby. Fugg off."

I chuckled and smiled. "Not a hope."

Daylight was fading by the time we had her out of the bath and dried off. When Chris wrist and ankle cuffed her and collared her with black leather, I managed to stay quiet. When he attached a metal leash, I fought not to explode.

Maybe part of this was that I also found her disturbingly sexy all collared and leashed. That scared me.

Being able to touch her and comfort her in the bathroom had brought a temporary serenity. Now, my sense of wrongness was on high alert. But unless I wanted to send Chris to prison, I had to figure out the right way to do this. I had to talk to her, as well as him.

The back of the house had a wide, sailcloth-covered deck that looked out through straggly scrub and trees over a beach. A circular, generously padded chair seemed the best place for Kat. Chris left her in there, curled up like her namesake, a cat, and apparently sleeping while we drew up and sat in chairs around a rectangular table.

Little anomalies piqued my interest. For instance, her leash had been clipped to a chromed steel ring on the chair.

Launching straight into a discussion about the obvious bothered me. We talked small – the power switch, and the weather, of all fucking things, and other unimportant stuff. Chris went to the kitchen, to perform his microwave chef duty with cans of stew and packets of nacho chips. Both of us knew we needed to discuss Kat.

The dampness from her underwear darkened the beige upholstery of the chair. A sea breeze swept the deck, riffling her hair and the leaves of the potted palms that sat on the deck's periphery. The rain must water them. With my forearms leaned on my thighs and my hands clasped, I studied our surroundings. This was a tropical beach paradise – what more could you want except a sex slave?

"Eat." Chris slid a plate of food onto the table beside me. "Scrim said he'll go back into town tomorrow for supplies now that the fridges are on."

"Good." I nodded and scooped food into my mouth, barely tasting it. "And her?"

"I'll give her something to eat soon."

I darted a look at him. Even those words had sounded tinged with threat. My imagination? "Good," I ventured.

"You're leaving tomorrow." He waved his fork at me. "Now you've seen I'm not murdering her."

"No. I'm not." I laid down my fork. "I go when she does."

"You'll go if I say you do. Scrim can take you with him. He'll organize a plane to fly you back."

"No. What you've told me so far, it doesn't justify this." I shook my head. "I'm not sure what would."

"Wrestle you for her." Chris tossed down his own fork.

"She's not a possession."

Then she stirred. Maybe our words had woken her, or the drug had finally worn off. The cascade of the dusk light caressed her curves as she raised herself on her elbows.

I swallowed, struck for a microcosm of time by the allure of indeed owning her. "She's not yours."

"She is now. She's mine."

God, I hated him. Gently, I stamped my fist on the table. "You can't own a person. Not in this time and age."

"You have no idea. Slaves are a reality as much as they've ever been in history. It's just a matter of beating the law. I told you before. Turn me in, or leave me be. This is something I want. I mean to have her." He sat back in the chair and contemplated Kat. "You're right, though. I can't justify this. What my friend did, yeah, he had some justification. Me? Put me back in history at Rome and I could be a rich man with a troupe of slave girls or maybe a sheik with a harem. Legal, even the pinnacle of society. Here, now?" His eyes shone dark in the dying light. "I'm just a bad man with a good sense of timing."

His blatant admission stunned me for a few seconds.

"A good sense of timing? Why the hell is this good?"

"She was going on holiday. Driving to the Outback. No one will miss her for a few days until the phone calls don't come in."

"Jesus," I whispered. He *had* planned this. This wasn't some distorted retribution. This was Chris being fucked up in the head.

"Now you know why you're leaving tomorrow. There's nothing more you can do."

"Fuck you," I muttered. "I'm staying."

"If I have to toss you out on your ear, I will," he grumbled.

"No."

"Motherfucking hell!" Chris stood, skidding back his chair.

I stared. I'd rarely seen him angry. There was no way I could take him on. Martial arts expert versus me – oil rig engineer cross stock market fiddler, and with a bad arm? Uh-uh. The fresh white T-shirt he'd thrown on after his shower shaped to his chest and made him look like a pissed off Colossus.

Face set like stone, he sucked in rapid breaths. "I don't want you being associated with this place…or with what I'm doing."

Associated with? What did he mean? Kat was on hands and knees and looking back at us through her tangled fringe. What he was about to do to her… I shook my head. "You're not just some Roman senator with a cute slave girl, Chris. You're a mean fucking sadist."

What did he mean associated? What was here? I eyed the metal ring on the chair's rim that he'd clipped her leash to. There'd been another like that in the bathroom.

His words came out quieter. "And she's always known that. She likes that part of me. Go. Please."

I was in no way convinced, but what was the use in arguing? Yet I wasn't handing Chris to the cops.

That day, out in the waves, when all around me had turned pink and red and water bubbled past my ears. I'd screamed then sunk again, flailing my good arm, twisting to see where my surfboard had gone. The shark was out there somewhere, circling to come get me again. My left arm, shredded and raw with pain. He'd saved me. He'd reached me before the shark did and somehow gotten me to shore by heaving me onto his board and paddling like crazy. My eyes watered a little. I blinked myself back to here, to the Daintree.

We'd been through some crappy situations. I'd helped him one night when a gang pounced on him outside the pub. Some of them had ended up in hospital. I mightn't have done much more than distract a couple while Chris smacked around the others, but we'd been a team.

"Staying." I nodded slowly. "I'm staying. Someone sane needs to be here." At least until I could get her away.

"Andreas…" He ran his palm through his hair, from front to back, then massaged his temples. "Shit."

I ached for him, sorry for the pain I caused him, but not sorry for the reason.

He walked around the table and went to Kat to say something quietly to her. Her answer was too soft for me to understand but he went behind her chair. Her head swung as she followed him. Then he picked up the chair with her in it and brought it over to set it down before me.

This close, with the lantern light above us, I could see twirls of red glinting in the strands of hair, the scatter of freckles on her cheeks, the rise and fall of her breasts as they threatened to spill from the cups of her bra, and the slow blink of her eyelids as she studied me.

If she could think straight, she'd know I was on her side.

"If you stay," he said reasonably, "You will see me hurt her. You will be seeing me dominate her."

At that, I swear her eyes went darker.

In a split of a heartbeat he reached down and took a fistful of her hair, twisting it round his fist. She whined as he bent her head back until he could peer down into her eyes. Though her hands were cuffed together at her front, she writhed on her knees and tried to grab his fingers.

"No, Kat," he said softly. "Let him see this." Casually, despite her hands clawing at him, he used his free hand to scoop each breast from the cups of the bra. The sight of her areolas shocked me. This was minor violence but so unexpected. I should leap up and defend her.

"My hair! That hurts, you bastard! Stop!"

I think my mouth had fallen open. The lure of this was sudden and undeniable. With her head back, her neck was exposed along with her nipples and the delicious curve of her stomach. Her muscles shifted enticingly as she struggled.

I'd never seen anything like this outside of a porn movie.

"Shh." Then he plunged his hand into the front of her panties and thrust a finger or two up into her. The guttural noise she made and then her squeals went straight to my cock which shot into lift off mode – painfully erect and bent around in my pants.

I should be telling him to stop but something about the absolute humiliation he was putting her through had hit every definition of lust incarnate in my dictionary. Worse than that, Chris was examining me with his mouth quirked up at the corner.

I guess I had gone stiff in more ways than one. I thought about swallowing but held it back.

"Hot?" He raised an eyebrow. "My only compensation is that I swear she'll like what I do, most of the time. Want me to get her to lick my fingers?"

"Go fuck yourself." Kat gasped, and I watched him take another quarter turn of her hair until her curses turned into one long whimper.

"Is that your way of telling me the valium has worn off?"

"You are a bastard," I muttered. But I dug up some of my missing morality. "No. Hell no. No finger licking."

Chapter 7

Kat

Shit.

After asking his friend Andreas if he wanted me to lick his fingers, Chris studied me. I couldn't do a thing, with my legs bent double under me, except look up at him, seething, hoping my eyes could set him on fire. My thighs hurt from the tension. His rigid hold on my hair left me no room to shift at all. I tried though. The man had fucking strength to spare and I hated him with every atom in my body.

I hadn't let anyone put anything inside me for so long. Fingers, cock, or dildos. For him to casually do it… Hate was too nice a word. I *loathed* him.

"Let go!" I croaked, feeling even the muscles in my throat struggle to move. Another inch backward and my neck would surely crack.

Panic.

He stared down into my eyes with that small knowing smile.

I couldn't help my other, sexual, response. It was nerves, anatomy, instincts…plus that thing I had for violent dominance. Not my fault. I'd never let a Dom do this, or bind me, for this very reason. Control. I wanted it. Didn't want to give it.

Tears gathered from the spiking pain in my scalp. I dug my fingernails into his forearm. "Fuck you!"

He screwed his fist in a little more. "Careful, girl."

Between my legs, he thrust his fingers higher. Moisture spilled from me. Mortified, I dug my nails in, deep as I could, raking them down his arm.

"Stop." Hard voice. Hard, straight-lined mouth. Meanness in every syllable. His blue eyes were glasslike.

The fear this invoked...Chris was not a kind sadist. I'd always liked taunting him with my list of limits.

Bad mistake. I slowed the scoring of my nails but kept them pressing in.

"Kat," he growled.

Fuck. I lifted my fingers, released his arm. My legs trembling, my heart accelerating, I closed my eyes to shut him out the only way I could. I wasn't ready for this showdown. So tired. Hungry.

His fingers stayed inside me. I felt them shift, and go in past the knuckles, widening me. The man knew too much about women's responses. He stroked forward with his fingertips, hitting the exact right place. I shuddered. I wouldn't come. I wouldn't. But the instant he'd entered me, I'd jellified. With his fingers jammed in and stretching my entrance, lust struck me like an electric tide. Now it spread, building and rippling outward until my nipples beaded and my breaths came faster.

He worked at me, coaxing to life my sexuality right when I wanted it to go far, far away. That other man, Andreas, must be watching. I'd thought he might be my chance. A friend maybe. But he said *nothing*.

I wanted to arch myself onto Chris's hand. Not happening. I suppressed a groan, my eyes rolling back.

Under the massage of the ball of his thumb, my clit stirred. Small lustful spasms shuddered through me.

At last, he let me go – extracted his fingers from my pussy, released my hair, and tossed me to my hands and knees. Locked in the echoes, I could still feel the drag of his fingers as they pulled out, and I clenched down there.

"This is almost too easy," he murmured from inches away.

I glared through the curtain of my damp hair. He was crouching and looking at me.

This time I made my words drip with nastiness. "Fuck you."

"I'm tired of those words. Say them again and I start punishment here and now, in front of Andreas."

"Let her be."

At last the friend spoke. I searched through hazy memories. He'd cradled me in the bath, gently. The man was good-looking, in a shaggy, laidback way. More importantly, he was saying no to Chris. I ran my tongue over my strangely numb lips, feeling the pains in my scalp receding. Maybe I could use him after all.

I contemplated Chris. Mr. Super-sleazy. Mr. Fake Dom who needed to kidnap women. For a second, my reply jammed in my throat. But I needed, *so* needed, to challenge him.

"I can think of new insults for you." My arms shook. Propping myself up on them wasn't a great idea. I sat back and went to pull my bra back into place so my breasts weren't exposed. "Rot in hell? Go masturbate a poodle? Eat hot shit mother...screwer?" I grinned even as my stomach rumbled.

Everything around me fuzzed in and out. Inside my head went white. A wave of weakness hit me and I swayed, aching and flushing cold. My fingers, so cold. While I was dealing with that, Chris anchored his hand in my hair again.

There was laughter in his voice. "Couldn't resist, could you?"

"Wait. Chris." Andreas's voice this time. I swallowed down nausea. "She doesn't look so good."

Warm breath on my face. I strained to see them, to raise my heavy eyelids.

"She doesn't, does she?" A palm touched my forehead, my arm. "She's pale and clammy. Maybe she needs food?"

Someone fumbled at my wrists and my hands were drawn behind my back. I was hauled onto someone's lap, and I slumped against them. Water, then food, pressed to my lips. I swallowed automatically. Head spinning, I fought to keep whatever went into my mouth inside me instead of spewing.

They wouldn't like me if I threw up on them. Serve them right.

Strength returned then awareness. I shut my mouth at the intruding fingers. Fingers? They were putting fingers in my mouth, not a fork.

I stared. Whose lap was I on? I swiveled my head to find Chris looking down at me.

"Back in the world? You've got more color." He slowly swiped a finger along my lips. "You had me worried. Andreas too."

Sticky. I could smell the gooey meat of an over-spiced canned meal and clamped my lips tighter.

"Not going to lick them?"

I injected determination into my gaze.

His chuckle made me jiggle on his lap. With my hands clipped behind me, the cloth of his shorts slid against my loosely clasped fingers. From the hard bump under my ass, he had an erection.

My memory of what he'd done to me returned. How dare he. I thought about cursing but swearing at him when I felt fragile as a twig seemed stupid.

Would it annoy him if I wriggled on his cock?

Maybe. Maybe too much. Being fucked out here on the table was also a possibility. Or spanked, or worse. If I riled him enough, Chris might do it. And this guy, Andreas, seemed likely to simply watch. Struck by the precariousness of my situation, I tried to recall the things Chris had pushed me to do in the past that I'd said no to. Anal sex, for starters. I hated the very concept. But there were far worse things than being ass fucked.

My courage sank. Without my carefully written-out hard limits, I didn't know how Chris would react. What were his kinks and fetishes? Especially the ones no one would do? Whatever they were, I might be his next experiment.

I'd be safer doing a naked chicken dance in front of a lion than annoying him right now.

I had to find my feet, get stronger, cleverer. Exhaustion wasn't helping. And I had to do more than taunt him. I had to escape.

Pick your battles. That saying came from somewhere. So when he nudged my chin and made me look at him, I merely blinked and tried to look placid.

The puzzled expression and corrugation of his forehead said I'd made him wonder.

"Are you going to behave now, Kat, while Andreas and I talk?"

My stomach tensed. This seemed like selling out to the Devil. "I'll behave," I said softly.

"Hmm." His eyebrow kinked upward. "Suspicious. Andreas..." He looked over. "This is when I know she's scheming."

"Really?" Andreas sounded surprised.

But I snuggled into Chris's shoulder even if it made my mind shudder. My skin didn't crawl though. Under the fresh shirt, he smelled...nice. Dangerous, exciting, yet nice.

God, I was losing my mind.

I'd always been attracted to danger.

They began to talk and with the side of my head buried against Chris, I half-listened with one ear and examined Andreas with one eye while I thought.

Chris said, "You understand now? If you stay you keep out of what I do. Plus it's one week, maximum. After that I guarantee I will bodily remove you. That should give you time to see I'm not going to permanently damage her. Agreed?"

The matter-of-fact way he assumed I would be his prisoner for as long as he wanted me to be...chilling.

Silence.

Chris spoke, "I promise you I intend to take care of her. I know she's a person not a thing."

"Okay. I guess if that's the best deal. Agreed."

"You won't be missed?" Chris asked.

"I quit the oil rig. I'm between jobs. I figured I'd make a go at making money from only the stock market for a while."

He agreed? What man would do that? Clearly Andreas wasn't in on this. He'd stumbled in somehow. How could he just agree to leave me? I wanted to sink my teeth into Chris in frustration. I wanted to scream at this Andreas.

You damn coward. Where are your guts? Where's your sense of what's right? I'm kidnapped. Not off on some forest holiday!

Chris offered me a nacho with cold melted cheese on it and I grimaced. "Eat."

I pulled a face. *Yuck.*

Reluctantly I bit off a piece, chewed, and swallowed. From then on, as he talked, he offered me food or sips of water and, once or twice, sips from a bottle of beer, until he suddenly decided beer and valium might be a bad combo. Again, I reminded myself that now was a rotten time to mess around. I ate, slowly filling up on this disgusting diet of nachos.

At least this Andreas seemed a little concerned about me. Deep down, he had a conscience, though I didn't understand what possible reason he had for allowing what Chris aimed to do, what he *had* done. Abduction, drugging me, sexual assault.

I felt like yelling at him, *there is no excuse good enough!*

Man up. Help me you stupid sodding asshole. I fumed while I nibbled and listened. Why had Chris done this? The answer loomed in my mind. I think my subconscious had worked it out already. Stephanie was another missing woman. I'd thought for weeks that Chris's partner in the Magnetic Island accounting firm might have been involved in her disappearance.

Oh you very thick person, I scolded myself. This must be what had made him take me. I'd gotten too close to the truth.

Where was Stephanie? Dead? Or someone's captive, like I was? I shivered. No one had seen her for weeks.

Chris wasn't a man who made many mistakes in life. Most likely he meant to keep me chained up somewhere, if not within range of his hands. My best chance seemed to be Andreas. The man with the piss-weak conscience.

He reminded me of half, no all, the Doms I'd met over the years – useless until you prodded them.

I did like the latent danger in BDSM. I even, theoretically, liked the idea of giving up control. But I didn't trust most of them. The way they all skipped around hard limits annoyed the shit out of me. If they wanted me to submit they needed to do a damn sight better job at dominating than I could. None had.

Not even this asshole whose lap I sat in. I'd never even let him tie me up properly. Never trusted him that much. If he thought kidnapping me would impress me, he was well mistaken. Now I despised him even more. Stupid fucker. The law would catch up to him.

The only Dom who'd done rope bondage on me was Damien and that was more a rope fetish act than dominance and submission. He'd ended up leaving me for a Domme. I sighed. Another wuss.

"So you're going to sit and watch while I flog her and make her beg. While I hurt her?" At that, I froze. He pulled me in closer and stroked my shoulder. "Andreas? You seemed intrigued, before."

"I'll watch. Don't start thinking I'm going to turn kinky like you. I may not hand you over to the law…but I'm not sure you're firing on all cylinders right now. This Scrim, is he safe? Can we trust him?" Andreas sat back in his chair and crossed one leg over to rest his ankle on his knee. Then he stared at me – watching me, watching him. Like I was something so unusual I needed a whole new catalogue name. A few black locks of hair curled over his forehead.

I poked out my tongue, amused at the waggle then rise of his eyebrows. If he had a sense of humor, I had a chance.

"I think so but I want you to stay away from him. Don't talk to him."

They drank their beers and discussed how surprisingly cool it was here, beside the beach at the Daintree. They talked things I didn't care about. I had other worries. The beer, the pleasant scent of the insect-warding citronella candles, and the soft murmur of Chris's voice next to my ear soothed me into the drowsiness of almost sleep.

Until I found my face grasped and turned upward.

"Cute. I never knew you snored." Then Chris kissed me lightly on the lips. "In the morning, I'll begin your training."

I merely grunted, too tired to do more than curse him silently.

His friend would help me. I'd tell him all about Chris.

"You'll be such a pretty slave." He stood with me in his arms.

That woke me more. I blinked sleepily then scowled.

Slave? I'll smother you in your sleep. He'd been an okay Dom. Better than some. As a kidnapper he sucked.

Chapter 8

Chris

Kat wasn't the lightest of bundles but I'd spoken the truth – she was a pretty one. The bedroom I'd chosen to use was one of three, all with king-size beds and private bathrooms. The metal restraint rings I'd noticed in the kitchen were here too. Walls, furniture…this house seemed determined to hammer home what had happened here in the past.

This was different. I had to remember that.

In my arms Kat seemed as innocuous as a kitten. Her hair had dried and gone that cherry red that screamed artificial. By the time I reached the bedroom door, her lips had parted, her eyes closed again, and her breathing was regular.

"Turn down the quilt," I murmured to Andreas.

"I don't think that's normal sleep." He squeezed past us on his way to the bed. "Can't be. Not with you carrying her."

"Me?" I held back until I deposited her in the middle of the white sheets. With my knee on the bed, I watched her while I answered. "You're a sleep expert now, are you? She's had a long, hard day."

A grunt was his only reply.

I grinned, certain that he was dying to call me out on that since I was the cause.

With her thumb near her mouth and her legs tucked up, Kat looked cute enough to be some Dom's little pet. Only this pet bit and scratched. The hair fanned out over her mouth and cheek tempted me, so I reached and rearranged the strands, placing them behind her ear. Whenever I caught her unawares, Kat's upturned nose, innocent eyes, and small chin made me think of someone from fairyland. All other times, I thought of a creature with filed-sharp teeth.

I searched for the clip on her bra. At the touch of my hand on her back, Kat's eyelids opened to slits. She growled so quietly anyone normal might think it a passing moth. I assessed her. Her hands were still cuffed at her back. My only real danger was a knee to the groin, or a head butt.

After planting my hand around her shoulder and pressing her an inch into the mattress, I leaned in and brushed my lips across her ear. "Either I unclip it and take this off the simple way, or I cut it off. Strange, I know, but I forgot to pack you spares."

Like a sniper taking aim, I zeroed in. Things amplified: the swallow at her throat, the slow relaxation of the muscle under my palm; the huff of her breath. Surrender.

"Giving up?"

She twitched her shoulder but said nothing.

"Good girl."

The tension provoked in her at those two words, made me smile. But she stayed quiet as I undid her bra. I didn't count my blessings or any such shit. This was the distant rumble of thunder before the storm. I shifted my other knee onto the bed and slid the bra straps down her arms.

Andreas was standing at the other side of the bed with his hands in the pockets of his board shorts. He cleared his throat. "No rape."

I ignored him, carefully undoing her wrists, taking off the bra entirely then doing up her wrists at her front. She let me. Not a single protest, curse, or wriggle. Of course, there wasn't a hope she'd win in a wrestle.

"I can tell you're waiting for your moment, Kat."

"Moment?" she murmured sleepily, nuzzling her face into the pillow. "No moment. Warzone, fersure."

"Oh?" I massaged her neck. "Go to sleep. Tomorrow is a new day. We're all tired."

Despite my claims about needing rest, her breasts were begging me to study them. Such succulent nipples, like little toppings on a cake – smooth and asking to be sucked or flogged, or any number of other things that made my head buzz with excitement.

"The possibilities," I murmured. Luckily she'd closed her eyes.

"Did you hear me?" Andreas asked, his baritone voice low in volume.

I raised an eyebrow then stripped off my shorts and shirt. "Yes. There is no rape happening that I can see. I'm keeping her in my bed so I can watch her. Her *breathing*."

"Sure you are." His gaze switched from her to me and back to her naked breasts.

"Don't trust me?"

"Not with her, no."

"You can either piss off to your own bed, Andreas. Down the hall, second room on the left. Or get in on that side of her. Take your pick."

He froze. "Seriously? With her like that? Naked?"

"I'm dead tired. Figure it out fast, Mr. Virgin Never-seen-a-naked-woman dude." I climbed into bed, settling in facing her and pulled the cool sheet over us, up to waist level. "And. Not naked. I swear she has panties covering her hot little pussy."

Her eyelids flickered. I smiled, wanting to stroke her cheek...to sketch around her lips with my fingernail. Maybe even to put a gag between those lips and do nasty things. My cock rose. Damn. Stop imagining, dickhead.

He cursed softly.

A few seconds later I heard him undress and his clothes fall to the floor, then the bed dipped under his weight.

"See you in the morning, Virg Dude."

He swore again. "Don't steal the fucking sheets, moron."

I smiled. His sense of humor was returning. Way to go.

No rape? Andreas was shaping up to be a party pooper. Not that rape was on my list.

As my eyes drifted shut, I checked her body again. Nice. All the right curves in all the right places and wrapped up in a ball of spitfire challenge.

"No, no rape. More fun to mess with her head...and all her other bits, until she begs for cock. Much, much more fun." I thought I'd said it too quietly for Andreas to hear but he replied.

"You're such an arrogant son of a bitch. Women do respond to nicer stuff too, you know? Romance. All that."

"Advice from the girlfriend expert?"

"My past is not relevant. Besides, I do have them, now and then. Haven't you ever heard of love? Of asking on bended knee for their hand?"

"You expect me to do that?" I smiled, she was gently snoring again.

"No, though I expect the sun shines out of your asshole."

I tsked. "Some women like it when men drive over the top of the asking and just *take*."

He was silent for a while. "And you think she's one of those?"

"Yes."

Think? I knew. The world belonged to the arrogant, to the sure, not to the meek. Not that I didn't have my moments of doubt, but I kept them to myself and that made all the difference.

I covered her small hand with mine. This woman was mine because I wished her to be. Not because she wanted it.

In time, she would want me too...

* * *

Something tickled my neck and slowly drew me from the void of sleep.

I snapped open my eyes. Kat's face was inches away, her mouth dropping open as she saw me waken, her pupils dilating with shock. The chain around my neck slid. Between finger and thumb, she held the tiny silver key that opened the locks on her cuffs.

She tried to throw herself away from me, turning at the waist, pushing up off the bed.

Damn. She'd undone the wrist cuffs?

In one smooth motion, I flicked the key from her fingers, and swung myself up so I was straddling her body and pinning her down. I sat more heavily on her hips and thighs, and by weight alone immobilized those dangerous legs.

Andreas was gone. She'd probably seen the opportunity when he went to the toilet.

"Get off me!" She went to knock my arms aside, but missed.

I intercepted one wrist then the other, transferred them casually to one hand then slowly I pushed them down – letting her see how little her strength counted. Teeth bared, she shoved and struggled.

"Can't get loose? You really think you have a chance?"

"Asshole. Let. Me. Go!"

I took her wrists a few more inches toward the bed, though she resisted. Muscles in her arms strained, until they seemed ready to pop, and she grunted with effort. The bed rocked with every twist of her torso and shoulders. Her tits jiggled too. Enticing as hell.

"Goddamn, you're hot, woman."

When she growled, I just grinned wider. "Go Kitty."

More struggling, more grunting, and she got exactly nowhere. "Fuck you. Ffff…"

When at last I had her wrists crossed under my hand and squashed into the pillow above her, I paused. Kat sucked in huge gulping breaths but kept up her game of pushing against my grip.

I smiled and reached down to squeeze one nipple as hard as I could until she squeaked and settled. "Thank you. Are we going to do this every morning?" The blaze of anger in her eyes said as much.

Her face was so flushed, I wondered if this wrestle had done more than tire her out. It had made my morning erection arrive with a vengeance. If I shifted a little, I could push aside her no-doubt wet panties and shove my cock in.

Still watching her for clues, I slid my groin down her body until she had to be feeling the tip of my cock below her clit.

The closure of her eyes then re-opening took place in a moment. A blink? I slid upward a fraction. The blink stuttered and turned into shut eyes. Her chest had stopped moving also then I heard the softest huff of breath. Pleasure. She was registering pleasure.

Ugh. I so wanted to fuck her. My thigh muscles tensed.

But, no, I exhaled slowly.

Footsteps said Andreas had entered the room.

"What are you doing?" he asked sharply.

"Not raping her? I'm pretty sure that's it. She got hold of the key to her cuffs."

"Chris, don't forget our deal. This is fucking…"

"What?" I glanced at him. He stood there foolishly, lost, like a waiter who'd misplaced his menu orders. "Sexy? You want a hobby, try wrestling naked women."

He frowned, not-frowned, frowned again, stuck in uncertainty. "Half naked."

I looked back at her. "The deal was you don't interfere with me and her."

Andreas made a tiny sound. "You can't…" His voice hitched.

She opened her mouth as if to comment and I lightly smacked her cheek. "Shush." It worked, amazingly. I whispered so only she could hear me, "Be good or I'll find a butt plug."

Her lower lip curled in and she bit it.

Cute. Was that a mannerism that said, hey, that scared me? I tucked away the memory.

At least she'd stopped cursing me.

"Run out of breath? Or insults?" I raised my eyebrows, while I groped and found the side of her panties.

"What are you doing?" she whispered. Her gaze twitched down.

"Fixing something."

Lace, so I could tear them with my fingers. I ripped the side through then switched the hand that held down her wrists, and tore the other side. Gradually, I extracted the panties from under her ass then found her wrist cuffs where they'd fallen. Though she resisted every move I made, I painstakingly re-cuffed her, separated the cuffs, and clicked each to the rings either side of her black collar.

"Shit. I'm not sure I'm comfortable with this." The upset tone in Andreas's voice made me look over again.

What was this doing to his head? I didn't want to mess him up. But he'd demanded this – to be here, watching. I wasn't turning back, not now.

I didn't quite understand his motivations. Logically, what I was doing was so bad it sailed off the edge of the morality world. Logically, he should have called the weight of the law down on me and gotten Kat free. He hadn't. We were friends like nothing else and I'd always known it would take an earthquake to shake us loose but this…this was a tsunami of wrongness.

I didn't care about logic. But…if I wasn't me, *I'd* have handed me over to the police.

Maybe I should give him incentive to go.

"Andreas, you don't need to be here. Even if you weren't, I wouldn't be fucking her right now." I trailed her panties across her mouth, enjoying the distaste showing in the twist of her mouth. Then I wrapped them tight across her mouth until the cloth forced apart her lips and her teeth. I tied a knot in the panties so they stayed in place.

"What do you taste like? I'm going to put my tongue in your pussy someday soon and get you off."

When she frowned at me, I stuck my fingertip in and played with her teeth and lips until she shook her head to dislodge me. "Uh-uh, be good." Then I pinned her down by the hair and played some more, painting the moisture around her mouth. "Can't do a thing, now, can you?"

I said, louder, "I'm happy to just fuck with her head at this stage. However, later, when she begs me to, I will fuck the rest of her, every hole I can find. Whether you're here or not, that is going to happen."

Kat grunted, glared at me, and wriggled.

Shit. A female wriggling under my impatient cock was not a good idea.

"Shh. Be still." I stroked her hair. "So. Are you leaving? I think it's best if you do. I don't want to scar you for life."

Andreas shook his head. Talk about eyes filled with fire, his looked alight. To my amusement, he wasn't looking at me. Was it the panties in her mouth? The drooling? Me playing with her? Something had set him off. I didn't generally stare at his junk but the man had a bulge in his pants to rival a gorilla's.

I wasn't sure what I thought of that.

It took fifteen to twenty minutes to get to the stage of breakfast in the kitchen. I kept Kat bound as she was in the bed, with her hands near her ears. It was demoralizing, I hoped, but it meant she could easily fall and hurt herself. Going to the toilet meant freeing one hand. Getting her to dress meant letting both loose until that was done. To my satisfaction she let me redo the bondage without fussing.

The panties were still in her mouth. I'd have to remove the gag soon. She was drooling all down her neck, and though I liked the idea of humiliating her a bit, she'd dehydrate if I left it in, as well as get problems where the gag pressed on the corners of her mouth.

I led her into the kitchen by the collar. Her face said she was itching to fight again, but her actions were subdued. The white beach dress I'd bought at a market was one of several I'd picked as being see-through enough to make me happy, yet likely to fit her. They were all vaguely Indian style with a lacy and loose material that fell from the shoulders but tucked up beneath her tits, accentuating their bounciness.

Andreas had followed us in and he sat on one of the stools at the breakfast bar.

The kitchen, like the rest of the house, was a mixture of modern, artistic, and pragmatic with kinky, if subtle, dungeon fittings. Open plan, it looked out over a living room that then looked out over the back deck and the sea. A light breeze whispered in from the deck. The counter tops were granite, and some of the stainless steel on the fridge and stove was going rusty – from the salt air, I figured. There were rings for tying women to everywhere, more than I'd noticed last night. Andreas had seen them from the way he eyed one on the nearby wall…and ceiling…and floor. So far he appeared happy with the BDSM club explanation. All I had to do was keep him and Scrim from talking.

I stopped Kat in the middle of the floor. "Turn around full circle."

After one long exasperated huff, she did so. As it swirled, the sheer material worshiped the shape of her body from those gorgeous thighs upward. No underwear so I could see the line of her slit and the dark circles of her nipples. My cock twitched at the sight. I took a half-step back and did another sweep from pretty toes to thighs to, well, everything worth looking at.

"Wow," I murmured then I toyed with the little bow under the bodice, and caressed the underside of one breast. Very deliberately, I held her gaze.

She blasted me with another nuclear-force glare.

"Taking off the gag is going to be interesting to watch," Andreas said, hooking one foot on the lower stool rail then fishing a tiny packet of cereal from the basket on the counter. He held it up and tore open a corner. "Have we got milk for this? Or bowls?"

Food was more important than looking at me dominate an almost-naked woman? Was he creating a distraction for himself?

"Bowls are in the cupboards behind you and yes, we've got some of that long-life milk. Is he right, Kat? Is this going to be interesting?"

She grunted indignantly.

In the background, I could hear cereal being poured into a bowl. I fiddled with the knot on the panties gag, loosened it, and took it off, then undid her hands too. I wasn't keen on binding her hands to her collar. The aesthetics weren't pleasing. I preferred the line of a woman's body when her hands were at her back. *"Don't* be interesting. If you play up again, I guarantee there will be consequences."

Kat licked her lips. "Why are you doing this?" She swung to look at Andreas while wiping her mouth. "Why aren't *you* going to the cops? Why the...everything, Chris? Why?" Her breathing hastened, her mouth pursed and, like a runaway missile, she launched. "I don't want to be your *pretty* slave or your damn anything! Consequences? Let me go or there will be damn consequences, from me!"

I waited then went right up close to her and wrapped my arms around her back. I kept my voice level and almost too quiet for Andreas to overhear. Almost.

"Done? You think that was good behavior? You're going to have to do better in the thinking department in future. I regard saying damn to me, twice, as bad behavior. Put that up here in your memory." I twirled her hair in circles above both ears. "Paste it in there this time. No further swearing, ever. Don't forget."

She tried to back away. Too late. I knew having me, a man more than a foot taller and much heftier, crowding her would give her pause. In our negotiated scenes, she'd reacted this way a few times, but I never did get to put the knowledge to use.

"You know why you're here, Kat."

After a few tiny gulps, she fashioned a reply. "Stephanie? Because of her?"

"Yes. Because of her. I was going to get you to kneel between us on the floor, with a cushion for your knees, if you were good. Instead...keep still for what I do next. Don't talk. If you talk, I will tie you up then string you up from the ceiling in here and beat you like a naked piñata until your screaming scares away the crocodiles for miles. Get that? Nod."

For a half a minute she barely breathed. Wide-eyed, she looked at me, then at the floor, her mouth working. Finally, she nodded, once.

I let my heartbeat slow from gallop to trot then I put both my palms on her back and caressed her while I had my nose in her hair, breathing in her scent. A minor victory, maybe, but I'd take it.

"If I have to, at meal times, I'll put you in the cage." I pointed with my chin. In the far corner of the living room sat a black anodized steel cage big enough for a human.

"Jesus." Metal chinked on china. Andreas swore a row of quiet curses then reached for a sponge to mop up the milk and corn flakes he'd spilled on the counter. "A cage?"

Though she ground her teeth, Kat let me lift her onto the breakfast bar. Once she was kneeling on a towel, I tied each wrist behind her to separate rings on the wall. By the time I was done, Andreas had picked up his bowl again. He wasn't eating.

"You finished?" I inquired.

"I guess," he muttered, eyeing Kat.

There it was again – he was looking goggle eyed at my captive. "If you look any harder you'll embarrass her."

Andreas sniffed then swiveled his stool my way. I grinned at his remorseful expression.

"I shouldn't stare, should I? Sorry, Kat."

The thoughtful look she turned on him made me get thoughtful too. "I'd prefer if you didn't apologize to her."

Though he tweaked one eyebrow upward, he nodded. He reached out and touched the one of the wall rings, scratching at it with a finger. "Something red. Is this a spot of blood?"

Jeez. Had they not cleaned up the place? I shoved over the sponge he'd used earlier and he rubbed at the metal. "Could be. Some kinksters get pretty hardcore with their play."

"No shit."

Thank goodness he couldn't see inside my head. I'd played that hard a few times.

Andreas wiped his hands dry.

"What you can do, is help me feed her."

"You want me to feed her my corn flakes?" He coughed once. "Really? I mean…really?"

"Yes. I'm going to get some too. We can both feed her." I added a pre-emptive statement, figuring Kat might decide to try a hunger strike. "She'll eat too, if she has any sense. If you're not strong, Kat, you won't be healthy, will you? I think even you can see the advantage of being healthy."

Her eventual curt nod came after a small spate of head shaking punctuated by an eye roll. I didn't remark on it. Body language control would come eventually. She'd learn.

By the time we were done eating, Kat had several spoonfuls of cereal and milk spilled on her outthrust breasts. She'd gasped and glared often but let us both feed her. Most of the spilled food was Andreas's mistakes. Some of the spillages had seemed deliberate. What the fuck was that about? Although…the idea of sucking it all off her was tempting. I smiled. How that thin lace clung to her curves like plastic wrap…sticky, messy, clear plastic wrap, with two erect nipples poking out like they wanted attention. And a few corn flakes.

Wet, suckable nipples…

If my balls ached any more I'd need painkillers.

"Fuck." Andreas was checking her out too and she was looking exasperated enough at our dual male admiration to rip loose from the bindings like some female superhero. I almost groaned as she again pulled with her arms at her back, making her tits pop out more, and her belly and thigh muscles contort in that absolutely delicious female way.

An image of Andreas up there on the counter with her shoved its way into my head – him licking milk and cereal off her tits. I elaborated, day dreaming, seeing her still bound, moaning, while he parted her thighs and drove into her.

God. I rubbed my forehead. This kidnapping was having unforeseen results. Andreas was getting ever more involved. No wonder, when a friend hitches a ride in your car while you're in the middle of the kidnapping.

I'd thought about what might happen, when abducting Kat first seemed a possibility. Sometimes I wondered why I'd become so obsessed with her. Other times I dismissed such thoughts because I wasn't sure why, except that she attracted me like no other woman. A timid, quiet, and fragile submissive meant nothing to me. Kat pulled me in like a wild lioness in the ring of the coliseum drew a gladiator.

That day at the beach, a week ago, we'd gathered for the munch. Us kinksters had intended to have a bit of fun swimming, barbecuing, and mucking around with beach cricket, as well as introducing some newbies to the lifestyle. Kat had been determined to figure out what Klaus was up to and had wanted me to go break into his house and check out his place in a search for Stephanie.

I'd done it for her because the whole idea fascinated me. Because Kat fascinated me. Not because I really thought she was correct, or because I thought my staid, if kinky, accountant partner had a girl stashed in his house. But she'd been right. That had floored me. I'd questioned Steph and discovered what she thought of her captors. Curiouser and curiouser, she'd protected them. Even lied a little.

A few hours later, after leaving Steph with Klaus and Jodie, I'd known that one day I'd get Kat like Steph had been…on her knees, submitting to me as her Master.

I'd researched it. Stockholm Syndrome, the psychology of captivity, how to break someone down until they believed anything you said, would do anything you asked. This wasn't the same as a Dominant/submissive relationship. I needed to alter my methods.

And here she was. Kneeling before me. Splattered with corn flakes. I almost snorted in amusement but darker thoughts hounded me.

Now I had her on her knees, the prospect daunted me. Maybe I was crazy after all. Worse than that, Andreas was intrigued. I'd seen fairly indisputable symptoms.

The spoon under my fingers began to bend. He was my rock steady friend. I'd never hurt him, yet here I was letting him become involved in an immoral criminal act that could see him in prison for decades.

"Change of plan. You don't have a week, Andreas. Four days. Then you're going and leaving me alone with Kat."

Chapter 9

Kat

Embarrassment had reached new depths. It was one thing standing in a room naked and getting whipped by a Dom you'd selected carefully and discussed your limits with. I had control over that. But this? Kneeling on the breakfast counter with my hands behind me and basically chained to the wall while wearing a wet, milk-soaked scrap of a dress?

I wanted to sink into the floor. Even more so since I knew having them do what they'd done – stared and treated me like a pet they had to feed, had turned me on so much I was afraid to open my legs. I could feel how slippery I was down there.

When Andreas excused himself and wandered off down the hallway to the toilet, I relaxed somewhat. One gone. Maybe now, I'd get freed. I braced myself for the evil I had to do, begging from *him*... Then I raised my eyebrows, in a hopeful fashion, at Chris.

He deadpanned back at me.

Shit. Did I have to whine? I was not whining. But I wasn't game to speak. Chris's suggestion of a piñata and the crocs hearing my beating had been ominous.

The stool scraped on the floor as he stood.

I managed a forced smile when he came to the counter and hopped up on it, sitting next to me with his legs dangling over the edge.

"You were very, very good," he drawled.

I blinked and tried to stamp down on my awareness of the difference between him, free, a dominant man and inches from me, and me tied up. It was electric. Chris was the epitome of alpha male. In the past, his pale blond man-god good looks had always steamed up my female sex goggles in milliseconds. I couldn't help holding my breath and giving my lower lip a tug with my teeth. Pure body reaction, I reminded myself, I still hated him. I did, I did.

His slow perusal of my breasts and the trail of milk and cornflakes down my belly made me both melt into a sizzle of goo and want to snap out something like…like, *I'm not your breakfast*. Noo. God no. *Need a spoon?* Fuck no, not that either.

Surreptitiously, I twisted one wrist, praying it was loose.

He spotted that movement and his mouth curved. "It's amusing, Kat. Watching you. Watching you and knowing I can touch you without you doing anything to stop me. Knowing you're aroused too."

"I'm not aroused," I ground out. "Andreas will be back soon!" My glare would hopefully turn him to ashes.

"You speak?" Gently he began to roll the dress up my thighs. I tensed and squeezed my thighs together. "Uh-uh. No hiding there. Open."

I glared some more.

Chris moved in and nipped my nose. Shock hummed through me as his other hand wrapped around my breast, squeezing tight. Big hand, hard grip, small pains that did *things* to me. I squirmed on the spot.

I hated possession like this – the casual owning of a woman bothered me, especially if it was *me*. But with his hand on me there, and the wrist bondage, with my arms pulled back out of the way, I had nowhere to go. Fuck. Hate you Chris.

Yet what he did fed heat into my groin.

"Open your eyes, Kat."

I snapped them open. Crap. I'd closed them without meaning to.

"I knew you were turned on because you've dripped on the counter."

Mild panic to mortified in one second flat. Knowing he'd seen my moisture coming from me... I stared at him. Amusement, lust, and the satisfaction of a Dom who's hit the humiliation and torture button flickered across his face. Bastard.

His thumb swept over my breast teasing my nipple as he added in a matter of fact way, like it was a done deal. "I'm going to make you come now, Kat. If you don't want Andreas to see, be good. If you're bad, I can stretch this out forever."

How did he guess Andreas watching would bother me?

"Good girl." He must have deciphered the consternation in my expression.

I argued with myself, tensing then relaxing. My nipple, desperate thing, poked up higher and ached. Don't tell him to fuck off, don't...because...

Because I wanted his hands on me. I throbbed in anticipation. Until he'd fingered me last night, no one had touched me there, skin on skin, for so long. *This is just a body reaction, nothing –*

Then his hand wormed between my thighs. I gasped.

Hand, pushing past my taut leg muscles until I had to relax. I shut my eyes. His thumb found my clit. The simple contact there made me shudder. I wanted, didn't want, but most of all I *craved*.

When his fingers traced the line of my slit and one, then two, fingertips parted my lips, I had to bite back a groan. When they forged up inside me and I could only kneel there taking it...my eyes rolled back and I arched my pelvis into the throb where his thumb perched, waiting.

Hate and want and pain as he dug his fingers into my breast. His thumb down there stayed mostly still while he slipped those thick fingers into me, then out and in again.

"That's it. Show me you want it," he murmured. "There's no one else. Just you and me."

I wriggled again, trying to secretly tell his thumb to move – like it wasn't his thumb, wasn't him.

He tapped his thumb once, circled my clit, once.

I let out a soft grunt of breath.

All of me was there, centered on the apex of my sex. Throb, throb. Him on me. The pressure, barely there, but I was so aware of it.

I wriggled again, pushing on him. His fingers stilled while thrust high inside, and my pussy clamped in on them...me panting, waiting, *fucking* desperate.

His thumb circled, once. "Say you want this, Kat," he growled. "Say, yes."

I quashed my rising sense of betrayal and breathed a choked, quiet, tiny, "Yes."

"Good."

After my confession he began to pump those fingers in and out, his thumb played with my clit in earnest, just the right pressure, just the right circling touch. I strained forward and his hot mouth engulfed my nipple, sucking on me through the material.

Unable to resist, I came.

I rode out the orgasm silently, jerking as waves came and went, my mouth gasping and open, aware he was there, that *he* had done this to me, and still not being able to stop.

When I opened my eyes, Chris lifted his head from my breast, and Andreas entered the kitchen.

Shit.

"What have I missed?"

My heart thumped an insane tattoo on the inside of my chest and I felt the intimate suction as Chris extracted his fingers. An involuntary post-orgasmic shudder struck me.

"You missed Kat having an orgasm, that's all." Chris let go of my breast and wiped his fingers on the bottom of my dress.

Andreas had seen something though. I could only bear to look up at him through the veil of my hair. Was that annoyance on his face or regret? Or both? Did he regret not seeing Chris…defile me?

That's what it had been, surely?

The dangling strands of my hair made it easy to pretend I was hidden from his view. I panted lightly, peering out with my head hanging low. I wasn't sure who or what Andreas was, but protector had been high on my list. Maybe I was wrong.

Chapter 10

Andreas

The little bay was deserted, as expected. Climbing over the headland rocks from the south would be a job and a half. Same for the rocks to the north. Kat and I were in a little rocky no man's land. There weren't enough tourists in Cow Bay to make visitors likely. Behind us, by fifty yards, was the wall enclosing the lodge – a small distance but far enough to make this seem like a different world.

Kat's leash wove across my palm then dripped away like a silver snake escaping. I'd sworn to Chris I'd mind her properly. He was off talking to Scrim about the recent power failures. This was the first time I'd been alone with her.

Although the battered little jetty only ran a few yards up the beach, it went far enough into the sea to make a great place from which to fish. A few sea gulls called out indignantly at our invasion then flapped off into the blue sky. Salt air. Wind ruffling in my face. The light sun of the early morning. The timber of the jetty underfoot. I sucked in some clean breaths.

Back there was different…dirty? Perverted. Nasty even. It didn't seem real half the time.

Below, the water tempted me with its clarity and coolness. I knew how it would taste in my mouth and flow crystal-cold over my skin if

I dove deep. But there was fear too. The teeth never went far away. I could see red in those waves.

Once upon a time, the sea had meant freedom to me. Now…it was a mixed bag of panic, leisure, fun, and pain. I'd long reconciled myself to never separating each of those threads from the others. The weight of the chain around my neck reminded of my vow to never let fear conquer me. I caught and held the silver-mounted shark tooth between finger and thumb, feeling its smoothness and the fine bumps on the saw edge of the tooth.

Kat cleared her throat.

I tugged on her leash, eyeing her and that tiny purple microkini.

Chris had retrieved it from a cupboard stocked with what he termed BDSM role-play costumes. The top was a barely two inch satin strip. The bottoms…I swallowed at how it showed the outlines of her pussy. The cloth delved up between her lips – she had to be dying to adjust that. Flimsy as a drizzle of rain.

If she'd had any hair left there after Chris had shaved her, I would have seen it through the cloth. That procedure had been something else.

Watching him shave her, with Kat strapped face-up to the spanking bench, had wiped my brain. He'd strapped her ankles to her thighs and tied her down so tightly she'd only been able to squirm her ass a quarter inch sideways at most. After he'd slapped her thighs a few times she'd ceased to do even that.

Fingers clenching. Her belly reflecting the overhead light. Her pussy lips glistening as he wiped off the last of the cream to leave her more nude than…nude.

I focused. *Ugh.* Having a boner while wearing quick unzip surf shorts when the person you were dreaming of was a foot away, not good.

Kat waited before me, hands cuffed at her front, for *me* to decide where we were going. Bemused, yet patient. I think she could see the wheels turning in my head.

Her gray eyes sparked with intelligence. I tightened my hold on the silver chain.

Through the gaps in the jetty timber, lazy waves slopped against the legs of the jetty.

"Sit." I pointed at the folded towel and pillow at the foot of the seat. I'd lugged this roofed bench seat out earlier. Even at eight thirty the sun heated metal. If we weren't in the shade, as the day progressed, the petite silver cuffs and collar he'd put on her today would sizzle against her skin.

She folded her legs and sat. Already drool wet the black rod between her teeth.

I also sat and rested my arms on my knees. The seat creaked as the struts adjusted to my weight. It was lightweight but the fringed canvas roof extended out a fair way, front and back – enough to shade us both.

"Hi." I nodded slightly and she did nothing except look back at me. How was it she managed to look so defiant despite everything? Must be the eyes. A compulsion struck me, to talk with her and discuss what was happening. "I don't know where to start...Kat."

She blinked and raised an eyebrow. A pretty, well-shaped brow like the rest of her. Wasn't I too old, and the wrong sex, for a teenage crush?

The last two days I'd watched the dance between her and Chris. He, aiming to take control. Her, dodging it however she could. She'd even kicked his shins at one point. I'd waited for him to flog her or something but he hadn't. Maybe he was waiting for me to leave?

"I have to go tomorrow. I'm sorry." I hung my head a second, and felt a need for something to occupy my hands. I opened the tackle box and began attaching a hook and sinker to the line of my fishing rod. Someone who stayed here had fished, or thought about it. My left fingers generally worked well enough for most things.

The rod and tackle box came from the storeroom under the house. I had my camera because the view here was to die for and I always took pictures. And for bait, I had pickled worms Scrim had bought at a store in Cow Bay.

I finished off tying the half blood knot, despite the fingers on my left hand going a little numb, and cut off the excess.

"I'm torn. There's the good moral me who wants to release you, rescue you. I guess you know that?" I smiled at her slight grimace around the gag. "He's warring with the other me, the one that's helping Chris – a man I'd die for...back against a rock while hordes of enemies shoot us chock full of bullets." I sighed. "I'm sorry I can't help you." I put aside the rod.

Shit. One-way conversations sucked.

And I'd lied a little. There was another me, the one that took over sometimes when I saw her and imagined getting her to do things she didn't want to. People said money made the world go round but they were wrong. It was sex. Dirty, nasty, glorious, romantic, soul-shattering sex made the world go round. When I was near Kat, the dirty and the nasty climbed up from the dark places of my brain.

The things that me wanted to do...to her.

That made me so uncomfortable, because it wasn't *really* me. It was some troglodyte throwback, some vestige of caveman.

I scrubbed my hair then crouched and clicked the leash to the leg of the seat before I reached for her mouth. At her flinch, I stopped. "I'm taking off the gag."

Kat remained still as I removed it. After I released the buckle, I let my fingers trail forward to her chin, sliding in the drool. Something, fuck, something weird about this grabbed me. Her helplessness? The look? I held her chin then let go. Even that small touch left me with blue balls. Not that I hadn't had those pretty constantly for the last few days.

Kat slipped her tongue out and across her lips and moved her jaw up and down. "Thank you," she murmured.

In the distance, a yacht appeared against the horizon. I made a note to watch it. The waters in the bay were littered with undersea rocks. Unless the skipper was insane, it'd stay offshore.

"You're welcome." We were being so civil. Strange, considering how often I'd imagined fucking her. "Water?" I offered her my bottle of ice water and watched her swallow some.

"What do I have to do to get you to help me escape?"

I shook my head. "Nothing. Because I won't. I can't."

"Why?" Her little frown begged me to smooth it out with a finger.

"Because. As I said, he's my friend." I spread my hands.

"What sort of man let's this happen to a woman and does nothing?" Though she didn't raise her voice, it shook. Angrily, she wiped under one eye, as if unhappy I'd seen her cry.

Good question. Reluctantly, I answered. "Me. I guess. Chris saved my life, years ago. A shark attacked me while I was surfing. He got me to shore. Stopped the bleeding. The whole way back, there was a shark in the water following us, or so they told me."

"That's it?" She rocked back and forth on her knees. The breeze carried strands of her hair over her shoulder, whipping them in her face.

So dismissive. Like it was nothing.

"It's enough." There was more, years more, of us being friends. I wasn't going to catalogue it for her. "He's not going to hurt you..." *More than you can take.* Chris had said she liked pain, right?

"Chris is a fucking sadist." Her teeth showed. Her eyes near glittered.

This was the woman I'd seen many times – kicking Chris, swearing, yet she seemed quieter now. Was she planning something? Did she want to appeal to me by acting sedate?

"I can't help you."

"Jesus. I have things to do, you know? A life back there. You can't do this!"

"Like what?" I was genuinely curious. "What did you do?"

"I worked with Child Safety Services. I've got kids in some really dodgy families who need me."

"They can replace you. Someone will do your job." It felt like I was the one signing her life away. What the hell? But, in a way, I was. By refusing to help her. Man up. Take it on the chin. It is my fault.

"No. They can't." She stared downward. "How can you say that? Just dismiss my life? I'm not disposable. I don't want to be his – oh fuck it. Can't you see what sort of a man he is?" Her voice rose. "He's an A-grade asshole! This is wrong!"

I felt sorrow, yes, and anger that it came to this. But…

Child Safety Services. I knew what they did. There would be thousands upon thousands of employees like her.

"I'm sorry. But there's nothing I can, or will do."

What would anyone do in this situation except say they were desperately needed? She wanted my sympathy. Kat wasn't stupid, I'd already figured that. There would be a grain of truth in this. Nevertheless, I was not betraying Chris.

She swore.

I frowned. No one was irreplaceable, especially not in a government job. Point made, but she kept going, cursing Chris and everything about him. I sighed and reached for the gag.

"No. Fuck you too. Don't!"

But I slipped the gag back on the way Chris did, forcing it between her teeth, and I did it up. When the buckle was fastened, I released her.

Silence, apart from the sizzle of the air heating from her glower.

"Uck oo," she managed through the gag.

I smiled, a little. There was something worthwhile, exciting, about my victory. Plus I loved the look of the gag in her mouth. Kinky as shit. A flash made me look outward, past her shoulder.

The yacht was still there, only closer. I snatched up my camera and zoomed in. They were zooming in on us, possibly. Binoculars.

And Kat kneeled at my feet, side-on to them. Cuffed. Gagged.

"Shit."

Inspiration hit me. And depravation. And an explosion of desire to do what I wanted.

I dropped the camera to the seat and leaned forward. My hand scrunched in her hair at the back of her head, buckle and all. I pulled her to me by that alone. How easy was this? How much control did this give me?

It was awesome. I pulled her up and onto my lap, her thighs parting to either side of mine. Her hands pushed on my chest. The leash stretched but made the distance. I was half aware that what they saw would be merely a man and a woman making out, but mostly I just wanted her.

The second before our lips met, I paused. Kissing was meant to be mutual, loving, a wonderful act. The very fact that I'd put the gag in her naughty mouth thrilled me. I loved the distortion of her lips, the act of surrender it embodied. It was grotesque and dark, primeval, yet to me it said triumph. With my hand in her hair she could do nothing except scratch at my chest with her fingers. Beautiful.

In her eyes, I expected to find that vicious challenge Kat so often threw out, instead I found them slowly closing. My awareness of her body expanded and I felt a softness in her muscles that hadn't been there a millisecond ago. I heard a barely audible exhale that was not a moan, yet it spoke of surrender. My hold on her hair just seemed *right*.

She took another breath and her thighs clenched. Her pelvis arched toward me, a tiny amount, as if she strove to disguise her arousal.

"You like this?" I said, amused. My male hormones sat up and roared to life.

Then I tightened my grip in her hair and I kissed her.

The gag made it interesting. As I took her mouth under mine, her lips strained as if she wished to kiss me back, and couldn't, not properly. I smiled at that. I could have forced in my tongue, instead I explored her mouth and her teeth gently. She answered with her own tongue and her breaths turned into a louder moan.

Gathering hair in fist, I tilted her head back further, kissing my way down her throat, biting the side muscle. Her squeaks through the gag were delicious as she writhed in my lap.

I pulled back, still close enough to feel the warmth of her ragged exhalations, to place my palm on her breast and feel her breathe. Slowly I let my hand follow the shape of her body to her waist. I'd never seen her respond to Chris like this.

I wasn't sure he'd ever kissed her. It made me wonder. "Are you doing this to make me help you?"

"What?" She opened those stunning eyes.

"No? How can I tell for sure?"

Aware now of my questioning and awakening from whatever spell I'd magicked up, she growled lightly.

"Tsk. Would you swear at me if I took out this gag again?"

A frown? Topped with a most dirty look.

"Jesus, you do ask for it. Now I know why Chris gets so fucking riled." Somehow, without me directing it, my hand had ended up on her ass, my fingers a mere slip and slide across her skin, through her moisture, to her slit. Those micro-kini panties were no barrier at all.

She tensed and dropped her gaze, as if waiting for me to enter her.

What in the world was I doing?

I hesitated and lifted away my fingers. No.

My fingers had registered wetness on her inner thigh, a long way from her pussy. And all from a kiss? Or was it the hand in her hair, or the gag, or just…me?

I stared down at her. Then I let her go.

This was so wrong.

But I couldn't wind back time and make it un-happen.

There was life before, and there was now. Now I knew I liked something more. I liked doing whatever it was I'd done, to women, or perhaps specifically, to Kat.

It had been so easy to cross from civilized to Neanderthal. Was I demented? I brushed some hair from her face, watching as she surfaced from wherever she'd gone to.

"I'm sorry, Kat. This won't happen again. It's just..." How kissable her lips were when wrapped around that bit. She couldn't answer me, of course, and I didn't remove the gag. I was memorizing how she looked, and I knew it, but couldn't stop myself.

When her tongue came out and swiped tentatively, slow as ice cream melting, along her mouth, I did nothing.

My heart went *lub-dub, lub-dub,* all regular like. That my cock was hard as rock meant nothing. Last time, ever, that I'd see this, so looking at her was justified. Totally.

I wished I had pictures.

Chapter 11

Kat

That afternoon, I lay in the cage trying to figure out what had happened. I didn't mind my new accommodation in a corner of the bedroom. It was big enough to hold a single bed mattress. After the first night when I'd stolen the key, Chris had tried making me sleep on his bed with my hands behind me. It had been extremely uncomfortable. Numb shoulder. Crick in my neck. If I had to stay awake, why not him? 'Sides, I liked keeping him awake.

I'd tossed and turned and complained all night. Seeing his red eyes in the morning had been worth getting a headache. So now I slept in the cage with a comfy mattress.

"Give me a laptop and wifi and this'd be paradise." I fluffed up my pillow and plonked back on it.

The men were off doing something to the power board, hopefully electrocuting themselves, though Andreas...

Tomorrow he was going. I didn't know precisely when but I could feel the tension. Everyone was waiting – me and Andreas, and Chris. He was waiting until he had me to himself. I didn't want to find out what he had in mind. I didn't want to be forced to service him. I'd been looking for a new partner for ages, slowly readjusting to the idea of a man I could trust again, whether vanilla style in my bed or all kinky on a St Andrew's cross, and now this? No.

Funny how he was holding back, though.

There'd been no threats, no whispered promises. Chris was losing his touch. If I had a sub like this, anticipating torture… I shuddered. I'd have mindfucked them into the ground. So simple to do.

Deduction: Chris was worried about involving Andreas. Could I use that against him?

The man hadn't made a real move on me since the breakfast in the kitchen. I screwed up my face and blanked that out. Wimpy bastard. It was obvious he didn't want to get Andreas in deeper than he was already.

Except Andreas *was* in deep. I didn't think he'd told Chris about what had happened at the jetty. Unless he was doing it now?

I'd done the ultimate in betrayal and disappointed myself.

I'd submitted to Andreas. Clearly, I had. Without thinking or anything, I'd just done it. I hated that.

Sometimes I responded to Doms I never expected to, though Andreas wasn't a Dom as far as I knew. An amateur. Maybe he simply had the talent? I had a thing about submission, about making any wannabe Dom work for it. The only other times had been after extreme S and m sessions when I hadn't expected it to happen. Once or twice with Chris the Asshole.

I chewed on a fingernail. If I let Andreas walk away, there went my chance of escape. I was going to need someone helping me, or a coincidence where the cops decided to knock on the door and explore the house. That was so not happening.

Okay, it was Andreas. How? The answer was staring at me. I cranked my ever-unco-operative brain into high gear. Logical step by logical step. Go.

If Chris was holding back from punishing me, perhaps he was scared Andreas would hate him if he went too far. I chewed a second nail. And if Andreas did hate him, what would he do? Or even, if he hated what Chris had done, mightn't he do something for me? Yes. That was it.

The house echoed with footsteps. They returned.

I had to risk it, had to provoke Chris beyond the point of no return where he'd do something vile to me that Andreas could not forgive.

I swallowed and eyed the door. I might like pain but there was a limit to it. Pain slut wasn't really my label. Be brave. I sucked in a breath. What could I do?

I played it by ear. When Chris told me to come out, I stayed in the cage until he hauled me out by the collar. When he declared his intent to teach me positions, I shrugged and refused. Even when he towered over me, took my throat and whispered mean things in my ear.

Jesus. Melt-time. Scary panty-wetting time colored with a little panic.

I remembered why I'd played with him in the past. I remembered how I'd resisted him then too. I showed him my A-grade fire-laden nasty look that could drop a flying bug into a screaming kamikaze dive. No one could defy like I could. Then I stomped on his toes.

The look hit me. No words, just the *look*.

Oh my lordee fucking hell.

He dragged me by my hair into the living room and buckled my cuffs to the top of the spanking bench so I was bent over with my ass out. My ankles he attached to the bottom rings on the Y-shaped legs. I still wore my light dress but no underwear and I was so exposed like this.

I watched him stalk away. From the way Andreas was hovering at the periphery – his face stern and arms folded, he too knew things had hit the fan.

Chris returned with a pile of weaponry.

The Iceman cometh with canes, and floggers, and other shit.

I could take the impact play. It was not being able to get up and walk away that scared me.

He rolled the light blue dress up above my shoulders, tucking it out of the way.

My throat closed in, but I wiggled my ass, almost feeling the sting before it happened. What was I *doing*? I didn't want this, did I? It'd been so long since I'd had a good beating. Maybe I did.

He started out firm and hurting. No preamble. Whacking into the backs of my thighs and my ass with something stiff. I screamed a few times but swiftly trundled into the land of the warm buzz where my skin hummed with heat. He switched implements. Each stripe of the falls of the flogger flared with a cutting burn that seemed to trickle down between my legs until I ached with a vengeance. A few times I squirmed as well as making involuntary sounds of pleasure.

I panted, draped over the padding, my butt throbbing with good pain, reveling in the afterglow. I shut up fast when Chris came around the front to crouch down and stare.

"What have we here? You liking this too much Kat? Want to come?"

Wasn't this punishment? I wanted to ask. I scowled instead.

Come? Hell no. Not in front of Andreas. Not when I wanted Chris to hurt me so much it was scary. Orgasms didn't say pain and suffering. Blood did. Screams did.

"No." I frowned. Maybe if I said yes he would do the opposite?

"I think you do." When he put his fingers near my mouth I snapped at him, teeth clicking next to his forefinger.

"Bad girl." He slapped my cheek lightly, carefully, like he was calibrating what worked for me. A gag appeared, dangling from his hand. As he leaned closer to buckle it on, I gathered my courage, and I spit in his face.

Demon face appeared. Blue startling eyes. Taut facial muscles. A glimpse of a twitch at the corner of his mouth.

Shiver. I blinked. Why the fuck had I done that? My pussy clenched.

With mounting dread, I watched the spit run down his cheek, the narrowing of his eyes, and the wetness on his palm as he wiped the spit away.

"You give bad a bad name."

I smiled sweetly. "I think you meant love. It's you give love a ba –" The bit gag was thrust in my mouth and I fell silent, apart from a few gargles, as Chris wrenched the strap tight and did up the buckle.

It was roughly done and he snagged some of my hair in the leather and metal. Then he started on me in earnest with a cane.

Wielded with smart, strategic blows across my upper thighs and butt, the cane's blows were as unrelenting as a force of nature. He wasn't holding back anymore, or not by much. I heard him counting, one, two, three, four. I cried out at seven and at nine, and at every blow after that until the numbers ran together in my head. Through the blistering pain I told myself over and over, you wanted this, take it.

And I did. I rode the storm until it carried me into the nothing place where the pain and the jerking of my flesh seemed so far away. I sagged, obliterating self, embracing it. Someone moaned and screamed, and I knew it was me. But I cared not. Me. Not me.

A hand rode over my body, tracing hollows and lines and a voice whispered. "Enough. Show Andreas this is more than pain. Show him."

A click and buzz was followed by a welcome ravaging pleasure between my legs that, within ten heartbeats, shot me into the place where lust ate at me, inexorably. The hotness of pain mixed with this hot throbbing hum.

My mouth opened, my eyes stayed shut. My toes scrabbled on the floor pushing my clit at my very center into that mind-shattering buzz.

Vibe, my brain communicated. Don't, mustn't...but the raw vibrations shook in and in, and spread, flooding me with an irresistible tide that sent me moaning and shuddering, that muscle straining, back-arching tsunami of ecstasy. I came and came until at last he removed the vibe, leaving me slumped on the bench, and blown away, in a million, million pieces, into the winds.

Chapter 12

Chris

That all-consuming kick that always took me when I gave a submissive pain was still lifting me when Andreas came over. His steps were quiet on the rugs in the living room. His camera swung from his fingers. A pro camera that one. Telephoto lens and all. He'd taken pics? I glanced at him then smoothed some more ointment on Kat's ass.

The raised welts were bright red. Touching some of them made her moan. I smiled, finding it hard to hold in the triumph. She was out of it, to a degree, staring down at the floor with her eyes almost shut. Kat would never show how much she liked this if she was totally compos mentis. Some dark blue stripes were forming low down near the crease where bottom met thigh, as well as on the back of her thigh.

I drew my fingernail down one blue line, absorbing the shudder of her flesh. So nice.

I could've done more, could've kept going until she was a writhing mess, untied her even, since she wasn't going anywhere with how she was right now, then done some smaller, focused intense pain, but Andreas was here.

"These are going to hurt like a motherfucker tomorrow." I ran cream down the welt and massaged it in.

Andreas only grunted. After I was done, he helped me untie her. I hefted her in my arms and looked down at her sleepy face. Spaced out, definitely.

"Is she okay?"

"Yes. Now you know how much she likes pain…if I do it right." I paced my way out to the deck, weaving around the indoor couches and the deck dining table. "Have you ever heard a woman come that loudly before?"

"No. But, you're saying she liked the pain before that? As well?"

I gently laid her on her stomach on the big red sofa. My hand hovered over the dress. It had gathered above her shoulders and her breasts. Eventually, I settled for pulling it down to her navel level, leaving her cute, if multi-colored, butt exposed.

Andreas cleared his throat. "Damn, Chris. That's fucking sexy. Even if you've turned her butt black and blue…and red. How do you *know*?"

I blinked and it took me a minute to figure what he referred to. "The pain?"

In the distance, the late afternoon wind was rustling the trees at the beach line. Getting darker here too, with the sun setting at the front of the house. I flicked on a standing lamp. When I stroked down her leg, Kat mumbled and turned her head to the side. "Stay there. Rest while we get dinner ready."

Andreas twitched an eyebrow, staring down at her with that slightly annoyed look that meant, well, that she puzzled him. I could bloody well understand that. Kat was not easy to figure out.

"I doubt she liked it when I first started. That was meant as punishment."

I thought back, remembering my reasons. I'd realized Andreas was watching everything and I'd scaled back. Besides, her behavior was unusual, even for her. Spitting on me? So damn provocative. She'd wanted it. Wanted hard punishment. I never gave them what they wanted if they were bad. Her initial squeals at the touch of the vibe had been thoroughly indignant. I was pretty sure she hadn't wanted *that* either. So making her come as well as giving her that punishment – icing on the cake, or on the butt, in this case. I couldn't help smiling at that memory too.

"You want to know if she liked the pain, ask her."

"Okay. I'll do that." He nodded. "I've put some scaled and gutted fish in the fridge. Are you up for cooking it? We should leave some for breakfast, though."

"I wondered how many you'd caught. Whiting? Bream?"

"Both."

With her collar attached by a long leash to the sofa ring, Kat wasn't going anywhere. I headed back to the kitchen with Andreas. "Show me what you want tonight. We've got mushrooms, leeks, cream, fresh garlic, and bread. I can whip up something good."

"Whip." He snorted and, as we stepped through, shoved the sliding door farther open.

I looked back. We'd be able to check on her from the kitchen. She hadn't moved as yet.

It was while I was sautéing the garlic, leek, and mushrooms that Andreas came up with his new proposal. Had I heard him correctly over the sizzle of the pan, and the surge of the waves and the wind? I stirred the food again, looked him in the eye. "Say again?"

Andreas had been staring out at Kat. He swiveled on the stool to face me. "What if you simply let her go? Get her to promise not to tell about –" He swept his hand across the air in an arc. "All this, you, me. Let her go home. I can see why you've done this. And…"

His focus went back on her, where she still lay on her stomach, bare-assed, asleep maybe? Pain took it out of subs and the breeze out there was soothing.

"And?" I gave the fry pan a stir. "And what?"

His jaw worked. "I can see the attraction, of her, to you. I can."

I frowned. That sounded more and more like Andreas was attracted to her, and in a deeper way than just appreciating her ass. "Keep going."

"Why?" He swung that dark-eyed gaze on me. "I can hear the fuck-off tone in your voice. I know you don't want to do this, to give her up, but you're going to ruin your life, and hers."

"You think?" More stirring. I threw in the fish fillets. "This, to me, is my life. It's something I want to do. Yes, it's perverted. Think of it as one of those life-affirming decisions. I want her, that woman out there –" I pointed with the spatula. "At my feet. As my slave, forevermore. Besides which, I can categorically tell you that you cannot trust her to do that. She'd have us all in jail before you could damn blink."

"Uh." He tapped his fingers on his thigh. "More than a passing hobby then?"

"Kat? Yes." I flipped the fish, inhaling the aromas of the dish. "This is like…" I stared out at her. "Getting married, only with added extras."

"And minus a few things like love, mutual commitment, and respect."

"Love, honor, and obey," I reminded him, waggling the spatula. "The last two are going to be mandatory. The first, we'll see." Funny but the idea of Kat loving me hadn't entered my equation. Maybe it should. Or me loving her.

"Beer?"

I nodded.

Andreas rose and went to the fridge, pulled out a couple of coldies then popped off the tops and handed one to me. "I've always thought love was the biggest part of those three. The others tend to follow. Don't you think she deserves love?"

"Deserves?" I took a swallow of beer, looked at him looking out at her. The man had some sort of fixation on Kat, already. I sighed. He hadn't noticed I hadn't answered properly and sat taking swigs now and then while I finished cooking and dished up the fish.

Tomorrow he was going. An emptiness was growing inside me and he hadn't even left. Yet him staying was a big no-no for me. I couldn't bear the idea of involving him in my perverted world. I was happy here. Not him. Andreas was honorable. He'd take a bullet for me, like I would for him. But there was no need for him to stay.

"Wanna come fishing tomorrow, early?" He waved his bottle toward the sea. "Not too early, of course. The crocs would be eyeing us off. I saw some of their drag marks higher on the beach today."

"Sure. Sure, we can do that." I didn't ask what time he was going. I'd drive him to the Cow Bay air field when we were both ready. I was going to miss him.

"I took some photos of you." His fingers wrapped and unwrapped around the dew-frosted bottle. "Of her and you. It was amazing. I don't want to ever do *that* to anyone, but..." He rocked his head forward and back a miniscule amount like the words were difficult to get out.

"But you liked it?" The moment seemed as taut as a violin string.

He breathed his answer. "Yeah. I did. I can't figure myself but I did. I liked watching you do all that. Most of it. Maybe not when she was screaming in pain. But the rest? Hot. Sexy. Incredible."

Shit. I stared at him. My fingers hurt from gripping my bottle too tightly. I had to get him away from her soon. It was weird even to me, but seeing Andreas fascinated with whatever it was that kinky scene had held for him was just too much.

"You're going tomorrow." That had come out snappy, but anger had surfaced from somewhere deep. "Make sure those photos you took don't ever get seen by anyone."

"I'll show them to you once they're on my laptop. If you say so, I'll delete them all."

Fuck. The trust he had in me and I was chickening out on trusting him. "No. Keep them. Just password the shit out of wherever they're kept."

"Okay. Thanks. No worries."

We were quiet after that. I gave Kat a plate of food and helped her sit up on a cushion, then we all sat eating and watching dusk arrive over the ocean. Even she was quiet. I'd found at least one way to silence her. Other men could work the flowers, the gifts, and the getting down on bended knee angle. I'd stick with turning her body into a jigsaw instruction manual drawn in red, giving her orgasms to die for, and getting her to do whatever I wanted her to.

I needed a T-shirt that said, *the things I want to do to you…*

Another flash from my imaginary graphic novel. Grey mostly, the side of a man glimpsed, his hand with a leash trailing from it. A woman on the floor, knees to one side, head bowed, with red lines all over her body. Plus maybe her shadow, a puddle of black.

I shuffled about the words. The things I want you to do? Shit, maybe just the image would do… Hmm.

Of course, I glanced at her, the real thing was far better than any T-shirt.

Chapter 13

Andreas

I closed down the photo and stock market apps, shut the laptop, and slid it away, careful not to put the precious thing in the middle of any beer bottle rings or bits of food. The fish had been delicious. I was full, tired, and more than a little disturbed at feeling so normal after today's events, after showing Chris the photos I'd taken of his big S and m session.

Though stills, with the photo right there on the screen, in front of my nose, I could hear her screams. I could hear her moans and the crack of the cane on her skin as if it was being replayed in video.

And, holy shit, I could hear those cute whimpers and gasps as she came for what had seemed like five minutes but had likely been only one.

Depraved? Wicked? I could take Chris being kinky but my own excitement was a revelation. I ran my hand through my hair, the curls flicking through my fingers. Same hair. I stared at my hand and the many lines crisscrossing my palm. Same me. But...who was I? I thought by thirty you were supposed to fucking *know*?

When I looked at her, Kat stared back at me. While we'd eaten at the table, Chris had let her stay over there on the sofa. From the fact that she'd decided to lie on her stomach again, she must've been hurting.

I stood and strolled over, feeling like some sort of creaking goliath warrior advancing on a slave girl in *Conan the Barbarian*. This was way too fantasy by far.

And she barely moved, lying there along the sofa. At least she'd pulled the dress over her ass. See-through dress though it was. Lilac this time? Purpley anyway. I could see everything, really. Worse than this morning. I swallowed, flicking my gaze from the slender arch of her calves, up to her face, managing to only vaguely stare at where her breast was squashed into the upholstery.

"Make room?" I gestured then sat at one end when she turned onto her side and tucked her feet up. "Are you okay?"

She nodded. "Approximately. Thank you for asking."

Nodding seemed infectious but I stopped after a few seconds. "I'm sorry that happened." Liar. No, wait. I was sorry. I just appreciated the view of her getting strapped down and made to come. Yeah that. If there was a sliding scale of voyeurism, I'd advanced a few notches above the average porn watcher on the net.

That I'd wanted to step up at the end and help make her orgasm too? A tied-up woman who'd just been beaten? Extra voyeurism points for that. I'd held myself back, but still, ideas counted.

Shit. I hated myself. Again.

There was a way to redeem myself.

I cleared my throat, wondering how it was that I felt awkward when she had virtually no clothes on.

"Did you want to say something?" Her voice lilted with suspicion. Her eyebrows crept up and she waited. And waited.

"I do." Chris was off having a shower. I had ten minutes more? Tops. Say it. "I want to help you get away, but I need to be able to trust you. I need you to swear to me you will not go to the police."

I had no way of being absolutely certain she would do this. But…Chris had been willing to go to jail. This was a lesser thing. Chances were, if we discussed it properly, she'd agree. Was I being a fool?

It's worth trying. It's better than leaving things as is. It has to be.

"Oh god." Kat swallowed, adding in a whisper, "I'll do anything to escape." Her gaze swept the living room then came back to me. "I will do this. I swear it. How do I convince you?"

Like at the beach earlier, the gray in her eyes seemed so pure. Guileless. Not innocent but without deception.

I didn't reply for a moment. I just breathed slowly, attempting to *see* the truth as I looked at her.

"Chris is my friend. You know that. A really close friend. I know he's been...wrong in this, but I'm correcting his wrong." The need to put some badass guarantee on this crept in and shook me. I tsked. Should I? Yeah, I should. "Do not cross me. Chris and me, we stand by each other. If you mess with me on this, or with Chris, I will not excuse you. I will come down on you like a freaking truck dropped from the sky."

She nodded again, wide-eyed. "Yes. I can see that. I understand. I won't go to the cops. I promise you, I won't."

"Good. Tomorrow morning, I'm going fishing with Chris. Before we go, I'll unlock your cage. Take the car keys, and the money I leave near them and go. Just keep taking those left turns until you hit the main road then go south to Cow Bay. Once there, it's up to you how you get home."

"Okay," she whispered. "Clothes? I can't wear these."

"Ah. I hadn't thought of that. I'll try to find some for you and leave them in the car. Okay?"

"Yes. Thank you, Andreas. Thank you, so much."

"You're welcome, Kat." I patted her leg. "Take care."

The fear in her eyes only reinforced in me that what I was doing was right. Giving in to my perverted desires was wrong.

Yet I fell asleep that night with sadness and guilt worming in my gut. What I was doing might be right, but it also was a deep betrayal of the one man I'd have by my side if the world ever decided to end. I lay in the dark in my room and put my fingers on my eyes and pressed in, hoping to murder the ache in my head. It didn't work too well. Dawn came and I woke bleary-eyed and sure that I was about to destroy something that meant everything for the sake of the welfare of one human being.

Like a man going to his grave, I pulled on my shorts and shirt then took out the two hundred and fifty in cash I'd kept for emergencies, and laid it on top of the bedside drawers.

I rolled my shoulders, blinking away the grit in my eyes. "You'd better be worth it, Kat. You'd better be damn well worth me doing this."

Chapter 14

Kat

When some noise woke me, I opened my eyes to see a man squatting on the other side of the cage bars. I gasped.

Andreas.

Oh my.

Some escape artist. I'd slept like a baby all night when I should've been planning. I remembered trying to think but my tired brain had shut down.

Andreas unlocked the padlock and opened the cage door. "You need to wake up damn fast, Kat. He's down at the beach already. I made an excuse so I could come back. Money and car keys are there on the bed." He jerked his head toward it. "The sooner you get moving the more time you have. I don't think the car noise will travel all the way to the beach but just in case it does, be quick. Open the gate first then start the engine."

I took his offered hand and crawled from the cage, sitting up on my knees and blinking madly. This was it. My heart accelerated.

At least my heart knew the situation even if my brain felt like someone had filled it up with hot fudge.

"Move!" He gestured, lifting his hand palm upward.

"I am!"

As I climbed to my feet, Andreas shot me a last frown then headed for the door. His black curls, olive complexion and dark brown eyes always made me think of a Greek tour guide.

Crazy words invaded my head. *Book now to get your next abduction cruise at a ten percent discount.*

Two deep breaths then I staggered to the bed. Aches had woken up too, and my ass and legs throbbed. Every step made me want to wince.

"God damn it." My ass could take a hike, to Greece maybe. I snatched up the keys and money, realized I had no pockets in my slave girl outfit and made for the door.

Something bugged me. An idea niggled. Think. I'd fallen into sleep while thinking about something, an important thing.

In the corridor I paused. Haste makes waste, even if being slow made Andreas have a purple fit. That made me think of what he'd made me promise. Something about that had been my last thought last night.

Don't go to the cops.

Shit. I stared at my bare feet. I liked Andreas, admired his honesty and that he'd risk his friendship to Chris to help me. I really admired that. Most people were douchebags when crunch time came round but he'd stood up under fire and come to my aid. But, no cops? After what Chris had done to me?

I let the car keys dangle from my finger. In the deserted house the jingle they made scared me. Frantic, I checked the hallway. No movement, no footsteps anywhere. No creaks. No one. Just me.

This was about me...and Chris. Not Andreas. Why should I have to compromise? Or lie? Why should Chris win? Because that's what this agreement did if I bent to Andreas's demand and quietly slunk away and did nothing. Give it a week and Chris might be back at work smirking whenever he saw me. Or halfway to China.

The laptop. Yes. Hell yes. That was the other last thought.

I straightened then padded to Andreas's room. If I was doing this, the more evidence, the better. Andreas had taken pictures. I'd watched him show them to Chris after dinner, last night. Passworded? Bullshit. IT experts could break into any computer given enough time. On a knee-high square coffee table, I found his bright red carry case, with the laptop inside it. Then I spent a few more seconds of my precious time staring, daring myself.

Go, chicken girl. Do it. I picked it up and tucked it under my arm.

The thing seemed as dangerous as a bomb. I guess it was. This laptop would help me fuck over Chris in a way that would make him think Hiroshima, 9/11, and the coming of the anti-Christ were minor incidents.

"Sorry, Andreas." I gnawed my lip.

I was sorry. I hated messing with friends and I considered him one. I was also fucking scared at what I was about to do. My heart stomped a clumsy tango against my ribs.

This needed doing. *Now* it was time to go.

Getting down to the garage was simple. They didn't even have the door locked that opened onto the stairs. I crept past the car. While still under the house and in shade, I peered out.

Outside frightened me. Open area. Past a stone fence was greenery and tall trees with chirruping insects and things making mysterious noises. The Daintree forest seemed a palpable, awe-inspiring presence. Another two story house stood inside the wall about fifty yards to the left. The gate was twenty yards ahead of me. Open that first, Andreas had said.

I looked down at my dress and could see my nipples perked up from the fear. Some super-secret spy person, I was. There'd be clothes in the four wheel drive, if Andreas had remembered. I went around to the passenger side door, undid the door as quietly as I could, and swung it open, praying I'd find clothes.

Thank god. He'd remembered. On the seat were silver-grey tights and a big white T-shirt that looked man-sized. They'd have to do. I slung the laptop into the foot space and put the keys on the seat. I dragged off my dress then, feeling terribly exposed, I hurried to pick up the clothes.

A man's hand clamped across my throat as he kicked into the back of my knee with a booted foot. I collapsed on that leg. My scream cut off. Fear of discovery rocked my shocked brain. Stupid? Or not? Who was this if not Chris?

I slipped, clawing for a grip on the car while also scratching at the man's hand. Was it Chris? It didn't *smell* like him. Sweat, acrid old sweat. His hands stank of engine oil.

He spat out one word, "Down!" as he dragged and shoved at my neck and twisted his boot round my other leg so I half-fell, half sagged to one knee on the concrete beside the car. Not Chris. I didn't know him. Grit scored my palm.

"Scrim?" I grunted out, venturing a name.

He kneeled on my back and ground my naked body into the dirt. Desperate, scared enough that inside my head was an incoherent scream of fuck, fuck, fuck, I scrabbled at the dirt with fracturing fingernails, pushing up with palms and, hopefully, legs.

Only his weight came down harder, heavier. The bone of his knee thrust, crashing into my spine. I coughed out air, sucked in more while wriggling. Then I opened my mouth, this time intending to scream full-bore, at sky-splitting volume, 'cause I didn't know who this was, what he'd do, where he'd take me. Anyone, *anyone* was better.

At the top of my inhale, he ripped back my head with a scalp-burning grip in my hair.

Instead of screaming, I whimpered.

Oh god.

Silence, just silence. Except for his breathing and a whispering, whipping rasp of something he manipulated. A bird sang somewhere far away.

He released my hair. Rope jammed up between my teeth and wrenched tight into the corners of my mouth, stretching my lips across my teeth. My tongue struggled to find a place to go in my mouth as it poked at the spiky strands of raw rope.

Efficiently, with no hurry, he found both my hands, took them behind me, and tied them with more rope. Tight. Several times he weaved it through and about my wrists then he knotted it. Though he'd shifted his knee down, what must be his whole weight pressed on my lower back. Pain was *everywhere*. Dirt pricked at one cheek, from my face being squashed into the concrete. My lips felt like they would split. My back was on fire. My breasts and belly hurt where twigs and gravel were caught between me and the ground. Already the blood in my trapped hands pulsed and swelled.

"That's better." His words rasped like waves churning over loose rocks. Then he hauled me upright by my hair and the rope around my mouth. "Now you look like someone owns you."

When he spun me and forced me back into the side of the car, I finally saw him.

Terror made him big as hell. Deep scars – one slashed down his cheek. Square face. Peppered stubble.

My eyes refused to close despite the smirk on his face and utter confidence in the way he leaned over me. With the hand holding my mouth rope, he propped himself on the 4WD. Slowly, he wound the rope in until it was taut and my head had to kink up to that side. Then he stood there, sedate, barely breathing hard, examining me.

Me, I was panting like I'd run a hundred yards, my chest heaving and drawing his gaze to it.

Fuck.

Naked, I was naked. At the small of my back, the cold metal of the car gave my nails something to claw. Overcome, I shut my eyes, mostly, eyelids quivering, unable to either look at him, or to lose sight of him completely.

It was one thing defying Chris – I knew him and his ways – it was another defying this man. Something about his rough handling of me, his casual violence, sent fear skittering through my veins. My downcast gaze spotted a knife sheath then an outline under his shirt, at his waist. A gun?

Sweat trickled down my spine. Cold snaked across my skin. Even the muscles of my face trembled.

"Pretty. What a pity I have to give you back." His mouth twitched up at one corner then he leaned in and gave a big, slurping lick up my cheekbone to my eye. He stepped back. "Be bad again, girl, hey? Then I might get to fuck you."

With his free hand, he fished a mobile phone from his jeans pocket and tapped in a number, put it to his ear while smiling at me.

"Hi, Chris. It's Scrim. Got you a present. Your girlfriend tried to escape in your car." He paused a few seconds. "No. Not joking. In the garage. Come to your front door and I'll give her to you. No. I can wait. Three or four minutes? Sure."

Then we waited.

He murmured small threats, all the while we waited, as if the words had been set loose now that he had me at his mercy.

"What's your name, pretty one? Can't talk? One day, I'll find out. Maybe while I fuck you. You think your boys in there are rough, wait 'til you see what we get up to with the loaners before they get shipped out."

What the hell was he talking about?

As though it were an afterthought, he pulled a long knife from the belt sheath. Slow as the coming of the night, he raised it toward my face. Light curled along the blade and the point, sharp as sin, rested an inch below my right eye. I strained to see it, as if by knowing it came for me, my eye could dodge out of the way. Useless. He had my head locked in place.

No single thing had ever frightened me as much as that knife point waiting…waiting for its owner to drive it forward and sink it into my eye.

It slid closer and I pushed with my toes, trying to climb up the car.

"That got your attention. Knives do that to girls, I find. You'd be surprised at where I can fit a blade, even a super-duper sharp one like this."

His words ran through my head in nonsensical threads that never came together. I was scared enough to want to see Chris again. Maybe even Andreas. Poor Andreas. I wasn't sure why I pitied him but I wanted to see someone sane again.

The tramp of people walking through the house above made him swivel then put away the knife.

I breathed again, in shuddering gasps.

When he reached into the 4WD and grabbed the laptop, my heart flip flopped. The laptop. Coincidence? Did he know…no, he couldn't. He couldn't know what that meant. Maybe they…Andreas, or Chris, maybe they'd just think I stole it. Maybe. I was so, so fucked, dead, stupid, *ohmigod*. They'd know. They would. I tried to keep breathing around the rope in my mouth but the oxygen seemed to go nowhere useful. My legs weakened and threatened to give way at the knees.

"Come on. Time to see your daddy again. I hope he knows what to do with you cause if he don't, I will be seeing you again, and I don't think you want that, do you?"

With the last few words, he'd eyed me once more. Then he pulled me out from the car, and towed me toward the stairs by the rope around my head and mouth. I shivered, and stumbled, going back to the men I dreaded seeing.

By the time the door opened and Chris saw me kneeling on the landing, I was numb.

"Can I keep the rope for a while?" Though he asked the man who'd caught me, his eyes never left my face.

"Be my guest." Scrim said, in an amused tone. "Give it back when you're done."

"I will, though that could be a few hours." Then he leaned over and undid the rope around my hands, took the end of the head rope from Scrim and pulled. "Don't get up, Kat. Crawl. Put your head down and crawl."

I sniffed, torn by my usual response to Chris to do the opposite to his command. Then my energy evaporated. I crumpled inside. Too much had happened. I was weary and I was scared and for once I saw comfort and safety in being with Chris. So I lowered my head and I crawled in until I was beside his leg.

"This is yours," Scrim said. "She was taking it with her." Something was passed over my head.

"Thanks." Chris shut the door. In the hallway, the echo of it shutting seemed muffled after the sharp sounds outside.

Another man stood a couple of yards away. Andreas. I could see his hand curl into a fist then uncurl. Next to his foot, he'd set down his laptop. "Hello, Kat. How…interesting to see you again."

I swallowed. Two men standing over me and I had nothing. I was all out of bravado and snark and defiance.

"I've made a mistake, Chris," he said slowly. "This was my fault."

The moment stretched and I wondered what Chris was thinking or doing but when I went to raise my head he pushed it down.

Andreas went on. "You're going to hear me apologize, and then you're going to hear me tell you why I want to stay. I hope you can forgive what I did."

Oh fuck. Yet I was giddy with relief in a strange way. I could hear Scrim going down the steps.

"I see." Chris took a deep breath. "Let's go into the living room."

"Can I touch her? There's something I need to do."

What was this? Again I tried to raise my head and was pushed down.

"You want to touch her?" Though sounding irritated, a moment later, Chris added, "Sure."

"Thanks."

The carpet was all I could see, and Andreas's feet coming closer. Then he wrenched up my head by the rope and I found myself looking at him and his very angry eyes. My mouth ached from the way he'd twisted the rope. I whimpered at the pain and at how he regarded me.

I'm sorry, I wanted to say, *ever so sorry*. But the damp rope in my mouth made that impossible. Tears wet my eyelashes.

"Kat," he murmured. "I can only think of one reason why you'd take my laptop. Shake your head if I'm wrong."

Confused and panicking, I pretended my eyes weren't watering, I wasn't gagged with a rope, and a man I'd come to respect wasn't spearing me with a *look*. Tentatively, I shook my head then froze when his face stilled, venturing into that territory of facial expressions where the apocalypse was just over the horizon.

"I know you're lying." His focus wandered lower and his mouth pursed. "Not getting the cops involved...that was the one thing I asked of you. Bitch, girl, that's pure bitch. Now you've got two men who want to beat your ass...and worse. Much worse."

Ice cold prickled across my skin, yet the longer he held me and stared the more heat mingled with that cold and gathered between my legs. My nipples hardened.

God help me. What retribution did Andreas and Chris plan? Despite my fear, I also felt relief. Scrim had gone. I'd do anything not to be in that man's power again.

Chapter 15

Chris

So many things had just gone wrong. I couldn't pretend I wasn't angry at Andreas either. I'd listen to his explanation but his actions had knocked me so off balance a small earthquake would've been an improvement.

Kat had almost escaped.

And Scrim had been face to face with Andreas, again. The potential mess from that, if Scrim accidentally said the wrong words, made my gut crawl. He'd brought her to the door looking like he'd dirty wrestled her on a bed of nails. I could see so many scratches on her stomach. The skin of her hands had been dark from the tie around her wrists – way too tight, obviously. Then there was the rope gag. Fuck. My balls tightened.

That part, I liked.

With the rope wrapped around her head and between her teeth, she crawled so damn obediently. It was also amazingly sexy. As we headed into the living room I couldn't tear my gaze away and did a last second dodge to avoid head-butting the door jamb. Behind us, Andreas chuckled. I raised an eyebrow when he too devoted a few seconds to watching her crawl. The sway of her plump butt would hypnotize most men.

"Stop." The chain-attached ceiling ring was above. "Stand."

I gave a small jerk on the rope to encourage her and watched as she sat up on her knees then rose shakily – her body and gorgeous long legs unfolding like some origami siren. If they'd had one of her for us boys to play with when we did Japanese at school, the teacher would've found us far more interested.

Andreas perched himself on the edge of the dining table.

The drool from the rope wedging her mouth open was par for the course but the tears tracking down her face surprised me. I felt, as I often did, that contradiction between wanting to cuddle her and shower her with flower blossoms and kiss away whatever had caused her tears...and wanting to do terrible things to her. Today was a day for terrible things. Today she'd almost left me and the need to hurt her was high.

I wanted cries and whimpers, and even more tears. As a Dom, vengeance wasn't tolerated, as her captor, I could do what I liked. I wound up the rope in one hand and wedged that hand across her throat in a *V*.

My voice was quiet but intense. "You are in so much trouble. You're going to stand here, very still. You're going to obey, unless you want to provoke me even more, and right now, flaying you with a butter knife is tempting. Nod."

In the past, it had always been rare when Kat obeyed me without fuss. When she nodded, I couldn't help that twinge of pleasure at the power I possessed.

"Put your hands behind your back."

Again, quiet obedience. "Good girl."

If only I could draw what I could see. The lines, the lines. I had an artist's eye but not the hands to render her on paper. Exquisite. Charcoal background with pastels for her breasts, her face, her body then maybe more fine black lines for the rope on her face. I held both her breasts in my hands, weighing them, enveloping them. "Mine."

She sucked in a quivery breath, her shoulder muscles rolling as if she debated the rightness of doing this.

Fuck, I could live on this elation for a week.

Once she'd settled, I attached the rope to the ring and pulled it through until there was very little slack in the rope. The piece of rope that had been around her wrists I laid across her chest just beneath her breasts, crossed it over at her back and brought it to the front above them. As I worked to create a harness, I sometimes brushed my hand against her breasts and nipples to show her I could do what I liked, when I liked.

I pretended to ignore her few shivers. Inside though, I exulted. No swearing, no garbled arguments through the gag – beautiful.

When I was at the stage of attaching the rope ends from the harness to the above ring, Andreas arrived at my shoulder.

"Need help?" Andreas rasped his palm across the stubble of his mouth and chin.

"No." He wasn't looking at me. The absolute mind-bending focus as he stared down at Kat made me tumble down that pathway I'd been avoiding for days. The man was spellbound. I almost ground my teeth. But, he was my friend. Maybe I could tolerate this if it were him. Another man I'd be ready to kill.

"You want her?" Can't have her, I wanted to say. Uh-uh. I should play nice. *Friend.*

Kat's breathing faltered and I scraped a fingernail up her arm, smiling at her predicament. Listening to two men calmly discussing whether they wanted to fuck her, or do other nasty things, must be unnerving.

Though I was thoroughly unhappy with what Andreas had done, I wasn't a man who dumped friends, or punched them, on a whim. If he murdered someone, I'd give him the benefit of the doubt. If he wanted the same woman as I did, I'd make myself listen.

"Do I?" he murmured.

"Difficult question?" I hadn't quite heard what he'd said to Kat earlier when he crouched over her, but he'd sounded pissed off. I had never seen him talk to a woman like he had to Kat. Never. Full stop.

While he thought, I finished the last knot above with a firm tug on the rope that jolted Kat and made her breasts bounce. Her feet shuffled as she adjusted position.

With my finger and thumb, I caught each of her prominent nipples and squeezed. "No moving."

That I'd forced her to move made me want to grin. I was like a boy with a new toy. I could do anything to her. Turn her fucking world upside down.

On both nipples, I added pressure, until she gave a tiny grunt. A little more and she whined and tried to escape my grip. Her nipples stretched out an inch then I saw the telltale way she brought her thighs together. I narrowed my eyes. She'd kept her hands at her back despite the pain.

For a second I contemplated feeling her pussy to see exactly how turned on she was. Very, I was certain. I could probably slide straight into her. God, I wished I could. I could almost feel the moist slide of her along my cock, opening up...

But Andreas was here.

Simmer down. I released her nipples and satisfied myself with watching her pant. Punishment first. Blue balls were staying blue. I stepped away, assessing my work.

Most of her weight now hung on the chest harness, making her tits pop out. Manipulating her nipples had made them nicely pink-red. And that downcast submissive gaze...

Pornography personified. The woman almost made me groan.

Shit. I needed to stop gawking. I stalked over to the TV and picked up a coiled power cord from the shelf. As I walked back to them, I let one end uncurl then doubled over a few feet of length. The weight was good. I flicked it lightly on Kat's lower thigh, making her jump.

Her tongue tip came out below the rope and again she did the whole body tremble. I'd barely done anything. What had happened when Scrim caught her?

"Can we talk now? Over there?" With a jerk of his head, Andreas indicated the kitchen.

"Yes." We had to figure things out.

I went round behind Kat then curled my fists about her upper arms – hard enough to make her skin twist. The hiss through her teeth and straightening of her fingers said I'd surprised her at least. She still had her hands clasped above that succulent, bruise-dotted ass.

"Is this hurting? What I'm doing?"

"Mmm."

"Good." I bent to growl in her ear. "While Andreas and I talk, you're not going to move, girl. Keep your hands where they are. You're in so much trouble that I'm not sure what the hell I can do that won't alarm the Piñata preservation society or Andreas." I flicked a glance across at him where he was dragging two of the red-topped stools to this side of the breakfast bench.

I took a step away then I made her turn so her body was close to full frontal toward the kitchen. No point missing out on the view as we talked.

Once we were both seated, I kicked back and propped an elbow on the counter – shifting focus between my delectable Kat and Andreas. Where the hell to start? I scrubbed at my hair, allowing some of that anger I'd kept bottled up to resurface. "Hit me. Do your worst. I'm guessing you helped her escape?"

He nodded.

"Shit." I struggled to keep my emotions in check. "Christ all-fuckin'-mighty, Andreas. Why? We're friends. I just don't understand. I told you, I'd rather you be honest. Why the sneaking?"

He nodded almost imperceptibly. "Yeah. You have every right to fucking beat me to death. I know I messed up but I didn't do it without thinking damn hard. Nothing, nothing, means more to me than you, mate." He stared out across the room. "I figured you just needed a chance to get back on the right side of morality. That she deserved freedom…"

I could see him looking at her. He was struggling with something. His own morality, probably. Right and wrong – such funny concepts. We changed our ideas on murder as soon as a war came along. Different circumstances and we'd be going, wait, maybe it's okay to do that when…if…

I brought myself back. "Why did you say you wanted to stay?"

"Because I'm a fool?" He stretched out his legs before him, leaning back against the counter. "You were right. I told her I'd let her go if she said nothing about you. But she had my laptop and there's no reason for that unless she wanted the pictures. She was going to the cops."

It didn't surprise me. I swore under my breath. "Though…if I were her, I'd have done the same thing."

"After someone asked you not to? After they said, agree to this, promise you won't do it? Because there was no way I'd have let her go just so she could send you to jail. I thought I was helping you. I'm sorry. Plain and simple."

I nodded, tapping the counter lightly with my fist while I thought. "And here I thought you were just trying to piss me off."

"No." He grimaced. "If she'd succeeded, I would have been charged too. Telling her to conceal what was done is definitely a crime and letting her go wouldn't change that. That's how grateful she was."

Time to end this. As if Andreas could ever be anything but a friend. "I forgive you." I put out my hand. "It's water under the bridge."

He leaned in and clasped my hand, shaking it slowly as he spoke. "Thanks. Next time I'll listen harder." He let go of my hand and smiled. "Doesn't mean I'll believe what you tell me but I'll try."

"Bullshit." I snorted.

Kat hadn't moved yet. The background light leant a luminescence to her skin. Naked and outlined in a halo of sunshine, she was the epitome of beauty to me. Maybe not to everyone. But I liked my women tied up and gagged, and at my mercy.

"If they were a friend and it was a vow made in earnest to them, I'd stick to my promise."

Andreas grunted. "My thoughts exactly."

I found the main point that bothered me. "But...you want me to let her go."

His deep inhalation sounded loud enough to pull his soul from its moorings. Out of respect, I waited.

"Not now. Not after she crapped on what I gave her. It's what I said before. I want to stay."

Where was this heading? "To stay and...I don't want an observer. That's done. Creepy bastard though you may be, I don't want you hanging about watching."

He didn't answer and the silence just stretched and stretched until I had to break it.

"You're tempted?" I looked at him from under my brows. Say no, Andreas.

"That makes me a bad man though..."

"Yeah. Sometimes you have to embrace your bad side to live with yourself. But if you can't live with that, you need to bugger off now. Run away, or stay where the big boys play."

I was taunting him but I didn't give a shit. He needed to get himself figured out. And I didn't really want or need him to stay.

"Asshole." He shook his head. "You want me to say it? Okay." He paused. "I want to fuck her. Even...watch you punish her. I think that's going to really make me happy. I know I'll find it hot even though it's kind of sick. But mostly I want to share her with you."

For a man who'd never been kinky, that was pretty amazing. Even if I didn't agree with the *sick* part.

I sat back and regarded him. "You're sure?"

"Yes. I'm sure. I'm very sure."

"I don't know." To have Andreas just drop in like this. Disconcerting. I was Frankenstein about to torture Mary Shelley. Batman with a naked Catwoman in his grasp. Sharing? I turned the idea over some more.

I swiveled on the stool and found our little captive squirming a little on her feet. Clearly she could hear us. This added another whole facet to things. Sharing her with Andreas? How would that make her feel? Even more overwhelmed? Both of us fucking her, mind and body. Eventually, both of us with the prettiest slave at our feet. I could see that happening in wonderful detail. I liked that. A lot. The things we could do...

"Okay. We can try it out. Where and when and how do you want to start?"

"How? Jeez. You know how to give me dirty ideas don't you?"

I shrugged. "No. It's not me. The one you owe for those is the woman standing over there all tied up...waiting for us."

Chapter 16

Andreas

No matter what Chris said, the ambiguity of this bothered me. I wasn't sure I'd ever figure myself out, but Kat attracted me like a moth to flame. Or maybe, considering what I wanted to do to her, I was her god. Make that *we* were. Call her a siren, a mermaid out of water, Aphrodite fallen into the hands of two men who knew just what to do to her…whatever, we were her gods.

When she'd trampled on the agreement I'd made with her, something had broken inside me. I didn't want to be restricted anymore by modern la-de-dah rightness, I wanted her. I wanted her in every way a man could have a woman. And I was more than willing to share her with Chris.

If anything, having seen how goddamn challenging she was, the two of us would make a good team at overwhelming her defenses.

I wondered if Chris knew how far I wanted to go with this.

"So it's a deal," I murmured, too low for her to hear. "We share her – but when I say that, I mean for more than sex." I cocked an eyebrow at him.

"Explain?"

"I mean we share responsibility for her well-being also. I'm not doing this to fuck her and leave her by the roadside…"

He frowned. "Me neither. This isn't a momentary fad, Andreas. You've stumbled into something that's..." For a second or two he studied her then he grunted. "She's my version of painting the Mona Lisa. And I don't think I'll ever finish this work of art."

"Painting?" Bruises stood out on her pale skin. "I wouldn't have called it that. I'm so glad Leonardo wasn't into kinky shit. But yeah, I figured as much." I struggled to say more about what I felt, and failed. I'd wait. So many words and feelings milled around inside me, and the ones I could decipher were mostly intrigue and a desire to see what it was like when you really did own a woman.

"No more calling this sick though."

"You're not doing this because you're sick and twisted?"

"Out of the goodness of my heart. You?"

A flippant answer.

We'd been talking quietly for so long that Kat was eyeing us surreptitiously, like she wasn't sure if she should be. I pointed. "She's listening."

"I noticed." Chris smirked.

"That gag." I shook my head. Why in hell did seeing all that rope on her blow my mind? "And us making her wait." I swallowed.

Chris chuckled. "That gets you going? And I'm sick? Tell me again why you're wanting our little rope bunny yours?"

"Rope bunny? Cute term." Why indeed? "Leaving aside the sexual thing."

"Yeah. Leaving that." He was still laughing.

"I want to understand her. She fascinates me. Crazy as it may seem." I grinned and managed to unglue my gaze from her body. She'd moved just enough to be partly side on, hiding that tantalizing part of a woman – the beginnings of the split of her sex.

"Fascinates covers a lot. So do spitting cobras on a nature program. Tomorrow you can go tiptoeing hand in hand through a field of daisies with her."

He was trivializing her. Me. I barely knew her but I wanted to know more. I'd never seen him with a woman he'd come close to wanting to marry. Did he only see Kat as an object to own? That didn't seem like Chris at all.

There was one other problem. "Scrim. He was with her a while. What if she spoke to him? Is it possible he knows?"

Chris stared. "That she's been kidnapped? No. I didn't see anything like that. He thinks this is deep role play. He's used to scenes like this. He'd never have given her back to us if he suspected."

"True." I nodded. It seemed right. "My other concern then is how rough he was. Kat has so many new scratches."

"Yeah." He looked across at her. "I've done worse. I'll talk to him. But she's not ever going to see him again, is she? She's never going to have someone open her cage and let her out again, ever."

What final words. "That's so medieval." I shook my head and frowned.

"Yes, it is." Chris put his hands behind his head and parked the heel of one foot on the toe of the other. "Makes me damn happy. I hope you wanted a slave, Andreas, because that's what she's going to be when we're done with her."

"It's just a label." I stood up and adjusted my jeans. Things down below were getting terribly constricted. "I want to see you punish her now." I cocked my head. "Or do we have to have a democratic vote on punishments."

He untangled himself from the stool and rose to stand beside me.

"Hell, no. Consider me the enforcer in this relationship."

Could I punish her? Hit her? I doubted it. "Technical question. Condoms?"

"I don't think we need to. She uses an implant. I use condoms with subs. And I get tested regularly. You?"

"Health tested before I could get the oil rig job. No time for girlfriends for ages. I don't do hookers. Tell me, though." Again I said this quieter than she could hear. "What does she like?"

His dumbfounded expression lasted all of a second. "Like? Sexually? Apart from some pain – she's close to a pain slut sometimes, apart from that..." He shook his head slowly. "I don't know."

"Weren't you a couple?"

"Nope. I was her Dom, sort of. Look, man, some of the subs call me the Interrogator because I get their secrets from them so easily. Her, though? No. I know what was on her hard limits but that's it. Elaborate bondage was one. A couple of times I did wrist cuffs."

"I'm not sure I know what a hard limit is. Not bondage? All that pale skin, those curves, rope looks so nice on her. You'll have to give me a run-down on the BDSM dictionary sometime."

"People have their different limits and things they like. They can change with time. But Kat with all her bratting and her limits, she was enough to make any Dom take up knitting instead."

"That makes her even more curious."

"Yes. She's like a Rubik's cube in a prettier package."

We ambled over to Kat and ended up one of us to either side. Wolves surrounding Bambi. I'd always been a guy who'd hold a door open for a woman and if I was ever on a bus, I'm sure I'd give up my seat, so why was being all predator-like with Kat such a thrill?

Somehow, I'd given myself permission to fuck around with her like this. Maybe because I'd seen, a few times, how she reacted to a man going all rogue male. Kat went soft-eyed and meek, well...mostly. She definitely spit less.

She shrank back the few inches the ropes allowed. A couple of red lines on her face... Bits of dirt still stuck to her. One deeper scratch on her cheek. There was even a row of parallel scratches above her nipple. If Scrim had been in front of me, I'd have been tempted to smack him.

While Chris recovered the cord from where he'd dropped it, I went closer and rested my palms on her shoulders. This whole idea of punishing a woman, in this day and age was an odd concept.

"You know you deserve punishment, Kat?" I wasn't sure what I expected. The rope was still in her mouth. She made some muffled noise.

Chris arrived behind her and from the quiver of her eyelids he was trailing the cord across her back or ass. "Lift your hands away, girl. I don't want to injure your fingers. Hold onto Andreas's hands."

Some visceral energy seemed to pass from her to me as she responded to his teasing threat. Enthralled, I kept my hands where they were, rubbing her shoulders, then Kat settled her hands over my wrists. This wasn't how it should be. I reversed it and held her wrists snug up to her neck. "Be good," I murmured, and she blinked at me.

"Look at all the dirt on you." Chris flicked the cord at her butt. Her flinch turned into a sway of her body. "I'm thinking we need to clean you up before I lay into you with this."

I studied her. Pale face beneath the smears. Trembles came and went in waves. "We could clean her up in the bathroom but here seems good."

"I'll go get a bucket and some warm water." Chris came up behind her and grabbed a handful of her hair. Her lips moved against the rope. That fucking sensuous rope. "When I get back, we'll clean you, and you *will* stay still for us."

As if she had a chance of going anywhere now. We were both several inches taller – enough to make Kat look small sandwiched between us.

He stepped away, and headed for the hallway.

So...innocent, those eyes. No wonder she'd taken me in with her trick. I watched her for a second then stroked my thumb along her skin above the rope gag. "There's a pretty woman under all this dirt."

Her eyelashes fell then rose. Soft veils. God, I could fall in love with her just from seeing those eyelashes. But they were mine now. All of her was.

A new thrill ran up my body, from my toes to my balls. *Ours.*

I'd said I'd take care of her. That freaky sexy gag had been on a while. Even if I didn't want to remove it, I should. I pressed my lips to her forehead. "I'm going to take the gag off. You're going to be good, right?"

Her grunt might have been indignant or just a yes, but I let go of her wrists and started to undo the knot. Though my left hand cramped up, I managed and unwound it.

"There. Is your mouth okay?"

"My jaw hurts." She licked her lips then said hoarsely, "I'm not good at being good."

"I noticed." Understatement of the year. "I think Chris plans to help you learn."

The man himself was coming up behind her, bucket in hand.

Fire flared in her eyes. "Him? Never. Asshole."

Over her head, I exchanged a smile with Chris. The woman was digging herself a deep hole.

"Oh fuck. He's there, isn't he?" she squeaked quietly.

Chapter 17

Kat

The realization that Chris was behind me hit like a scene from a horror movie. Sneaky. God. I didn't know what to do. What I could do. I'd exhausted all my avenues. Escaping had meant Scrim had actually grabbed me again and brought me back. To my own chagrin, I felt guilty over what I'd done to Andreas.

Which sucked. He had that stupid look on his face that said he knew I'd been caught bad-mouthing Chris. Yet, I liked him.

Those little black curls looping over his brow made me think naughty school boy. But he was six feet. At least.

Someone male with an erection, Chris, who else – I resisted rolling my eyes – pressed up against me from behind. If he tried to put that in me, I'd do more than scream. I'd kick his balls in. I'd...

I breathed out, mind going nowhere, feeling, eyes closing.

Inhaling made the rope around my breasts tighten. God, that was nice. Only it shouldn't be.

I hated being trapped even if I loved it when I could tie up women, or when I could watch someone else suffer. Yet, with Andreas to the front and Chris behind I was involuntarily melting. Every breath reminded me of man.

Stupidly, I pushed back at Chris. He grabbed my wrists and hung on even when I tugged.

"Let go," I muttered, teeth clenched, and trying not to hiss like a snake.

"Why'd you take off the gag?"

"I figured she'd had it on long enough." Andreas still had that smile on his lips, full Greek-looking lips…yeah, if ever I went on a Mediterranean cruise I was ordering one of him. "She's also been calling you an asshole."

"You bastard," I mouthed to him. That he smiled wider gave me unexpected hope. Why had I thought that? Just because he smiled nicely? I didn't understand my own logic.

I felt and heard the scrape of metal and the click as Chris linked my wrist cuffs. "That'll stop you clawing at me."

A hand lifted my chin. Andreas. In fake bravado, I twisted up one side of my mouth in a what-the-hell-do-you-want kind of look.

"We're going to clean you up, Kat. You have dirt all over you. Some blood even. Poor thing."

Emotions spun about. Tears leaked. The sheer caring I saw there in his actions undid me. I hated him seeing and I blinked madly. "I can do it myself. A shower, you know?" My hopefulness embarrassed me.

"No. We're doing this. You have to understand that from now on, you're ours."

Chris slid his hands up my arms, gripping them above my elbows. "You're like a blank page for me to draw on." He said the words to my ear, quiet yet harsh, like he'd sieved them through his teeth. "Just that one bird tat, here." He bit my shoulder where the flock of ravens took flight.

I whined, scared, praying he'd let go soon and gasping when he did. Chris was a little the wrong side of crazy, couldn't Andreas see that?

My world was splintering. I knew what they wanted to do with me, had known for ages but had barely gone there cause it was wrong and scary. My mind veered. What I didn't know was if I could handle it. My breaths came shorter, shallower.

I hung my head, tried one last desperate plea. "I can do this myself."

Their conversation came to me like some distant recording. I couldn't bear to look up anymore. I'd held out for days, kept myself sane by being angry at Chris and now they were what, cleaning me? I struggled to understand my situation. My…everything.

They want to hurt me and fuck me. The hurt, I could probably take, so long as Chris stayed sane, but…I didn't fuck anymore.

It'd been a few years since I'd had sex with a man, since I'd gotten off anytime except at the touch of a vibe or fingers or tongue at a play party from a Dom. The wrench from the warped relationship with Erik the Uber-sadist had messed me up. My heart had never recovered; my sexuality was, but slowly.

A warm cloth soaked my shoulder and meandered down my spine, while another gently slid across my face. The water ran in little trails down off my breasts and dripped off my nipples. Already the rug underfoot darkened from being wet.

"Hey." The finger beneath my chin encouraged me to look up. Andreas's brown eyes seemed full of sympathy but also latent lust. Without warning he leaned in and kissed me, his lips sliding over mine, awakening a burn where the rope had been. When I tried to respond to his kiss he moved on, putting small kisses on my throat.

"Stay there."

I gritted my teeth at his assumption but couldn't follow as he went lower with the cloth, circling, going to one knee and circling my nipple like it was some holy grail.

"Don't. It's not…" Not what? Even I wasn't sure. Not his?

Chris laughed. "This is where we're going? Why not? Let's fuck her first."

Andreas pressed his mouth to my nipple and for a moment I could feel the slide of his lips and soft tongue as he sucked on me. But he went lower, shifting down, wet cloth then lips circumnavigating my belly button, traipsing over belly muscles to… Oh god…my mound.

I arched, just the tiniest amount, not wanting to show I wanted him there. I should've known I'd lose. With these two men I always did. But that instinctive response I fought to the last until I gasped and arched more. His tongue needed to be *there*.

Fascinated, I watched his head slide, felt the tiny suction of more small kisses. God, he *was* going to kiss me on my clit. Then he did. My awareness expanded, scintillated, shivered into *pain*. Chris had bitten my back at the curve of my waist. Warm wet ecstasy at my front, nibbling teeth at my back. Teeth met on my ass, and I squeaked. He'd gone from cleansing arms and fingers to biting. The multiple sensations flurried across my body, twining, intermingling.

"No," I gasped. With bound hands, I tried to grab Chris's hair. He growled, and sank his teeth deeper, hanging onto my ass until I desisted.

I weakened, relaxing into the ropes, closing my eyes. A tongue met the divide of my bottom and slid down, nipping, licking. Two men down there, playing with me and I was their little puppet being bumped to and fro by first one licking then the other biting.

Fuck. Fuck. Fuck.

I stirred, lust rising, pumping slowly through me. My clit swelled. The throb of my blood. The rhythmic rasp of air in my throat. The silence when my body locked momentarily in its climb toward climax. Hands were on my legs, on my hips, the ropes, the leather…I couldn't get away. Loved that. Then, it stopped.

I whined, just a little. Though Andreas softly teased my clit for a second more, the lapping of their tongues, the nipping, ceased, and I heard them stand. Transfixed, unable to believe, and one glorious moment from coming, I opened my eyes.

Beads of sweat coursed past the outer limit of my eyebrow.

"Beautiful." That was Chris and he kissed my mouth.

"Yes." Andreas delivered a gentle kiss on the other corner of my mouth.

I was so close to begging. The ache lessened but never left me and I twisted my hands around the metal linking them.

"Eyes down." Chris pushed on my head.

The curse I meant to say locked in my throat. I hesitated then lowered my head.

As they undressed, they touched me – shoulder, waist, my hair, and someone's fingers trailed across the divide of my ass – as if they wanted to remind me they were there. Their clothes sifted to the floor and I watched their feet. Large feet. Men's feet. My gulping breathing slowed. But my heart pattered faster.

Men. No choice.

They surrounded me again, not knowing how fear was fluttering in.

"We're going to fuck you." With his hands at my waist, and chin on my head, Andreas's words drifted to me. "We're going to make you enjoy this."

I smelled him, so close, so warm. The muscles of his chest bumped into my bound breasts, stirring electric tingles.

"Chris. We can't both take her at once."

I listened as they discussed me, knowing I'd scream if they were violent. Knowing I'd likely hate them after if...if... I needed something. I hadn't fucked a man, or been fucked, for so many years. I'd run away for so long that I hadn't known how to stop.

Tears teased my eyes. I blinked them away.

They had me at their mercy. I hung on the edge of enlightenment, fumbling for an answer inside the mess of my thoughts.

Shock. A cock slid in my juices, from back to front, the full length of my slit. I groaned at the exquisite sensation, and at the man at my back holding my hips. Then I jerked my hands, trying to get them free. I flip flopped from awareness of rising pleasure, to panic, and back. I *needed* something, something more.

He slid the head of his cock a half inch in. My entrance opened only a fraction. But I was wet. I'd almost come, it was no wonder I was wet. Nothing to do with him entering me. Trying to. I gulped. Nothing at all.

I could feel him, *there*, in me, poised.

"Tight," he grunted. Chris had won the first go at me.

In a weird effort at misdirection I murmured a taunt. "You lost, Andreas?"

"No. Hell no." His voice rocked with laughter. "You dare tease me with his cock in you?"

There was a pain where Chris stretched me, prodded. Thoughts screamed in circles. Stop, stop, stop. If he moved in deeper, I'd tear.

His thrust jarred me forward and I bit back a scream at the hurt. Had his cock moved? At all? Had I torn?

"Fuck. Relax, woman. How can you be this tight?"

"You won't fit!"

He snorted. "I will. I'm big but not that big."

I choked air in and out, spasming still. I wasn't telling them. Not them. Not why. That was me. My past.

Andreas caught my hair, sending fire into my scalp as he twisted his grip.

Oh. I shuddered.

His mouth engulfed mine; his tongue sought mine. I answered timidly.

The hum in his throat spoke of desire. I wanted him, and in that moment I wanted the cock that was in me. I wanted it delving higher, fucking me, until the darkness made me yearn to get away. *No.*

"I want to do this again with rope in your mouth." His lips breathed the words into my mouth. "I want you, your sexy red hair, your body, your love."

Love? An anchor. A good one. I scrabbled to hold onto the *good*. I felt that foreign object, that invading cock slide inexorably inward.

Hurts. Hurts. Hurts. But all I allowed out was a tiny scream that grated on my throat.

"There. Yes. Fuck, yes." Chris rammed in, sliding, hurting me again, hitting somewhere high inside. A luscious heat spread, aching. Pain interwove with lust. My mouth was forced to bump into Andreas's while someone's fingers searched between my legs then found the nub of my clit.

I moaned.

"That's it, Kat. Let yourself go." His fingers were stone entwined in strands of my hair.

"Oh god," I whispered, on the verge of nirvana, of letting go...

His cock must be forged of iron. My walls clamped down harder as if to push him out of me.

Then he shoved in again.

No.

Mayhem erupted, rampaged through my consciousness. I struggled crazily, feeling pain where I wrenched at rope and hand, making nails scrape across my thigh. I couldn't get free, couldn't lose the fierce hold on my hair.

"No! Stop! I can't...can't –"

They closed me down, instantly – their muscles were bigger, stronger, their grip fierce. Drained and sweaty, mind swirling crazily but my body irrefutably theirs, I sucked in needed air. I quivered.

No pause in the rhythm of their fucking. Chris locked his arm about my upper arms. Death grip.

Fuck. My worries shrank to a back-of-the-mind blot then to nothingness. My thoughts were only of what they did, where they touched me, forced me, thrilled me, opened me. My pants became a litany of sexual grunts.

I clenched around his cock, my body bowing backward in a remorseless desire for more. The liquid slip and slide of him inside me spoke of my arousal. I shut my eyes, finding heaven forced upon me.

Harder. More. My pussy squeezed in. I was theirs. No choice. None.

A hand twined in the harness at my front, winding the rope ever tighter about my breasts. Fingers strummed on my clit.

The storm erupted, unraveling its quota of lightning, the orgasm seizing me, shaking me to my core. I cried out, mind blank as I gasped over and over. The cock in me slammed in harder. The man's body slapped against my ass, then he grunted and the heat of cum swelled inside.

I wound down, my legs trembling. I had *his* cum inside me. Distaste vied with the glorious mind-fog of an orgasm.

By the time the ropes and ties were off me, I was shattered. I crumpled toward the rug then was caught and held. Someone caressed me. I was lost, fractured. I'd given far too much. Would I ever find myself again?

Chapter 18

Andreas

When Chris undid the last of the rope, she collapsed onto my chest. I wrapped my arms around Kat to stop her sliding to the floor, frowning at the contentment filling me. All because I had Kat in my arms? I shook my head, despairing at understanding me, let alone her.

Judging from how much of her weight I carried, her legs had pretty much given way entirely.

Kat sighed and muttered, "He's still an asshole."

My chuckle made us both jiggle and Chris pulled a worried face at me. "What?"

I snorted and shook my head. "Later."

"Let's get her in the shower."

I lifted Kat into my arms. "Shower. Then let her rest somewhere? What you did to her yesterday, and Scrim, and now this...she's dead on her feet. You'll have to punish her tomorrow."

He raised an eyebrow. "Perhaps, though she's tired, not dying. Punishment is best served up on the same day. Leave it too long and the effect is less."

I bent and nuzzled her hair, inhaling. Whatever she'd been up to, no matter how exhausted she was, she smelled exactly like a woman should. The rest of her...as I paced to the shower, I checked that out too. With my arm wrapped under her in support, my hand was next to her breast. I stroked her there with a finger, smiling when she stirred and peeked up at me.

"I can stand."

I growled and she flinched and shut up fast. That flinch bothered me, even if I'd caused it.

Those lips were a huge temptation. I stopped walking and lowered my head.

There were rope indentations across her face and around her tits. Somehow that made her look hotter. Maybe I was way, *way* kinkier than I thought? I kissed her, exploring softly at first. The give of her mouth under mine and her small whimper made my cock stiffen.

"What the fuck." Chris threw in few more curses. "Keep walking and stop getting an extra taste. And don't drop her."

"I think this is my payment for doing the grunt work and carrying her. You're scheduled for the next kiss." It was an amusing concept – sharing her like any other possession.

Chris lightly smacked my shoulder. "Maybe I should stick a timetable on the fridge."

Her eyes seemed to grow larger.

I kept the kiss going with deeper tongue, forcing her head back, and opening her mouth underneath mine until she moaned and wriggled those hips. Nice hips. Those and the just-right plumpness of her ass, the scent of her arousal and Chris's cum, said *fuckable* to my balls in a universal language. I swallowed and readjusted her weight, regretting that I'd let Chris take her first. But I wasn't making her have sex again so soon. Not when she'd been ready to keel over.

"There room in the shower for all of us?"

"Absolutely." Chris grinned. "Don't take too long getting there." He set off down the hall.

Being kissed or released from the bondage, or both, had revived Kat. She struggled in my arms. "I want to have a shower by myself. I never agreed to you...either of y –"

"Quiet. This isn't a democracy. You don't get a say anymore. Get used to it."

When she swallowed, and her mouth quirked down at one corner, I smiled grimly. "Now you got the message." I kissed her forehead.

"I don't –" She stared to the side.

"Shh!"

Just knowing I had this woman at my command made my dick grow two sizes bigger and my toes curl. Funny. Her obedience pleased me, but the flighty eye contact made my stomach clench. I wanted her to look at me. You could see inside someone's soul through their eyes.

"Fuck," she whispered and took a ragged breath.

I let that one go.

Where was I getting this from? Was this me? A *me* I'd never dared explore? I thought about it as I went the last few yards to the bathroom door. With Kat it simply seemed right. Now that my anger at her dishonesty had diminished, I realized something else. If I became completely and absolutely certain that she hated me for doing this, I would stop. I couldn't go on…no matter what Chris wanted.

It would break me to keep going if there was only hate.

From the sounds of it, Chris had the water running.

In some freaky way, I was enjoying the fact that she'd not spoken another word, that she'd snuggled herself into me after giving in. When she took a breath, with her nose on my chest then hummed contentedly, it was like seeing the hint of gold on the horizon at the rising of the sun. That's when I knew. This might be illegal, immoral, and grounds for going to hell for eternity, but in that moment, I *knew*, we were meant to be together this way.

I sighed. If only that moment were guaranteed to last. I also knew nothing was ever certain. Doubts were just around the corner.

Going in sideways, I nudged the half open door.

The ivory-themed bathroom had a big tiled area with a glass wall separating the shower from the rest of the room. Mist rose from the steaming water. Outside a long, narrow window, the fronds of a brilliant green tree fern curled and tapped against the glass, shaken by the outside breeze.

I set Kat on her feet, steadied her when she wobbled for a second, then I guided her into the shower area where Chris waited. He stood at the edge of the shower. Water cascaded over his startling white-blond hair then down his body, the rivulets carving out the landscape of his muscles. For an accountant he sure had the badass vibe going. The man had a lot more bulk to his shoulders, chest and thighs than me but he trained like mad at his martial arts.

When Kat slowed and hesitated, I wondered if he scared her. I put my hand to her back. "In. He won't bite."

"Does," she muttered but after a moment of tension, where I could see the muscles of her arms and back tighten then relax, she walked in. That exaggerated roll of the pelvis only women could do had me watching her ass.

The slow up and down wander of Chris's gaze said he appreciated the view from the front.

"Stand there." He pointed to a spot under the shower.

Again she hesitated, though her head was down. Bravado, maybe. This wasn't the place for wrestling and from what I'd just seen of her, this weary version of Kat would give in if pushed slightly. So I urged her forward with little steps until we were both under the shower spray. Then I turned her body and pushed her into Chris's arms.

I smiled when she went without protesting. Tiredness or maybe she was accepting her fate, or both? Either way, though I'd have loved to hug her some more, this way I could observe everything he did to her.

She'd closed her eyes already and relaxed into his hold.

It was the first time I'd seen her surrender when she wasn't bound. Nothing held her there except for her own mind. Chris gave in to temptation. He wrapped his arms across her chest beneath those luscious breasts and began to caress them.

I grabbed a second bar of soap and helped lather her skin. Her nipples peaked under our roving hands. Every curve of her was smooth and soft and led my palms up or down to yet another feminine slope.

I knelt and soaped her thighs, letting my hand run down their length, squeezing her muscles. When I reached her feet, I played between her toes. I looked up at the little waterfalls coming off her nipples and the triangle of her mons.

Water flowing over a woman's body was an orchestral composition played by heavenly powers. Or some sort of fancy shit like that. I could've watched her all day.

Chris was whispering something. Whatever it was, she didn't reply. Since he was preoccupied, I claimed a favorite spot and soaped her pussy. Pushing my hand and fingers between her legs evoked a gasp.

She lunged for me. "No!"

"Uh-uh." Chris grabbed her wrists and she wrenched her upper body about trying to free them. The possibility that she'd kick me ran through my mind, but I didn't hold her legs, I simply waited.

I had a strange faith that if she didn't kick me it meant something…something good.

After a short tussle she quieted.

"I'm not going to finger fuck you. Not now, anyway. Stay still while I clean you." I placed my palm over her mons and waited for her breathing to calm. "This is mine. I do what I want." If I said it often enough she might come to believe me.

Languorously, I ran my fingers back and forth between her pussy lips. There was that restrained challenge in her face and in the tightness of her leg muscles and the wriggle of her toes. So I took even longer to do what I was doing. When she did nothing but glare while I teased her with my fingertip, I was satisfied. A minor triumph.

My kiss directly onto her clit made her squeak. I smiled as I rose.

"Have fun?" Chris asked.

I just cocked an eyebrow.

"Now you're going to let us wash your hair, girl." He forced her to put her head under the stream and she grumbled indignantly.

"Quiet!" The smack on her ass as Chris spanked her there, once, was loud in the small room. Water splattered everywhere.

She was halfway through turning and speaking a harsh word when she ground to a halt and stood there taking deep shaky breaths.

Chris and I shrugged at each other and proceeded to wash her hair. This was more fun than I'd thought it could be. When I shut off the water, a red handprint still showed on her butt over the other marks.

"How's that?" I grinned down at her while Chris foraged for towels in the shelves. The look she shot me was ferocious and I tsked.

"Here." He tossed me a big blue towel.

"I could let you do this, but…" I took great delight in covering her with it then drying every wriggling part of her I could find. The muffled shriek or two made me *tsk* again. When I was done and removed the towel, her red hair stuck out everywhere.

"You turned her into a witch!" Chris chuckled.

I shook my head. Behind the frazzled and twisted curtain of damp hair, a malevolent gleam showed in her eyes. "Uh-uh," I murmured. "More like a tiger."

"Well this tiger isn't getting any food until tonight."

Now, finally, she spoke, and it was low and angry and through her teeth. "I'm not going to ask why, Chris Wessex. It'd only make you think you're important."

"Meaning you disagree?" He reached through her dangling hair and took her chin with finger and thumb. His instructions came out like they were timed by a clock. "Andreas and I *are* the most important people in your world now. Starting tonight, you get punishment. Before dinner, it's the electric cord. Ten strokes. Before you are allowed to eat, you will beg for it by kneeling and waiting for me to administer it. Hear me?"

Her shoulders slumped and she nodded, in a short up and down jerk. I guess escaping had taken away some of her fire, at least for now.

"Good." He thumbed down on her mouth, stretching open her lower lip until I could see gum below her teeth. "Because if you don't, it will happen anyway, but with more force, more strokes. Remember, I don't give a shit if I make you scream."

I think my heart stopped beating for a while. When she added nothing more, I breathed. Sometimes Chris scared even me.

The reflection of light along her lower eyelids, were those tears?

If it was, she never shed them.

Sometime soon, I needed to work up the courage to talk to her, even if I didn't know if I could handle what she would say.

True to Chris's word, we locked her up in the cage with water but no food. Toilet breaks and water were going to be it until around six pm.

Breakfast was cereal. There weren't a lot of options around here. I stuffed another spoonful into my mouth, chewed noisily on the crunchy stuff and swallowed. "What's your plan with Kat? You have some sort of training in mind?"

He leaned back in the canvas chair. "Yes. You'll see. Repetitive things to do each day. Things that make her say yes in small increments so she doesn't quite get up the guts to protest. Doing things to her that emphasize our dominance. Instilling automatic responses to certain events. Maybe if I have to, some sensory deprivation. Mostly, you need to reinforce what I say and do."

"How long do you plan to stay here?"

"Four weeks, tops. Klaus is selling his half of the accountancy practice to me but he can cover for me for that long."

This casual discussion was weird, even if it was necessary.

"Isn't this the busy season for tax accountants?"

"Not yet. He's hiring a locum to fill in for me. What about you? Last I saw, you were following stock market trends."

"Still am. You've got internet here. Phone coverage." I ate a few more spoonfuls then pushed away the bowl. With Kat starving, my appetite was less. "I've been watching my stocks even here. Plus I've saved a ton of my salary from my oil rig job. I don't need to go back to work immediately."

"So you can help me break her?" Casually, he spread avocado on his toast.

That word jolted me. *Break* her. Fuck. I watched the green stuff cover the bread, thinking inanely that at least Scrim was of use running about getting regular groceries, even if he had a tendency to forget things we wanted. We had two bottles of BBQ sauce and no orange juice.

"Andreas?"

"Sure." I nodded. "Break her just seems so nasty."

"It does. It is." He sat forward and leaned his forearms on the table. "I'll show you again, tonight. In case you forgot. Kat likes nasty."

"To a degree."

"Yes. To a degree."

Not that I thought Chris would go too far, but his sadism unnerved me at times.

"I know when to stop, Andreas. But..." He frowned down at the table. "If you ever think I need reining in, say it."

The concept that Chris might need stopping from doing something to Kat had occurred to me. Him saying it though, planted that seed even more firmly in my brain.

"You? Reining in?" I tried not to look skeptical. "I will. You've got my word on that."

"Good. I've never had a woman who I could do anything to. Blood play, extreme sadism has a certain addictive quality, gives me a huge power rush. I should be fine." He grinned. "Don't look so worried."

Should? Blood play? I must have fallen into Picasso's world where the clocks melted and people ran about with faces like jigsaw puzzles. This was so surreal.

That night we had fish and chips waiting for us in the oven. Scrim had decided to buy takeaway food despite the fresh fish I'd caught and given him. The man seemed to like going back and forth along the potholed local roads. Perhaps he was practicing for rally driving.

At six pm the bugs were chirping out in the forest and the coolness of evening was settling in. Past the circle of our lights there was darkness and the strange noises of night creatures stirring. Leaves rustled mysteriously. A crack and series of thumps heralded the fall of a tree limb down through the foliage.

At least I hoped that's what it was. The crocs liked to patrol at night, I'd heard, despite their reptilian systems meaning they were slower. I didn't plan to test the theory by going for night walks beyond the walls. The forest could keep its creepy nighttime secrets.

The tread of feet made me turn to face the living room.

Chris led Kat out by the long chain leash. The whole visual concept had me swallowing. The collar at her throat. Her being brought out like a pet – our pet. Black leather cuffs at wrists and ankles and she wore another delicate low-cut dress that flowed down her curves in a rain of steel-blue lace.

As they came closer, I suppressed a groan. The cloth concealed nothing – not the peaked darkness of her areolas, nor the shadows of her navel and slit. Her feet made soft scuffing noises on the polished timber. Chris had her stop before me. Her head was bowed.

I wondered what he'd said to her before she came out here. Had he threatened her with worse punishment if she was disobedient? He must have.

Yet I caught the flare of displeasure in her eyes.

"Kneel in front of Andreas, Kat. Facing him. Then pull your dress above your waist."

Her breasts swayed before me as she did so. Agony. Already my cock was straining at my board shorts. I adjusted myself. Chris got to look at her naked butt. Maybe I could make use of her mouth. The idea of that, of making her take me in her mouth, nearly set me off.

"Give him your wrists."

Chris stepped over to a chair where a coiled power cord rested over the back.

She looked warily at me for a second before she held her hands up. I took them, wrapping one hand around those slender wrists then pressing them to my thigh. The brush of her fingers across my erection made me twitch.

"Fuck, woman. Take care," I hissed.

Slyness surfaced in the curve of her mouth.

"I'm going to make you suck me off when Chris is done, pretty thing," I murmured while I traced a slow gentle circle on her face, my finger dipping and rising as it bumped over the edge of her lips.

Kat gave an odd little noise. Was that annoyance or fright or something else? The fluorescent lighting cast such curious shadows. Whatever it was, it vanished to be replaced with blandness.

Chris came over and squatted beside us. With a hand in her hair, he turned her to face him. "Didn't I tell you that you'd kneel for me, little Kat?"

After a few seconds, she swallowed.

"Answer me."

Her chest expanded then she exhaled. "Yes. You did."

Behind us, the sea washed into the beach. So peaceful, those sounds. The salt smell carried a long way. I held her wrists down, waiting.

He looked at her sharply, until she shifted nervously on her knees. "Ten strokes, since you've been good. Say thank you."

Silence.

"Make that eleven. Say thank you, Kat."

This time she huffed but added a quiet, "Thank you."

"Ahh." He patted her head. "We're getting there. Good girl."

From the rigid curling of her fingers she'd still knife him given half a chance. I grinned and wondered if I risked getting my dick bitten by asking for her to suck me off.

Chris uncoiled and doubled over the cord while Kat nestled her head between my thighs. This was foreplay, I decided. I didn't dare blink. There was so much sexual energy bathing the place. When he laid the first few blows across her ass, she only gasped and shuddered. The next five made her shriek...and yet she raised her butt toward him. Only an inch or two but Chris saw it and smiled grimly, then increased the power of the strikes. The cord blurred.

Those two, she screamed.

After the final whack of the white cord, she stayed low, face buried, breathing with big chest-shaking gulps.

"Done." Chris wiped his forehead and tossed the cord onto the long red sofa before he stepped back in.

He ran his hand across the wheals, watching Kat twist and squeak. The man was a predator with his prey writhing under his paws.

"These are very nice. Each night, I will give you ten hits with whatever implement I pick, until the night you kneel and say that you are sorry for what you did, and that you accept us as your masters. Understand? Understand me?"

"Yes." She mumbled weakly, nodding, her hair rasping against my shorts, and the top of her head rubbing my balls.

I grunted. "I'm at one minute to lift off if she does that again."

Kat lifted her head and gaped at me. "Oh."

Her abrupt backward knee-walk was halted by Chris stepping in behind her.

I anchored my hand at the back of her neck "Fuck no. You're not leaving now. Unzip my pants."

After a brief inner struggle that showed in the way she chewed her bottom lip, she gave in and put her hands on my shorts. Slowly she began to pull down the zipper. Fuck. My eyes were growing stalks and probably glowing.

"Faster." Still, she was slow – one frickin tooth of the zip bumped past per minute. "Keep teasing and I'll get Chris to add some more lines to your butt."

"Way to go." He grinned.

Did I just say that? I'd threatened her. Goddamn. What was I thinking?

But she didn't look at me and unzipped faster. I scrunched my fist into the hair of her nape, angled her head back, and examined her.

Wide-eyed. Tongue playing with her lip. Fast breaths. Did she like that order?

I thumbed away some strands of hair from her forehead.

"Girl, you fucking kill me." I slipped the tip of my thumb into her mouth, pushing past her teeth, thrilled at the curl of her wet little tongue over my skin. "Suck on that."

She did. Several small sucks on my thumb tip. A pulse traveled straight to my cock. I kept my voice steady. "Now do that to my dick. Wrap those lips around me and suck." Fascinated, I pushed my thumb in and out.

I pushed her head down and watched her pull out my cock, wrap one hand around the base and take a single taste. Crap. That gorgeous tongue again, curling around below the head of my cock then licking up to the eye and poking about, sliding down the whole length of me.

I gripped her head in both hands and she sucked most of a ball into her mouth.

"Jesus." I half-closed my eyes. Her saliva cooled on my dick in contrast to her hot little mouth as she went up and down the shaft and the head, intent on painting me with her drool.

Then there were her teeth. I'd been worried about biting. Seemed like I was right, for the wrong reasons.

"Careful," I growled when she pulled at the skin below the head.

I'd had enough. Her open mouth was close enough. I plunged my fingers deeper into her hair and twisted then directed her mouth until my cock was prodding her for entry.

She whimpered once but I shoved her down onto me, pleased at the muffled sound she made when I was inches in. I sat up and for a while I fucked her mouth, going deeper, hearing the slick sounds as my cock rode on her mouth moisture.

"That's it, Kat. Be my little mouth whore. Fuck, that's good." The throb built slow and steady, peaking each time I drove all the way in. She was adapting to my rhythm, grabbing air when she could.

On a whim, I looked up at Chris while in as deep as she'd let me in. A couple of inches more and I'd be balls deep. "Damn! I've never…" The power rush from this was immense.

He smirked then went to one knee. "Let's get her really helpless."

After making a funny choking noise while still on my dick, Kat tried to get up. I grunted at the bolt of sensation. My cock pulsed, and my toes curled, but I kept my grip on her hair. She got nowhere as Chris did what he had when we fucked her, locked her upper arms together with his arm.

I pulled out to let her drag in a breath. Her eyes had rolled up when he'd locked her down. "You like that?"

She gagged and spat out some saliva but seemed oblivious to my question.

Well, I liked fucking her mouth. This time she put up no resistance when I plunged in all the way to the back of her throat. The explosion came within seconds, my cock jerking as I came way down inside her throat. I pulled her off and listened to her swallow rapidly then suck in a long spluttering lungful.

I sagged back in the chair, petting her. *This* was ownership. Seeing her lying there in my lap with her face covered in drool and tears, and her mouth still open from being fucked.

My heart stumbled back into a slower rhythm. I leaned up then cradled her and kissed her softly on her forehead. "Thank you."

Though Chris shook his head at me, I gave him a lopsided grin and a shrug. "I'm learning too, you know. We can't all be experts at the slave talk."

That set him off laughing. Good to see – to know he still had that sense of humor.

Later that night Chris was intent on putting her back in the cage to sleep. Such a pity. I convinced him to allow her into his bed to be cuddled for a half hour or so. It was late, nearly eleven, and we were all tired, but I was determined to find out more about Kat.

She was on the quilt cover between us, wrists cuffed together, and not even wearing a dress this time, only panties and a bikini top. Wearing a dress in the cage wasn't too practical. When she crawled the dress caught underneath.

In the light from the bedside lamp, I studied the swirls and specks in her gray eyes.

From the buzz of his snore, Chris seemed to be asleep already.

"Thank you," she whispered.

"For?"

Her shoulder rolled as she shrugged. "Letting me up here. The mattress in the cage is uncomfortable."

I drew in a breath, thinking, stirring the curls of her hair where they fanned across the pillow. "Generous of you. I think I'd be trying to spit roast me, if I was you. Are you trying to get on my good side?"

Her eyelids flickered closed, then she opened them again, "I'm having trouble hating you. You seem...nice, apart from being *his* friend."

I wondered how genuine that statement was.

I reached down to play with her hands, running my fingertips over the sides of her fingers. So tiny, so feminine. "Not going there. I figured you needed human contact that wasn't just sex and ordering about. Cuddling is good for the soul. People need to touch people in a loving way or their immune systems go downhill and they curl up into a ball and fade away."

She smiled, watching my fingers toy with hers. "I'm glad you didn't want me to fade away."

"I might have done this for any woman Chris decided to keep."

Kat paused to study me. "I guess you might, at that. You're too good to be here. You should run away. Go, while you can. This won't end well. I'm going to make sure it doesn't."

Amazing. "Are you threatening us? Seriously? With him behind you? After tonight?"

That shut her down. She looked at her wrists. This time I was sure those were tears reflecting on her eyelids. "Hey. No crying allowed."

She coughed and swallowed. "You're fucking kidding me?"

"No. I'm not." Face what you did, man. "Just because I made you give me a blow job you doesn't mean I want you crying. The opposite, in fact."

"Tough shit." She sniffled. "We don't always get what we want."

I narrowed my eyes. "I did. I wanted you." My heart did a hard tattoo, reminding me of her attractions. Lying as she was, things were squashed together. I glanced at her cleavage then ran my fingers down that sexy valley and along beneath her breast. "I got you."

"Still can't stop me crying."

"Huh." I kissed her softly then pulled away. "Tell me about you. Tell me…" I needed to know. I plunged into the deep end. "Tell me why you had bondage as something you wouldn't do and yet whenever Chris and I hold you down, you react…well."

Like some sort of arousal button that had seemed to be. I was curious. I hadn't seen that happen before. Maybe I'd just needed to try it on a girlfriend?

Kat went quiet for a long time before she muttered, "Fuck. You don't get to know everything about me. You just don't."

"True. It's up to you. You can keep as many secrets in your head as you like."

I waited while she took some deep breaths and blinked away more tears then raised my eyebrows.

"I had a boyfriend, a Dom. I thought –" She twisted her mouth. "He was like the best at first. Knew all my buttons to press, I kneeled at his feet, adored him, and then I went home with him and I became his slave. Voluntarily. Things changed in a way that made me doubt what happened. I thought when things went wrong, when he found fault with me, that it was automatically my fault. But for six months he used me like some girl who was his experiment at mind control. I know now it was abuse, not kink. Getting out was like escaping from a prison camp."

"Go on." I pulled down her top on one side and played with her aerola.

"Hey. You can't expect me to –"

"Keep going." I ran my nail around the circumference and smiled at how her nipple popped up.

Kat wriggled. "Stop doing that."

"No."

She frowned. "Erik... He used to like to tie me up and put a knife to my eye." She made a funny choked sound then paused as if suddenly aware she was telling me too much. She twitched her eyes sideways. "Don't tell *him* that. Please?"

"I won't."

Chris had stopped snoring but I wasn't pointing that out.

"After him, I wanted to still be involved in the BDSM community, but I just couldn't bring myself to do some of the things I...I used to..." Kat's lips twitched.

She was scared to, in other words. This was a revelation. If I could just be sure of what to do with it.

"Like?"

"What do you mean?"

She seemed to be being deliberately dense. Or was I reading something in that wasn't there?

"Like what didn't you do?"

"I don't know I want to tell you."

I screwed up my mouth. "You already admitted one of them."

"Huh." She paused a long while and, when she spoke, some of her words seemed as if they stuck in her throat. "I still do pain. It helps me, if anything. I just didn't do anything where I felt trapped, or heavy dominance or..."

I waited.

"Did you enjoy it with us?"

Thunk. The very air seemed to die. Wrong thing to ask. Obviously.

"I said enough. Why did I say that?" She shook her head fiercely against the pillow. "Why? To you?"

I kept my hand on her but let her outburst go.

She'd liked it. I was sure. But was all this reason enough to do what we did to her? Making her do kinky stuff she'd become scared to try? No, of course not. Chris and I were keeping her here just because we wanted to and we could. I took a breath. We were kidnappers, and...we were rapists. I hated that word but it was true.

I put my hand to her eye and drew a wisp of a line under her eyebrow, imagining how cruel a man must be to put a knife there when he knew it terrified her. "I like you," I said softly.

"You like me?" She coughed out a laugh. "Andreas, you are a one of a kind. I guess…I like you too."

"Guess?"

She shrugged. "In the circumstances, I think that's pretty good."

Not the best answer but she had reasons to be coy.

If she ever truly showed she hated me, I was leaving so fast I'd have burn marks from the air friction. If that meant leaving her with Chris, so be it. Though since I wouldn't help her escape, and I would never betray him, I'd be caught between two bad decisions.

Shit. I'd cross that bridge if I ever came to it. The flip side – if she ever truly showed she cared for me, I was never ever going to leave her.

Chapter 19

Chris

I listened to Andreas and Kat softly talking for a long while, about her past and sometimes about his. I knew he was touching her and from the small movements of her body that it aroused her. Some of what she told him, I knew. Some things surprised me. I'd known of Erik, but not of how he'd affected her. The man was a respected Dom though he'd left town ages ago.

Maybe that's why she'd never said anything about him? Maybe Kat had been too traumatized to say? It explained her behavior, gave me ideas on how to train her. I'd have to be careful with knives. I'd be careful, full stop. Total panic was never my goal.

Drifting in and out of sleep made it difficult to be certain of the time. I couldn't see the clock but their talking surely went on past midnight. Andreas finally helped her to the cage and went to his bedroom.

I lay there fully awake, listening to her move about to get comfortable, and to the swish and rattle of trees outside. The wind had picked up. Perhaps it would rain tomorrow? The air smelled damp.

I replayed what had just happened.

The more I'd listened to them, the more my chest had hurt, like someone had stuck a claw in me and was slowly extracting strings of my flesh through the incision. Why? Annoyance? Jealousy? Maybe a bit of anger even?

I thought I'd adapted to Andreas asking to share her with me. Now, though, after he quizzed her like some guy on a romantic date – fuck. I was envious. I never intended for love to enter into the equation between Kat and me, it wasn't realistic. No matter what I'd said to Andreas. Devotion, submission, yes. Not real romantic, gooey love.

Yet here he was, heading down that path, or that's how it seemed.

I knew he wasn't going to run off with her. Not Andreas. Not physically. But he was, in a way, stealing a part of Kat. It fucking bugged me.

Let it be.

I turned over and punched the pillow into shape. Then I closed my eyes and made sleep my bitch.

When I checked my emails in the afternoon, there was one from Vetrov.

I heard about the attempt to leave prematurely.

Damn. That would be Scrim reporting about Kat. What else would the man do except report it to Vetrov?

The chat icon was on so I logged in.

C: It won't happen again.

V: Your friend was a risk. He still may be. Though less so now. I gather he is also helping you with training?

Scrim was good at watching.

C: Yes, he is.

V: Good. You are almost family. He is not. Remember that.

I loaned the house to you on the proviso there would be no risk. I tell you this as a longtime friend. If the incident is repeated the person will accompany my next shipment. I cannot afford risk. Understood?

Crap. I wiped my hand over my head, smoothing down my short hair, and dug my nails into my scalp for a second. Steady.

C: Understood.

I thought a moment, my mouth dry as dust. I'd rather a MMA bout than this conversation. The man was talking about taking away Kat and sending her wherever the fuck Vetrov sent his sex slave shipments. Overseas, somewhere, I was fairly certain. I wiped my hands on my shorts.

C: *Everything will be fine.*

V: *Yes. It will be. Expect a shipment in the next week or two. Stay out of their way and they will stay out of yours.*

A shipment? What the hell? That had never been mentioned before. I'd have to check with Scrim.

If there were somewhere else I could have gone to that was safe, I would've gone ASAP.

Andreas would be the main problem – keeping him oblivious of the human trafficking going on. Shit. I sat a while, staring at nothing. I'd have to lie to him. More than I had. So far it had been by omission.

Shit, shit, shit.

Why hadn't Vetrov told me about this shipment? I guess, in his business, things might not be certain, or run on timetables.

For years I'd kept separate from this, ignored the knowledge David had accidentally tossed about on those drunken sessions. Now, I was going to have to confront something I'd heard stories about. I'd buried it, walled it off. This was the cancer inside of me that I'd pretended wasn't there. One of its tentacles had finally wriggled out and was waving about in daylight. Black, dirty, sickening – a part of me. Fuck.

I could've done without this.

Once upon a time, I'd wanted to do something but I hadn't. I'd gone back and forth, back and forth, swearing at myself. But I'd never done anything. I'd been afraid. Afraid both of what might be happening to the girls, and of how much that lured me.

* * *

I wriggled my back into a better spot on the beach lounge, drank the last inch of orange juice, and set down the glass to the merry clink of the ice cubes. The sand grated under the buried plastic legs. A few miles out, the sky was a porridge of a thick slate gray and the sea reflected the darkness. Closer in, at the sea's edge, small glassy waves curled in like nature's clockwork. The water was a blue so clear that even from twenty yards back, I could see fish flitting and curving through the water.

A thunderstorm hovered out there, maybe thinking about rolling landward.

Kat lay on her back before us on a towel. Her body shimmered with light and sunscreen. When she shifted in any way, things did a dance – she was a living wet dream from a porn site. Anticipation was giving me the biggest hard-on.

Andreas was flaked out beside me on another of the long, white lounges. Plenty of time to move back to the lodge if we had to. An hour of sunbaking left in the afternoon. The beach was still a great place to be.

Vetrov could go fuck himself. Compartmentalizing was the answer to keeping life under control.

I'd taken precautions. Kat's ankle cuffs were joined with a chain and Andreas had her long leash. No one could see us, and anyway, no one would think anything except that we were kinky. Kink wasn't illegal. Though the iridescent bikini I'd given Kat to wear should be.

I'd almost like her to try getting away again. It'd give me an excuse to get creative.

Andreas's lounge was semi-reclined. He cranked himself up higher, on one elbow. "Fuck. That's enough. I'm warmed up enough."

"The sun?" I shaded my eyes with a hand.

"No. Her. Time to catch a mermaid." Andreas tugged on the leash making Kat look up, startled. Then he began to reel in the leash. The metal tinkled as it knocked on the lounge. "Come here, girl. I need you to sit on my lap."

From the small mountain peaking up Andreas's shorts, the man was in a bad way.

Kat had a crinkle on her forehead that came and went. Would she do this? When she stayed put, I sat up and added some tension to the leash.

"Move. Unless you want to test out some of the more gruesome toys I found, out here, in the open?" I gave her my best mean stare but found I was hoping she'd defy me. Doing stuff to her after she was bad seemed better than just doing stuff, full stop.

"I got it," Andreas growled and hauled on her even more until, half-pouting, half-frowning, she lurched toward us.

"Go for it." I lay back down, smiling. "You're a quick study."

Watching her resist just enough to delay the inevitable, electrified me. I compared this to her previous performances. We were getting somewhere. She was truly my work of art in human flesh and mind. I'd never forget her mind. Getting inside there was as important to me as getting inside her pants.

With a few more tugs, he made Kat crawl up the lounge until she straddled his lap. To either side, her knees rested on the blue padding. The ankle chain would be cutting into him.

"Key?" He held out his hand for it.

She wasn't going anywhere while sitting on him with me inches away. I took the key off my neck and gave it to him so he could undo the ankle chain then looped it back around my neck.

Andreas caressed her cheek with his left, leash-holding hand. "Hello, pretty thing." His other hand, he slid between her legs, two fingers distinctly pressing upward, back and forth, working the bikini into her slit. She squeaked in one involuntary breath then bit down on her lip, as if trying not to look aroused.

I smiled and turned over onto my side so I could watch properly. Already the swell of her labia pushed out the cloth. "You're more adventurous than I remember. Outdoor sex?"

"Mmm. What gave you that idea?" His finger sneaked aside the cloth and did that little dance sideways that said he sought her entrance. "I haven't been in here yet, have I, Kat?"

His finger sank in an inch, two, and kept going up inside.

She clutched at his arm, trying to pull him away. "No," she gasped out.

Andreas shifted his left hand to grasp the front of her throat. The reaction that triggered made my male hormones go into overdrive. She arched forward, her eyes closed, her mouth dropped open then she wriggled on top of him. This time her hands seemed more to guide him to drive his fingers deeper.

"Oh fuck," she whispered.

The sinuous movement of her tanned thighs, and the jiggles of flesh as her tits nearly escaped from the top was enough to make my cock spring up some more.

I tsked at her grabby hands. "We can't have that." So I climbed off the lounge and pulled off my swim shorts. My erection sprang free.

"You keep that away from her pussy this time." Andreas nodded toward my dick. "In a second, when she's wet enough, I'm fucking her."

Kat opened her eyes then opened them wider when she saw my cock. "No. Wait –"

"You're telling us, to wait?"

Though she didn't answer me, she struck at the arm pinning her throat. Andreas grunted. His arm dropped away for a few seconds before he recovered and recaptured her throat.

I straddled the lounge at knee level with my feet in the sand then grabbed both her flailing hands. "You okay?" I asked him.

Her panting wound down a little.

"Yes. She got me where the nerve's damaged. I think Kat's channeling that shark."

A little frantic, she looked from him to me.

I stared her down until she dropped eye contact. "Leave your hands where I put them while I tie them. Tonight, you'll learn why you shouldn't have done that. Now, I could just use your cuffs but this is sexier."

I ripped the bikini top ties and freed her tits, happy to see she kept her hands clasped behind her, though her fingers were white. Worried? "You obeyed. Very good."

"Please." She appealed to Andreas. "Not both of you at once."

"Why not?" His eyes were hooded and he pulled her head down a bit lower. "It's going to happen sometime."

While I was tying her hands firmly at the small of her back, he removed his fingers from her pussy. Before I could rebuke him, he plucked at, and pulled open, the tiny bows that tied the bikini bottoms together.

"Because..." She tugged with her hands, testing my knots. "I don't do anal." But as she spoke he dragged her ever nearer to his face. "Andreas!"

I snorted, having figured out why her voice had gone high-pitched.

After pulling open the bows, he'd put his arm around her and his finger to her little asshole. With his hand coated in her juices, he was steadily introducing the tip of his forefinger into that rosette. Already the finger had disappeared an inch inside.

Kat whimpered and squirmed. "No. I don't –"

"That's going in easily for someone who doesn't. Let's see if she can take more." I cocked an eyebrow at Andreas. "As in my finger."

"No!" she squeaked. Then she shuddered again as his hand visibly tightened on the back of her neck.

I leaned in closer. "Have you been fucked anally before?"

"Not..."

"Not what?" I licked her ear then bit.

"Ow! He only used butt plugs on me, but I...um..." Her voice stuttered to a halt and I bit a little harder. "I...I used them sometimes when I got myself off."

"Thank you for answering honestly." Andreas brought her in for a quick kiss then clamped her head to his chest so she was fully bent over and exposed. He smirked at me.

"You might not have been fucked here before but you soon will be. You're getting a cock in your pretty little asshole today. And you're going to love it." By steering around his hand, I slicked up my fingers, riding along the groove between her soft engorged lips. "Damn, she is turned on." While I held her wrists to her back, I pushed a finger into her pussy.

One very annoyed Kat. While she still scowled, I shoved another finger in and massaged high and fast inside her toward the front. The change in her face…

From the jerk of her body and clench of her walls, I'd found somewhere close to her G-spot. I planted my hand on her back to hold her in place, and kept going, jarring her with the violence of the massage. At her prolonged moan my balls started to ache with a vengeance. Fuck this. I needed inside her soon.

"You like her gagged, Andreas?"

He cleared his throat then chuckled. "I do."

"I'll use the bottoms."

I slowed my massage then removed my fingers, amused at how our little Kat had slumped forward.

"Abracadabra." I dragged the scrap of cloth out from under her.

While he held her upright and still, I centered it across her mouth. Her gray eyes watched my every move but her teeth remained together.

"Open." I waited. "Open or tonight we will have a triple punishment."

"Sir, plea –"

Though the completely voluntary *Sir* had made my heart do a hop, skip, and jump, I wedged in the cloth then tied it at the back.

"Now, let's see what you can take. There's no sand here, okay. And you've got plenty of moisture. Relax, girl." Slowly I began to wriggle my fingertip in beside Andreas's.

"I won't move mine," he murmured.

Apart from a few squeaks, Kat held her breath like someone internalizing their enjoyment. Her little hole expanded and contracted, allowing me to penetrate her without fuss. Two fingers. What the hell size butt plugs had she been sitting on? When she shuddered, clearly taking pleasure from the act, I was sure I could fuck her there.

"She likes that." I kissed her shoulder. "I'll go get a condom and some lube. Keep her happy. Two minutes, tops," I added to her. "Then we'll see how much we can get you to come while we both fuck you."

The wideness of her eyes and the submissive, accepting look in those pupils made me take her mouth softly. I caught her lips in my teeth then kissed her again, "Don't go anywhere."

Chapter 20

Kat

Chris had gone. I waited a little longer until I heard the slam of the gate in the wall – half because I wanted to be sure he was far, far away, half because Andreas still had his finger in my ass and I was so ready for sex I wanted to hump him. Only the cloth of his shorts, then him. Naked him.

The length of his cock rested between the lips of my pussy. I could feel it there, as clearly as if I was touching him with my hands, running my fingers along it. But I didn't want him inside me. A vibe, I just needed a vibe. A man inside me, *no*, especially not Andreas or Chris.

I needed to get away, *now*.

My wrists were a little loose. I twisted them.

Plan B – escape.

Fuck it. My head was screwed on the wrong way. His shorts must be so wet from me.

Though I was aroused, him doing it to me, here on the beach, or indeed anyplace, that concept made me feel so off, so wrong, almost ill. I didn't need this man to complete my life. I wanted to go back to how I was, me, myself, and I, easing back into sex, with an occasional kinkster with a flogger, a vibe, or sometimes a tongue. I was getting there all by myself.

But, god. It wouldn't hurt any to move. I ground against him, eyes closed, and listened to his chuckle. Sitting on him with my wrists tied by my bikini top, gagged, his hand wrapped around my neck, and his finger up inside me. My clit was going to pop if it poked up any more.

"Like that, do you." He pulled out his finger and grasped my hip. Not a question. The man was amused I was horny.

Despite the gag, I tried to voice a no and it came out a messed-up gargle.

His hand tightened on my neck. Shit. Loved that. I hazed out. For that moment in time, I was nothing. *His.*

Andreas let go of my neck. "Let's get my pants off so I can get you nice and worked up before Chris returns. This can go back on later." He pulled the bikini bottoms out of my mouth.

I heard the tinkle when he took up the chain of my leash. I opened my eyes. Left hand. Left hand on leash, remember? That's good.

"Hop off so I can pull these down, then you can suck me a little before I fuck you."

I gaped at him.

"You're slow." When I still hesitated, he sat up, took my breast in the half-circle of his hand. At first he sucked and the hot suction and alternating lap of his tongue undid me in seconds. I groaned and wriggled on his cock. Teeth clamped on me. I shrieked but wasn't game to move in case I lost my nipple.

He let go and smiled evilly, the skin around his gorgeous dark eyes wrinkling. I wished I could draw my finger along his black eyebrows and down to his mouth so I could see if he would nibble my fingers.

Beautiful man.

Prettiness did not make a good person, or especially a person you should stick with when they were doing immoral things to you. Here was the oddest enigma of my whole life – that I could so enjoy submitting to a man who was forcing it on me. I struggled with it every time he touched me. I guess, I trusted him still, that might be the key, though not enough to ever expect him to free me...again. He wanted to make me have sex with him? Deal breaker.

I sighed, regretting what would never be.

"Come on, girl. Move!" His slap on my ass had me dismounting from the lounge between it and Chris's lounge. A glass rolled over my foot, the dregs of orange juice dribbling onto my toes.

I reined in my heartbeat, assessed everything. Hands, check. His left hand on my leash. Check. From my collar to his hand, the metal chain swayed in the sunlight.

"Undo my hands?" I suggested. "I can take off your shorts."

I tried to look innocent. I was almost loose anyway. The last loop fell away while I waited. Chris had made a mistake. Bikini material stretched.

Lazily he checked me out. "Nice teeth marks." The saliva from his bite cooled on my nipple. It throbbed, but so did my pussy. "Untie you? No. I like having you my...our little prisoner." He put his right hand to his waistband and lifted his hips as he pushed down the shorts.

God. I was going to do this. Hope. Fear. A bit of panic. And a tinge of guilt. Stupid maybe, but I didn't want to hurt him.

I have to.

This could go so badly, but I had to try. They wanted to be my masters? I rallied anger. Fuck them. I hadn't asked for this. I'd seen that small weakness. The forest was only another twenty yards away. Now or never. I crouched down and licked my lips as if eager to taste him. My traitorous pussy spasmed as I smelled him, *man.*

Such a waste. His cock, freed from the shorts, waved under my nose. I almost moaned.

Weakling. Snap out of the sex fuzzy zone.

"Go on. Suck." He said, hoarsely, tugging on the leash. His right hand was still on his shorts.

Thunder rumbled and the sky grew dark. A spot of rain hit my shoulder. Way to go, ominous weather.

He looked upward at the sky. "We might have to go indoors."

Do it. I reached down, picked up the glass…it bumped on the lounge on the way up and I almost dropped it…shit! I jabbed the glass into that white scar on his arm. Only, that musical crack I'd heard had been the glass chipping. Red spread across his arm and he cursed. His arm flopped, lifeless. He twisted to grab me with his right but I'd jumped the lounge and was sprinting away.

Another curse as he tried to get up but was entangled in his shorts. The forest. What had I done? I made him bleed! *Run, fuck you, run. You do not want them to catch you.*

I had a fifteen yard head start on Andreas, the man I'd just cut. He'd kill me if he caught me. Wait, no he wouldn't. But Chris might.

My internal monologue scrambled my head. *Shut up.*

"Kat! Kat! Stop! Fuck it."

The shouts made me run faster. I'd made him bleed.

Trees. I entered the tree line, stumbling through the small shrubs. Deeper in, the undergrowth thinned. As I ran, I frantically tucked the leash around and around my collar. If that caught on something, I'd break my neck.

Chris was shouting now too. Then they went quiet.

Bad, that was bad. Meant they were coming fast, too fast to yell, or they wanted to be silent.

I ran. My legs pelted into the sand, then into harder sand and dirt and twigs that hurt my feet as I went deeper into the trees. Dark, dark, darker. More grumbling thunder. Rain started smacking down through the trees, whacking into the big leaves, jostling the tree ferns.

Panting, big breaths sucking my chest apart, I paused with hands on knees. Change direction. Go somewhere they won't expect.

I went deeper. Ran. Pound, pound, pound into the rainforest dirt. *Ow!*

"Fuck." I staggered into a tree, caught my foot, and hopped. Bit my lip to stop the hurt from turning into a loud curse. Somewhere near, I could hear them running. Damn, still close.

I peeked at my foot, praying it wasn't bad. Just a twig. I plucked it from the notch it had scored in my sole and gingerly set my foot down. The trees here mostly went up straight to the sky, seeking light. Thick roots snaked across the ground, green with moss. A curious little bird swooped in and buzzed past to perch on a branch sending it rocking. It angled one pristine-blue eye at me, then the other.

Through a gap, I saw water below, smelled the dark fungal aroma of a rainforest creek bed, and heard the gurgling notes of water running over rocks. Something had slid down the muddy bank recently. I could see the smears and scratches on the roots and in the soil.

Frowning, I peered down a slope dense with rotting trunks and ankle-snaring roots.

Claw and slip my way down that embankment or... If they came close and I threw a rock over there, to the opposite bank, maybe I could send them away? The water wasn't that deep. They could cross, so potentially, I might I have. That smear of dirt would make them think so.

A huge gnarled rain tree, yards in diameter, dominated a thicket to my right, its branches and roots twined about, as if a giant had twisted the tree's trunk in his hands then shoved it in the earth. The tree ferns and the palms gathered about its base made a place I could hide. Footsteps came closer, crunching wetly on fallen leaves.

Quietly, I weaved my way into the plants, trying not to leave marks, and I crouched on the opposite side of the rain tree's trunk. I wished I could stop breathing, for each time my chest moved the harsh sound seemed louder than before. I pressed my mouth to the back of my hand to muffle it.

Andreas stalked into view, silent, vigilant. My heart, frantic, thumped into higher gear.

But also...relief. He was okay, though as naked as I was. Fresh blood shone on his forearm. I wrinkled my forehead, straining to see. He'd not tied anything on the wound but from the quantity of blood I hadn't hit anything major.

The ache in my ribs ebbed. If anyone deserved being cut it had been Chris, not him.

His erection had gone. A man without pants on always looked a bit silly to me – their genitals never seemed made for running about. Everything wobbled. But then my tits did too. I looked down as I registered a small tickle there, jumped in fright, but caught myself. Bug. Green. A baby praying mantis? On my boob. Ugh. I flicked the pretty creepy crawly away.

Where was Chris? Where the fuck was he? I needed to know. Andreas turned away from me and took a few slow steps toward the creek. As he peered over the edge, a few yards away from him, the fronds of a low plant shivered. I glimpsed reptilian scales. Gray green. Fuck. Crocodiles liked water. We were near the sea. He'd said there were drag marks at the beach. No. Calm. It's a lizard. *Just a lizard.* There were big monitor lizards here.

Crocs could move fast.

I bit my lip as the thing beyond the leaves moved nearer to Andreas. How fast could they move? Could they go a few yards in a second? I stopped breathing, recalling a video of a nature show where a croc leaped yards into the air to grab a dangled chicken. Yes, they could move fucking fast.

What to do? What *should* I do?

They'd done bad things to me. Served him right. Except, no. Not Andreas.

I wiped at my eyes, started backing away, farther into the undergrowth. I couldn't do this. The thing rattled some leaves. More reptile showed. Big, damn big, not a lizard.

Andreas was a good man, sort of. If you subtracted the kidnapping. The rape. What was I *doing* forgiving him?

Scream, and run. Scream. Run. I sucked in air. God, this was dumb.

"Andreas! Behind you! Run!"

Then I spun around and did the same. Feet again thumping, jumping, I shoved aside leaves. A noise to my left warned me. Man. Oh shit, oh shit. I dodged, leapt over a root. Feet pounded after me. Shit. Don't look. Don't. *Run!* A hand snagged my arm, whipping me about. I staggered and put my palm to the ground as I swung and ended up sprawled and rolling across the ground.

Free again. A chance. Go! I scrambled to rise and was tackled down, face first. My chin scraped into leaves.

"Got you!"

A heavy body landed on me, knee in my back.

Once before, Scrim had done this. Learn from that! Don't. Sit. Still. I squirmed madly, crazy with fear, just plain crazy, feeling mud smear into my body. But my hands were caught, wrenched back as I strained the other way. I gasped at the force on my shoulders, at the iron grip that didn't give no matter what I did.

I spat out a leaf and dirt, grunted as I pulled and tried to jack knife. Fuck. The man was heavy, like a damn gorilla sitting on me. I sagged. It wasn't fair. It was so not fair.

The click as he connected the cuffs made me stiffen. I sobbed, heard the crackle and rustle as he rose. His foot landed on my back. I lay there, defeated, still sobbing, in an effort to both gain enough oxygen to live and to expel some of my panic. It didn't do much. After sliding down my nose, my tears dripped onto a leaf.

More padding footsteps and a man's foot arrived next to my face. His toes flexed.

"Fuck, she can run." Chris.

"Yeah." Andreas. The foot next to my face lifted and came down, gentle yet firm, on the back of my neck. "That was stupid, Kat. There's two of us and we can go faster than you. Even if you did try sticking me with glass first."

I gulped in air, sniffled. "I didn't mean that. Just to hit you. I never wanted to cut you."

"Shit. Really? Too bad, girl. I'm pissed at you now. What are we doing with her, Chris? You're the punishment man. The enforcer." He said the last like it was some sort of stamped-on title.

That did not sound good. Fear and dread tightened on me.

"You mean do something here? Like whip her with a stick maybe?" He laughed, damn well laughed as if this had been a morning stroll. "Sure. Why not? I can hang her by the cuffs from a branch. Be a good lesson for her. She needs punishing. We're on the opposite side of the wall to Scrim's house so her screams probably won't reach him."

Ice shivered up my spine, raising goosebumps. He won't hurt me that much, not with Andreas here. Won't, I repeated in my head, half-convincing myself.

Why'd he mention Scrim and the house? I was that close? Had I run in circles? Couldn't have, could I? Shit, I couldn't even run the right way.

A memory jarred me. I twisted my face to one side so I could be heard. "Crocodile! I saw one behind Andreas. Back there. Please look." I feared Chris but a croc was far worse.

"Was that why? Why you yelled to me?" Andreas lifted his foot and squatted beside me, studied me closely. With leaves bunched up around my face, I could only see him with one eye but he almost looked...relieved? "Thank you. So you don't hate me?"

What the? "Crocodile?"

"Chris is checking. Do you hate me? Don't lie, little Kat. It's important to me." He stroked my cheek then down the side of my damp nose, as if following the path of my tears.

I blinked at him. More tears leaked. Jeez. What a question. Did I? Should I lie? I was such a mess I couldn't figure it. But I shut my eyes, unable to take more of this. I was trapped again. Run down like some forest creature, tied up...again. I wanted to go *home*.

"No. Maybe. I guess not," I whispered. Not him. It was true still.

"Good. I told myself that if you ever truly hated me that I'd leave."

I stared at that leaf, caught in a dilemma. If he left, there'd only be one. It would be easier to escape if there was one man. I was stuck, half about to spew out something about lying, that I hated him, but I couldn't do it. He wouldn't believe me anyway – not so soon after what I'd said.

Besides, Chris would be the one left. Chris, alone with me. That made my skin crawl. He always seemed one breath, one step, one *something*, away from doing something wicked to me.

"So...you don't hate me. You even risked getting caught again to try to save me. That counts in my book. That's, yeah..." I felt his fingers at the collar then he carefully turned the collar to unwind the leash from my neck. His nostrils dilated as he took a long breath, as if what I'd done meant more than its face value. "That's good."

Him and Chris were both giving me the creepy vibes.

"The leash. Good thinking. I can use that." Chris had returned.

Though there wasn't a lot of point in resisting, I had a go at kicking him when he hauled me upright. I shouldn't have bothered. He just had Andreas hold my legs while he undid the cuffs and tied them to a low branch with the leash. Since it wasn't a branch with any give or resilience and he calculated wrongly, I ended up having to balance on my toes, half the time. It was that or strain my shoulders when flatfooted. So I varied from one to the other. Then I caught him staring avidly.

Ahh, what was I thinking? Not well, that was for sure. He'd done it deliberately.

"Asshole," I muttered under my breath.

"I am that. I can lip read that much, Kat." He swished the whippy branch he'd found through the air. "Lucky for you I'm feeling lenient over swearing. Swear away. What I do is going to happen anyway."

"I don't fucking care. Do what you want to." I showed my teeth, too fed up with being his willing victim to pretend. He'd do what he aimed to do anyway.

"I will." Then he stepped in and flicked it across my left breast. The smack was sharp and unexpected.

I hissed and couldn't stop myself checking my nipple. Another half inch... Shit. Blood beaded along a scratch.

Then the rain began again. Overhead the steady patter became a low roar. A stray raindrop made it through the overhead foliage to spat onto my forehead.

"It's still there. Your nipple." The smile was vicious. I should've thought him ridiculous. Stalking about in this storm darkened forest, circling me, naked, his dick half-erect with Andreas watching. A scene from a B-grade movie. Rain pouring down between us. Obscuring him.

Then I saw myself through his eyes. Whipping a naked woman hanging from a tree was probably his ultimate turn-on. The leather cuffs squeezed along my wrists, getting wetter by the second, I blinked away the water. Cold. My nipples poked out, hard and also frigid and I shivered, feeling more rainwater run down my flanks.

As it dribbled down my face I remembered why he'd gone missing. The crocodile.

The stick flicked out again and pain striped my ass. Damn him, he was making this last.

"The crocodile!" I said aloud.

He said nothing, circling me, and Andreas prompted him for an answer.

"It was a lizard. Probably. You saw a monitor lizard."

He hadn't found it then? I twisted to follow him. Or was he messing with me? If I asked and he was, he'd mess with me again. My heart drummed. This wasn't worth making a mistake over. In the shadows around us I imagined that the rain rattling the shrubs and palms was disguising the first move of a croc.

"Are you sure?" I asked, as nonchalantly as I could.

His smile mocked me.

I waited. Waited. He striped my other breast and I spun on the leash as I tried to escape. My feet slipped on wet leaves.

"Are you sure?"

No answer.

"Andreas?" I appealed. Apart from a quick glance at Chris he did nothing except to fold his arms. "Fuck you both."

More strikes from Chris left me bleeding from multiple scratches on my stomach, ass, and breasts. I danced away as much as I could.

"He's going to hurt me permanently, scar me," I said to Andreas. "Do something!"

He shrugged, a gleam in his eye as he surveyed me wriggling, exposed, being whipped. I shut my eyes a second, wincing at the four or five rapid hits on my back. I almost daren't turn, but I did. The rivulets of rain stung as they meandered down me. Cool against the heat of the strikes.

"You can't." I bit my lip, suppressing a gasp as Chris took the opportunity to stripe my breast.

"I can. Andreas won't listen to you. He knows you're wrong and I'm right. I know what I'm doing." He side stepped, going behind me. "Apologize to him."

Say I was sorry? Was that all it took? I wanted down from here. Away. If something lunged at us, I was trapped. They'd never get me down in time. I kept checking the periphery of my vision. I knew he saw what I did. After all, he was hitting me, crisscrossing me with pain, and I wasn't watching him anymore. He knew, and he stopped awhile.

"Worried, Kat? I told you there was no croc. It's him that you should be worried about." He flicked his gaze upward. I followed.

Above me, two yards up, a snake coiled about a large branch, sinuously revolving around the tree, on his way down, toward me.

"Shit," I breathed, my throat stoppered suddenly with dryness. "Get me down."

"No," he said quietly, dreadfully quietly. "Now."

Now what? I couldn't think with that up there. And I still didn't know if the croc really wasn't anywhere near. If it was, I hoped it ate him first. The python flicked out its tongue, all pretty in its glossy green and lemon scales.

"Please get me down." I said in a hushed tone, hopefully loud enough for Chris to hear. I didn't take my eyes off the snake. I knew they could strangle people, even crush your ribs if given a chance to wrap themselves around you.

"Apologize."

My eyes were drying out from not blinking. Water hit my eyes... Yeah, except when the rain dripped straight into them. I shook my head, water went flying. My soaked hair whipped about my head, flailing into my neck.

"I'm sorry. I'm so sorry, I –" What the hell had I done? "I'm sorry I cut him. Get me down!" The snake eyed me. Maybe it thought I looked tasty. I swear I could hear it slithering over the noise of the downpour pattering on the upper leaves of the trees.

"Not yet. Andreas? Still want to? I'll watch the snake." Earlier, he'd taken my bikini bottoms, and now he tossed them to Andreas.

Fuck, fuck, fuck.

Andreas had a gag fetish.

Want to? Want to what? I had a good idea what he meant but couldn't face it. When Andreas moved closer, I backed up a little, almost swinging off my wrists as my feet slipped forward again. With the rain running down him, sluicing off his muscles, he looked surreal, a man from a dream, or a nightmare.

Snake. I looked up. The damn thing was watching us. Me. At least it had stopped moving.

Andreas wrapped his arms around me from behind, burning to life all the tiny scratches. On the edge of my vision, something hit the ground and rolled a foot or two. A bottle? His wet cock slipped along my cleft, searching, prodding. I froze as he put his hand down there and guided the head to the right spot – the entrance to my other hole. My ass tightened instinctively.

He wanted in. I didn't but what could I do?

"No," I gasped. "No. Not there. Not after all that happened. Don't. Please."

"Oh? All of what you just did makes me even more determined to fuck you there. Relax and let me in, babe. I chucked away the lube and the rain's washing it off my dick real fast. Open up."

While I was concentrating on where his cock was going, he put the bikini bottoms across my mouth and gagged me.

Relax? The burn as he tried to enter, as my anus dilated, had me grunting through the gag. I put my head down, going up on tiptoes in a futile effort to get away from the pain. But he kept pushing, moving himself into me as carefully as someone threading a needle with a damn tree trunk.

I attempted to say *I can't* but the gag turned my word to a guttural grunt.

"Open, Kat. I'm going in there. I'm fucking your ass."

He hauled my hair back and whispered instructions to my ear that I barely processed. All my desperate thoughts were on where he was down below and how I wanted to stop him and couldn't. Another quarter of an inch, another stretch. My protests became a constant whine.

Chris laughed and I snapped my eyes open, watched him saunter up to me and slide his hand down my stomach until it cupped my pussy. "I'll get her excited for you. Then she'll let you in easier."

"Go ahead," he rasped back. "She's so tight right now I may have a permanently squashed dick."

"I guess we got her all worried. Hey, Kat?" He studied my eyes and I shook my head as much as Andreas's grip allowed. I'd deny anything he suggested just on principle.

At that he started to rub his fingers on my clit. I strived to calmly meet his eyes, to show nothing. His fingers strayed further and massaged over my pussy lips then found my clit again, circling, playing. Fuck him. He was torturing me by making me like it.

"Would you spit on me again, Kat?" His eyebrows rose and fell. "I bet you would."

I grunted my disgust but, even so, the heat of pleasure stirred me.

Chris. My tormentor. I jerked up my knee but he'd come in so close there wasn't room for more than a deflected bump into the side of his thigh.

He kissed me over the gag, softly, exploring my lips around the cloth. "I bet you hate the idea of me getting you off with my tongue."

My clit grew bigger, pulsing, making me want. My neck bowed back under pressure. As my resolve wavered, my eyes broke contact with his.

Stupid sexual response. I wanted to head butt him. But couldn't. My scalp stung from the fingers entangled in my hair. My neck muscles strained. My tongue strayed and brushed the inside of the gag. Yuck.

"Do it. Lick her off. I want to feel her come while I'm inside her." His cock went subtly out then in again, slick, hot.

No. No, no. Above, I wrapped my fingers around the leash, wanting him to stop, but also, abruptly, wanting him to go all the way *in*. By scalding, stinging, fractions of inches he was making that last part of me his.

I squeaked and writhed a little, but my ass was pinned, my hands locked above. My body was theirs to toy with. Trapped.

I felt myself open, and my next breath cut short as I processed the feel of him there. Every time I opened, he took advantage, shoving in like he knew I'd force him out again given the smallest chance.

I half moaned, half gasped at the next intrusion. *Push out* turned into his cock sliding, slipping, thrusting, in. I twisted on the pivot of my overhead hands trying not to show my appreciation with more betraying noises. He could fuck me there, but he couldn't make me –

The snake! I looked up, only to have another thrust hit me and my eyelids slammed shut. If the snake was still there, I didn't care anymore. I whimpered. Heat, pain, lust. All three built in my groin. A crazy, explosive mixture.

"I think she's liking it now anyway." He nuzzled my neck, licking me then nuzzling me again with his nose. "You're going to like this, girl. Chris punished you. This is just me, us, saying, mine, that you're not getting away from us. Accept it."

I felt the trail of sensation down my front as Chris went to his knees, his big warm hands brushing my frozen nipples, my belly, my hips, then his mouth fastening onto my clit. And sucking.

I arched involuntarily into that hotness, and Andreas pushed in. More of him. In. Me.

"God, yes," one of them said.

Pleasure arose from all their touches, their forced entries into my body. Someone's fingers wiggled into my pussy then worked up and down. Chris flicked the flat of his tongue on my clit before he began to suck rhythmically. I shuddered and arched, crying out as an orgasm burst through me. My legs quaked. Andreas grunted once and shoved his cock all the way in.

He stalled there a second, with my ass spasming onto him, cursing like he wanted to hold himself back. When the sucking on my clit ceased, my climax wound down. Chris jammed his thigh between mine, spreading my legs.

Lust flared back into being as his cock rammed into my pussy.

Both of them were inside me. The stretch from their two cocks squeezing in was almost painful. I pried open my eyes. Chris glared down at me.

"I wasn't going to, but you're like hot fucking catnip." He bared his teeth as he alternated his thrusts with Andreas.

A few seconds later, he picked my legs up, elbows under my knees, carrying some of my weight. They both fucked me. Full. Taken, thoroughly overcome with their possession, I swayed there, my body rocked to and fro by the force of their passion. Nothing I could do, no escape, even when it hurt enough to make me shriek into the gag. I saw only the insides of my eyelids, absorbed in the sensations, in the pain, in the rough, animalistic ritual of sex.

Then I felt them strain and grunt as they came.

One of them bit the join of shoulder and neck, the other my breasts in many places. Chris again. He dedicated an especially hard and brutal bite to one nipple. Exhausted, I whimpered and prayed he'd let go. A few seconds later, he did then he kissed the mark.

We breathed raggedly together. Rain pattered onto leaves and dirt. Sweat, rain, and something warm that no doubt was cum, dribbled down my legs. They hugged me, still inside me, a part of me.

After they withdrew and ungagged me, I could only hang there, spent and limp, heart thudding, waiting to be cared for and released, when they willed it. This act had seemed so final, momentous even. I wondered how I'd ever separate myself from them when they'd had me like this.

Just as I thought them done, a hand arrived between my thighs, finger and thumb pincered onto my clit. Hypersensitive, I jerked my head up, trying to get myself free from the grip. Chris. He applied enough force to make me almost swing off my feet. His other hand, he anchored on one of my nipples, stretching, pulling my nipple out like it was rubber. I was forced to tiptoe a few inches toward him, and whimpered as he kissed me.

"Let go!" I pleaded.

"Uh-uh."

Then he simply observed me, his mouth straight, his eyes flickering as he checked my reactions. He twisted his fingers on my nipple and clit, smiling as I hissed at the pain. "One day, soon, you'll submit to me, Kat. Of your own volition. On that day, I have plans for these. So you'll never forget who owns you."

I closed my eyes in relief when he left me alone. Everywhere throbbed or hurt. The snake had stayed up in the tree, and no crocodile had arrived, but I had my own monsters here, with me, in the form of men.

Chapter 21

Andreas

After taking Kat down, I cuddled her a while as Chris watched. He'd joined in for all of a minute before stepping back. The man needed to get more up close and personal with her at times other than kink and sex unless he only wanted to be her jailer. I'd have a talk with him later.

The rain was no more than a fine drizzle. The storm clouds had passed to the west.

I attempted carrying Kat back through the forest, but my arm gave out. The cut wouldn't need much more than a bandage for a few days, but my left arm always had suffered from weakness now and then. Whacking it with a glass hadn't helped. I set her on her feet, the bikini bottoms I'd retrieved from her mouth were balled in my hand. I could've given them back, tied up the bows at the side…but, no.

She eyed me warily, not speaking. I guess us dominating the shit out of her had shut her down for once.

Naked. With all those fine red scratches across her tits and belly, her back and thighs. Bite marks. One on her nipple – that'd be Chris. Having run her down and double penetrated her, Kat was even hotter to me than she'd been on the beach.

I cleared my throat. "You left your mark."

"Yes. Like it?" He smiled as he too assessed her. "I do."

Kat looked away. We'd left her hands clipped together at her front. Such a pretty little captive. Mind explosion moment. How the fuck had I gotten to here? Admiring a woman who was... Who I'd... I lost momentum. Accept it. This is it. Enjoy.

My balls tightened. My dick resurrected somewhat. I'd gone from wanting to carry her, to pitying her, to wanting to mark her body with more of that red.

"Fuck, man, you're corrupting me." The rain had made his blond hair darker, though the shortness meant it stood up like some kid's anime character. "You still look evil, even when wet. How do you do that?"

He shrugged. "Practice. Want to make her walk faster? Here. I don't think I can conceive of punishing her enough today. You hear that Kat? Today was like a fucking milestone in badness. If you wanted me angry, you got it. If you wanted me ever more determined to break you, you got that too."

Though she couldn't have missed hearing that, she kept her head down and said nothing, did nothing except stare at the ground, as if she wanted it dead.

He handed me the whippy branch he'd used earlier to make those scratches. I swished it, stared at her. Then I whacked it across her butt and smiled when she jumped and uttered a curse.

"Take care, Kat. No swearing. Move." I switched her again. She glared but turned and started walking.

Wow. I glanced at the stick. Power. And in something so small.

"Don't get too wrapped up in causing her pain," Chris said as he passed me. "That's my job."

"The fuck it is." I followed after that enticing, red-marked butt. He was right, though, it wasn't the pain I liked, it was seeing how wrong she looked. Okay, wrong word, it was seeing her dirty. I liked the cum on her legs, the mess that we'd put on her. I liked the looks she'd given us that said, *I don't want this.* I liked her, sometimes, not clean, defiled, violated, and I loved that I'd helped do it to her.

I was as fucked up as Chris, maybe, just different.

I remembered the list. This wasn't that new. I always had...dreamed.

Chris stepped up the training after that. Determined not to let her have an opportunity to escape, he kept the order in place for her to kneel each night and, in that way, ask for punishment. Though she never, in words, asked for the ten strokes. He varied what he used on her, sometimes using an implement that barely seemed to sting. When she'd recovered from the last bruises, he went at her hard again. I could see it frustrated him that Kat still didn't truly give in. He wanted her to beg, in words, to say sorry. And she didn't.

I think he wanted more from her than I understood.

A week and a bit had passed. It'd been scary but fascinating to see the news reports on her going missing. Chris had been stunned but pleased when her car showed up near Alice Springs. Since then the investigations had been skewed by the assumptions she'd either been abducted there or somehow walked off into the scrub and died. How her car had gotten there, he wasn't sure.

Perhaps it was a car thief? I got the impression, he thought there was more to it than that. But I didn't ask. Some things I didn't want to know.

Chris had more patience than me. He amped up the begging for pain so she had to wait with her head down and her ass in the air, or get more strokes. We started protocol for kneeling if one of us entered a room and also calling us both Sir. A cleaning regime was instigated, so that she had more to do, though supervising her was essential. A broomstick could be lethal if used well. We couldn't trust her. Still.

That baffled and, at times, infuriated Chris. I was sure he'd once told me that a good Dom rarely showed anger and never punished while angry. Maybe the rules were different with kidnappers?

Mostly, she was good. Now, though, just now, I think she'd had a brain spasm.

Sunset, and the deck was awash with faded colors in that in between phase. Chris had dropped his plate of food on the floor, and demanded Kat clean it up. She'd refused. I was still in shock. He'd stalked over to talk and something he'd said had sparked her off. She'd spit in his face. Again.

I'd seen the spark of defiance in her eyes, the gleam of I-dare-you-to-do-something. Like she expected his worst and didn't care. Like she wanted to test him. It had scorched into my head, riveted me. If a nuke had exploded on the horizon, I might have looked away. Might. I'd been holding my breath. I wanted to see what he would do.

This was going to be good. In a fluid move, where she barely had time to squeal, he had her down on the floor. Knee on her back, her wrists there too.

She couldn't have expected to win. Who was being tested here? Him or her?

"Come here, Andreas." It sounded like Chris was ready to snarl and eat some prey.

I walked over to them, ten feet high. Fuck, I wanted to see how this ended so much my hard on was already taunting me.

"Hold her while I get some gear. Do not let her up. Keep her face in the floor."

I crouched and took over, pinning her with pressure on her back and neck.

Chris stalked away.

"Are you crazy?"

I knew that while Chris fully intended to hurt her, he was never going to do something so terrible she'd be permanently damaged. That added a certain potential to this scene. Fun. Voyeurism with a big V.

What the fuck was going to happen?

"No. Not crazy."

"Then?"

"Shut up. I don't care. You're almost as bad as he is."

"Careful." I squeezed on her neck and she tried to shake loose but couldn't.

"You've been so good lately." I sighed melodramatically.

"Don't have a baby on the spot, Andreas. He can do what he likes. I don't care. This is nothing."

"Oh?" I bent down and bit her nape, held her firmer when she tried to get away. "It's Sir, not Andreas."

"Fuck you too," she muttered.

Though amused, I wanted to show her she had to toe the line with me too. I started undressing her. I clipped her cuffs together and shimmied her panties down, touching her where I was sure she didn't want me to, feeling her cunt, pinching her. Definitely fun.

"Fuck," she whispered. "Not you too. Stop. Fuck off!"

All the days of saying Sir had gone in an instant. Yet underneath, I sensed this was her testing us. I guess she expected more of the same. Some pain, some fucking. I had a feeling Chris was too annoyed to stick with same ol' same ol'.

"What are you trying to do, Kat?"

"Piss you off?" she grumbled, struggling against my wrist hold.

"Well you achieved that."

Chris came back with rope and some black leather strappy objects. "Here. For the dress."

He gave scissors to me and I cut the straps of her lacy white dress. Once I was done, Chris straddled her legs and undid her wrist cuffs.

The furious attempt she made to shake us off meant flailing arms, swearing, and her grunting, as she tried to get out from underneath. I'd never had the opportunity to overwhelm a woman with my strength before Kat. Exhilarating. Together, we weighed three times as much as her. We had her under control in seconds

"Fucking octopus, you are." I grinned down at her and she glowered back.

Her little growl made Chris sit back on his heel.

"Enough." Then he tugged back her neck to stare in her face and grab a handful of cheek. "You want to challenge me? You got it. How long will it be before I get you to scream?"

At that, she went quiet.

Chapter 22

Chris

I slipped both her arms into the black leather sleeve and zipped it up.

Not a hope she could get out.

Andreas whistled. "That is devious."

"Yeah. It is. It's an arm binder." The leather was like a long stiff holster for her arms, shiny buckles galore, evil looking to a T. I smacked her butt, smiled at the instant handprint, and rolled her onto her back. She hadn't done anything more than hiss. "Do what you like to her while I restrain her legs."

Kat muttered something but not loud enough for me to understand. Feeling frightened at last? I checked her face and her gaze slipped away from mine. Good. She'd invented entirely new levels of bratting. I'd been kind for long enough. No matter what Erik had done to her, she needed taming.

Andreas lay down with her, staring at her face to face but upside down, with his legs stretched the other way. I put on the suspension ankle cuffs and attached them to the spreader bar, while listening to him menacing her with crazy suggestions about what I might do. So crazy, she'd know he was lying. I grinned and wondered what she'd be making of that.

Even with me sitting on her legs she was still struggling, her muscles twitching. Unless it was what he was doing? I looked over my shoulder while I pulled the rope through each cuff's buckle.

"You're in so much trouble." He had hold of both of her pretty pink nipples and was slowly flattening them. That explained the squirming.

"Here." I slid the red ball gag along the floor toward him. "Put that on. Let's shut down that foul little mouth for a while." I waited until he'd strapped it on. "Let's see if I can make this girl scream. After I'm done with her, maybe I'll toss her in the sea for the crocs to find."

Saying that was evil. So fucking evil. But the hitch of her breathing and that stark expression was like ten thousand kilowatts zapping through me. Nice non-lethal, sexual kilowatts. *Here I come, Kat. Here I come.*

I had to stand on the table to get the rope through the anchor point on the canvas ceiling's steel frame. Then I pushed away the table. "Ready?"

Andreas nodded.

With him steadying her, I hauled her up in the air until she was swinging with her face at groin level.

I circled her, wondering if she'd finally figured out how stupid her meltdown had been. The timber floor creaked underfoot. Waves shushed in the background above the sound of trees shaking their leaves in the wind. I was barefoot and in shorts and T-shirt. She was naked except for the bra that Andreas had thoughtfully bunched beneath her tits. I pulled on one nipple until she tilted forward, hissing.

"Not quite naked." I tsked. From among the gear on the table, I found the knife. I squatted beside her so I could slit both shoulder straps, undo the clasp at the back, and slip the bra off. "The more skin, the better."

She flinched when the steel went near her face. I stood, examining the blade, pressing it on my finger. Sharp enough. Clean. No jagged parts.

A knife had so much potential but…I shut my eyes, recalling how knives bothered her. Yes? No? Reluctantly I went to place it on the table. "No knives?"

After squeaking past the gag, she frantically shook her head.

"Ahh. The girl made a noise. What about you make some more?"

I reached down and swung her toward me using first one nipple then the other. They stretched and her breathing hastened like she'd become a steam train. I let her go and turned her into the sexiest pendulum ever. No knives. A pity.

"Wish I could see some blood tricking down you." The graphic novel in my head would really come to life then.

Her eyes were so big when I looked. The ball gag wet. Her tits so scrumptious I bent and nipped them and did the sexy pendulum again, and again, until her eyes betrayed her. "Tears?" I wiped them away. No screams though.

I spun her, watching her hair swish in an arc, watching her swallow and try to keep me in view.

The length of her body gave me so many ideas.

"What first?" I paced to the table. "Cane, flogger, paddle, tawse. Clothes pegs?"

I placed a few pegs down her sides. And of course, couldn't neglect her nipples.

She made a tiny sound.

"At last, a whimper." I shook out the flogger I'd chosen, sent her spinning slightly.

The flogger had thin falls. Too many. Using them all wouldn't hurt. I wrapped most of the leather strips in my hand then went to trail the remaining falls from her cunt downward. Flicking lightly made her skin slowly change to pink. Increased tempo and force, made it sing, made it sting. The paddle was thuddy but wasn't fun. Not on her. The clothes pegs flicked away by the leather gave me broken squeaks.

The pegs scattered and skipped across the floor like fleeing beetles. The leather whipped nastily on nipples and breasts gave me gasps.

Red-pink. Sweat. The scent of a woman's arousal and pain. I was sure I could smell pain. But no screams.

Blood spots rose. Bruises. Little kisses of pain. Cane, next. It whistled in the air.

Tapped on her thighs and ass gave me nothing. Smacked harder... Ahhh...she flinched and squirmed.

"You're like a worm on a hook," I murmured. Idea. *Hook.* Where had I seen one?

No screaming still. Patience. I had plenty of that even if I'd turned most of her a scratchy, patterned red.

When she tried to twist away, I steadied her. "Stay. You seem better at spitting then screaming. You're staying until you learn to scream. Then maybe we can both fuck you."

She craned her neck to glare up at me for a second before her neck muscles tired and her head flopped down.

Her pussy was just below my head height. With her legs wide apart, I could see everything. Moisture shone along her slit.

"What's this? After all that sadism? I'm disappointed." Intrigued, I slid a finger along, gathering her juices, teasing her. Then I drew a wiggly wet line down her stomach.

"Are you liking this too much? That's *not* good. I need to make you hurt." Her whine made me smile and I crouched to be eye to eye. "If I don't think you've screamed enough, and properly, Kat, I'll use the knife."

She blinked then shut her eyes. Fear. Fantastic.

But I needed more pain. Or maybe some humiliation would bring her around to my point of view?

The hook, and...her feet looked fine. Upside down was still okay.

"Keep an eye on her, Andreas. Bite her here and there for me. I'll be back."

I found the anal hook and returned. The big silver ball at the end snuggled down into that rosette orifice like it had found a new home. I used both hands to sneak and wriggle it in further.

"This is lubricated, girl. It's big, but lubricated. And fuck that's cute." I stared at how the thick silver shaft disappeared down between her butt cheeks and into her asshole. "I could almost stare at this all day."

I roped the eyelet at the end of the hook through the ring of the arm binder and up to her hair after I manufactured a ponytail. Then I plucked the rope. Working the hook in and out made her shudder.

I talked to her again, face to face. "Last chance. Let it out. Scream or it's got to be the knife. Give me your fucking screams." I toyed with the drool on her lips then grabbed the cane again.

This time, I let loose. Being nicely directional I could do everywhere within reason, if I regulated the force. Ass, thighs, upper back. Breasts, and the piece de résistance, her inner thighs and her labia. With her legs spread, I could hit her there. Not exactly recommended, but I had good aim. Then, at last, *finally*, she started screaming. Beautiful, sobbing, half-choked gasps and screams. When she sounded gurgly, I unclipped the gag and watched her drool on the floor and writhe and cry like her world had ended.

Fuck. Task done.

"So, the girl finally does as asked to. Now you're going to suck my cock."

I didn't even bother mentioning not biting. I knew she wouldn't, not now. Not when she'd surrendered. I kicked my shorts aside and stepped up to her face with my cock in my hands. She sniffed. Her last sob died away.

"Suck." I touched the head to her lips and watched avidly as she choked on the first thrust. A long, wet, slide in, an all-enclosing hotness as I hit the back of her mouth. "Gorgeous. Fucking gorgeous. Keep going, pretty piñata."

When I grabbed her hair and she squealed, I recalled the ass hook. I chuckled. "Sorry."

Then I made sure to tweak it some more. Pressure built in my balls, my dick felt twice as big inside her mouth. I sped up, taking time at the back to get her worried about breathing, then letting her inhale some precious oxygen. Fucking Kat's mouth seemed like dessert after making her hurt and scream. I came as far down her throat as I could go and watched her spit most of my cum on the floor when I withdrew.

"Never mind." I toyed with her open mouth. "It's difficult swallowing upside down. Andreas." I beckoned him over from where he'd been sitting on the couch. "Come fuck her mouth too."

Watching him do it was nearly as good as doing it myself. Kat was butted back and forth by the force of him shoving his dick into her mouth. The man must have been overwrought because he came within a minute or two. Another pool of cum and drool collected on the floor under our gently swinging girl. Before I let her down I kissed her belly.

"Good girl."

That I'd spoken to her belly didn't seem to faze her. She was far gone, staring into space, her eyelids at half-mast. I was pleased with the results. Taking her spit in the face had been more than worth it.

Chapter 23

Andreas

I got a hard-on just thinking about what he'd done a week ago. He'd not allowed her any pleasure. He'd strung her upside down and whipped her until she was pink and red and screaming. He'd fucked her mouth then invited me to do the same.

What a memory. I looked to the living room. My toes curled, thinking of it. I was waiting for her here, at the back steps that led down to the sand of the back of the lodge. The beach, the waves, a stroll in the forest maybe.

I shut my eyes, rubbing my face and trying to reconcile how much that face-fucking scene had aroused me, remembering the feel of her mouth on me, the look of my cock disappearing into her mouth, and her tied up with her hands in the black leather arm binder. I'd fucked her mouth with Chris's cum still dribbling from her lips, using my grip on her head to drive myself into her throat.

I'd never come so hard, so fast. When I pulled out she'd drooled and choked for a few seconds. Even that had made me stare. I wanted to do it all again someday. Almost wanted her to misbehave as an excuse. Hell. Next time I'd make her come first…or at the same time.

I murmured a few expletives. I was so thoroughly into bad guy universe I doubted I could find my way back. Fucking a girl in a plain ol' ordinary way would be like eating cardboard.

I looked up as I heard footsteps and there she was walking toward me, swaying. A gold gossamer dress over a white bikini. An angel, a kinky angel who I could make do so many dirty things. I could bend her over the railing, the couch...

Beach, I reminded myself, swallowing. The fucking beach. I smiled and levered myself off the railing.

When she stopped before me, the urge to give the hand signal for kneeling was so great that I had to deliberately make myself not do it.

"Come here." I wasn't going to let her walk freely, not outside where she might run again, but I didn't want to restrict her too much. "I'm putting this on your collar." I eyed her as I fiddled and clipped the leash on. The other end was attached to a cuff around my wrist. "I'd like not to have to, but you know why."

Kat shrugged. "I understand, Sir."

The Sir always resonated for me. She said it now, without thinking, or seemed to. I wondered if inside her head she resented it. Even after all these weeks, I didn't know her well. If anything she'd shut herself off more after she'd run and we caught her. Today I was going to start us on a new path.

Keeping her didn't mean treating her like dirt, or an object...

That upside down scene flashed to my mind. Yeah, except when I wanted her that way.

We stayed in the edge of the shade where the sand met the forest. I took her hand and held it, amused, in some ways, by the resemblance to two lovers out for a stroll. I stared out across the white sand to the rolling surface of the sea. Three in the afternoon. Great weather for swimming – a little cool, but the ocean was a few degrees warmer since we were heading deeper into winter.

I'd braved the bay a few times, in the middle of the day. It wasn't mating season for the crocs so we were fairly safe. Chris and I never swam if the water wasn't nice and clear.

"It's beautiful out here," Kat murmured. "Wish I could swim.

From the rueful quirk of her mouth and the way she gazed past me toward the bay, her words seemed genuine. Long ago we'd decided we couldn't allow her to swim. "It's dangerous."

"Crocs?" She pulled a doubtful face and stopped walking. "I know you swim. You don't trust me though, do you?"

"No, we don't."

"*You* don't."

Why the emphasis? "No."

Her nod was distant, like I'd only confirmed a suspicion.

I tilted her chin up with the back of a finger. "If I knew you better, if you behaved better, I might trust you."

"Behaved?" Again with the big stare of those gray eyes.

She wouldn't fool me again.

"Tell me about yourself."

"So that's an order, Sir?" Then she turned away and looked up into the high trees, as if she wasn't being bad by turning away while we were talking.

By tone alone, I made my reply an admonishment. "Kat." Chris had trained me too. I jingled the leash.

She turned back. "Sir?"

Close to the bone. I let it by. Day of talking, being normal, remember?

"What were you looking at in there?"

"A bird. See?" She pointed. A yellow bird hovered beside a tree, its curved beak either probing for insects or nectar. "I think that's a sunbird."

"It is."

She frowned at me. "You know your birds?"

I waggled my head. "I've been googling while staying here. And I've walked through there a few times. That's a yellow sunbird."

"Ah." Her fallen expression told me I'd struck a nerve. "Can we go in there? Sir?"

That last Sir had been slow, reluctant.

"Sure we can." I took her hand again.

We entered the forest. Both of us were barefoot so I didn't plan going deeper where there'd be even more forest debris. We went in a few yards before walking parallel with the juncture of the trees and the beach. So, she liked creatures? One small fact learned.

I kept an eye out for more animals or birds. We chatted as we went on, falling into a gentle rhythm of spotting the small birds, a lizard, even a rifle bird that called its signature whip crack noise for us before flying away. Two minute green tree frogs sat on a moss-covered log and took a few hops when we crouched to look more closely.

"There was an adult in the toilet a few days ago," Kat said quietly.

"I know. I fished him out and let him go near here."

"Oh." She looked disappointed. "He was pretty."

My voice rose in disbelief. "Living in the toilet? No." Slowly I shook my head. "No way. I'm not being surprised by a frog each morning when I go to the toilet."

"Wuss," she muttered.

I chuckled. "Careful what you call me, miss."

"Huh." She smiled, actually smiled. "I'm a brat, that's the official kink term."

"It is?" I ventured into dangerous territory. This was such an artificial situation. It was hard to know what to talk about. Friends, family, job – all were off limits. "You can teach me some more of those, or anything about kink, if you want."

Kat snorted and switched into hostile mode in the hitch of a breath. "Me? You're fucking joking. You can learn all of that from friendly Chris. I'm not teaching you."

Swearing at me? I hesitated, cranked back my response to minimal. "Sir."

Her eyebrows rose. "...Sir."

Maybe we could have that heart-to-heart talk I wanted, needed. A clean fallen log from a gum tree made a convenient place to do this where it curved up a few feet from the forest floor. I sat down and pulled her to stand between my knees. "What's bothering you?"

"What do you think?" Cheeky, bordering on outright disrespect. She hurried on before I could pull her up on that. Was that two or three infractions? *"You* can walk free in here, I can't. *You* have access to computers, the world, I don't. You have a life. I don't. Lots of small –" She held up finger and thumb so they were almost, but not quite, touching. "– weeny insignificant things like that."

The front of her gold dress heaved as she sucked in an indignant breath. Angry little thing. I narrowed my eyes. The tiny embroidered roses scattered across the bodice were shaped in and out by the hills of her breasts. I almost stuck my tongue out and licked her cleavage. Fuck. Riveting. My cock was responding.

I wrenched my gaze to hers.

My words tumbled out before I censored them. "You're being a brat again. Disrespectful."

"I'm what?" Incredulity twanged in the pitch of her words. She was seething, eyes glaring, teeth showing.

This was the first time I'd walked with her alone and now I regretted not having Chris here. He'd named himself well. The enforcer.

"Didn't you learn anything yesterday?"

Ah. *Now* she went red and a moment later she looked away. Kat nibbled on her lip. "I'm sorry. Sir."

"Are you? Maybe I should make sure of that."

I shouldn't go further, not if I wanted this on a vaguely normal level, but I undid the bow of her halter neck bikini top, then I gathered her dress up at the back until I could slip my hands beneath. Up over the curve of her wonderful luscious ass…

I watched her eyes, enthralled, did what I needed to by feel alone. Smooth back. Soft skin. She winced a few times when I guess I nudged bruises. Apart from that, she stayed stock still, only rocking if I moved her body, I found the back bow of her bikini top and pulled. The top fell away to the ground. The see-through dress revealed her…

I inhaled, caught by her sexuality, her beauty, as I was every single time.

Under the dress, I moved my hands and cupped each breast. My palms weighed their fullness. "These are pretty." I thumbed slowly across one rose-pink areola. "Soft as petals." With the pad of my thumb, I traced around and around one nipple while I checked her for a reaction.

She opened her mouth and I could see the underside of her tongue as she touched her lip, then the slow blink, until for a moment her eyes were closed, only to open when I stopped my finger moving. The breeze from the sea sent strands of her hair swirling into the air.

"I want to suck on you whenever I see these."

"Oh?" she asked huskily, swaying toward me. "Bad man."

I smiled. "Yes, I am." Turned on already?

Chris had said it would become automatic with time. We were training her to become aroused quickly, at our touch. I liked that. My cock did too; it was prodding at my shorts already, trying to get out. As if she knew, her focus dropped to my lap.

Memory. The feel of her mouth on me. I almost groaned aloud.

Yes, no, should I, shouldn't I? Normal was rapidly deteriorating into let's fuck her simply because I can and I want to. Let's do it in a way that I like and maybe she doesn't.

Or...I could kiss her first. Foreplay and whatever happens after that.

"Fuck no," I growled.

Her eyes widened at my threatening words. "Andr – Sir? Wait." She splayed her palms out before her. "This is wrong, you know this is."

"Uh-uh." Using the leash, I reeled her in and forced her over my lap.

She wriggled but not enough to bother me. I had her wrists in one hand and an arm leaned over the lower curve of her spine. "Think I was weak, Kat? I'm not, you know."

She huffed and her muscles slackened. "I didn't. You're a man. I know you're stronger."

My ego liked that – her acknowledging me as her superior.

Her dress had stayed hitched up nicely. Convenient. I moved my hand lower to the lush mound of her ass, pulled down her panties, and let them fall away past her ankles. Pure joy, being able to do this.

"I could check you out all day. With your pussy where I can see it. There's so many possibilities, when I have an ass like this to play with."

"I guess." Her words were almost lost; she'd lowered her head and murmured that to the ground. With her hair hanging in a swathe over her face, I could see the faint lightness at the roots.

I'd clicked her cuffs together, so I let go of her wrists to instead comb my fingers into her locks at the nape. "Like water. You have beautiful hair. You're blond elsewhere. Why turn red?"

Her shrug was slight. "Truthfully, I bleach myself blond everywhere else."

Definitely being a brat this time.

Methodically, I unlocked and disconnected the leash from us both, dropped it to the ground. The thing was going to get in the way. Then I delivered a few heavy swats to her butt. They were hard enough to make her squeal and squirm, to make her skin blush pink.

"Wow." I looked at her rear end more closely. There were old bruises but my handprint stood out. "I can see my fingers in the marks."

"Good for you. Whoop-de-doo-dah," Kat muttered. "Do you want a cake or fireworks?"

"Neither. I think, with those words, you earned what I'm going to do next."

Her meek silence made me grin. I laid her over the log, ignoring her curses when she worried about bugs and dirt and shit. I pulled my shirt off over my head, then took off my shorts and set them on the big log for padding and I moved her so she draped over my clothes.

I clipped her ankles together. Now *that* made her nervous. She turned her head to look at me, suspicion written all over her face.

With her legs together, she was perhaps thinking anal. I let her think what she wanted.

"Sir?"

Fuck. That word again. It made me hyperaware of how vulnerable she was.

"I can't breathe." Kat wriggled on the spot.

All her weight was on her stomach where she draped over the log. I redid the cuffs so she could rest her hands over her head, on the ground. Since she was still ass up and at knee height, I was happy. Even happier when I dragged the dress fully over her head until it caught under her armpits, and was inside out, then I used the dress itself to knot it firmly around her arms.

She wriggled madly for a minute or more while I smiled at her struggles and held her hips down. At last, she stopped and lay there panting.

"Now I've caught you." This was a little homemade net and trapped inside were her upper back, her arms, her head, and that pretty mouth.

"Let me out of here. Please?" Her words were barely muffled and hoarse. "I don't like being all tangled up!"

That prompted me to run my fingers down her spine, beginning from where the fabric turned up, to her ass, and then along the back of one leg to her knee. She squeaked when I tickled her there.

"No! Please. Let me out. Please."

I gripped her knee in my fist, thrilling at how I had her at my mercy with such a simple act. "Shh. No words. Only noises are allowed. If you talk I'll find a nice branch to flog you with and I don't know what the hell I'm doing with sticks. If I were you, I'd keep my mouth shut."

Kat whimpered once.

Those little noises of hers went straight to my cock. This was the first time I'd rendered her helpless all by myself. I liked this, a lot. Sexual power with sprinkles and caviar on top. Dominating her was so fucking addictive it was burning holes in my veins.

I sat on the log beside her and put my hand on her back so I could feel her warmth, feel her ribs expand and the thud of her heart.

I leaned down. I could see her looking back at me through the rose-dotted cloth. "In a minute, when I've looked enough, I'm going to rip a hole in this dress, and use your mouth like I've been dreaming of doing, little fucktoy." I trailed my fingers down into her cleft. "Or maybe I'll use one or two of your other holes first."

She stared, dark-eyed, back at me, but said nothing. Now this, *this* was power.

I'd deviated from what I'd intended to do but I had all the rest of my life to learn about Kat. She wasn't going anywhere, anytime soon, unless I let her go. That thought made me pause. I used to be the man who conspired against his best friend to free her. Now I couldn't bear the thought of letting her go. Did I still admire, or even like, myself?

She'd told me this was wrong. Words and more words.

I could go round in circles thinking like this. I had done on a few days. Men had done things like this through the centuries. I didn't hate what I'd become. I'd grown used to this concept of owning Kat. As long as we treated her properly and this didn't become some sadistic exercise in torture and slavery, I was fine with it. Full stop. End of argument. This was me.

"Let's see what I can get you to do."

This was where I realized the pleasures of having her all to myself. With Chris about he tended to arrange what happened and what we did.

No woman had ever sat still for me to explore her body at my leisure. We were in the shade, both comfortable. I examined how I had her head down, ready for me to touch her. Well, I was comfortable.

I parted her legs as far as the link on her ankles allowed and spent all of five or ten minutes simply playing with her pussy and making her wriggle and moan. I skated my finger lightly around and around her lips and dipped, ever so slow, inside her to the depth of the first or sometimes the second knuckle. Torture in a way, but a good sort. I slowly stretched her with more fingers, and watched her lips swell, fascinated by how desperate her noises became when I also toyed with her little swollen clit.

I stopped with two fingers half their length inside her, with her panting and beginning that gorgeous arch of back muscle most women did just before they came. Moisture welled up around my fingers. Her breathing came fast and deep.

"I hope you aren't going to tell me you don't like this, Kat, because I can see the evidence." She grunted as I slowly pushed another finger in. "That's three fingers I'm fucking you with. One day…I might try fisting you. I like that idea. I've heard women can have incredible orgasms with a fist in them."

Her generally unhappy noises rose in volume and made me look down at her obscured face. She shook her head vigorously.

"No? Take care. Get too loud and I'll do it now." Dead fucking silence. Hah. "Much better. If I do decide to try fisting, I'll make sure you like it. I'm not into pain by itself."

I'd worked that much out about myself.

With her on the edge for so long it might not take long for her to come. I thrust those three fingers further. When I wedged them in, while still thumbing her clit, she began to shudder, and her hands clawed at the ground.

I'd never seen Chris train her to come on command but it wouldn't hurt to try. I kinda liked the concept. If I said it often enough, maybe it would eventually stick?

"Come for me, Kat." I gave her clit a thorough treatment, rhythmically, softly, rubbing round and round, while I whispered sweet words. A minute or so later, she screamed and her body stiffened. "Come for me, *now*." This time she did. Her deep and frantic gasping and the clench of her on my fingers made me wish my dick was inside her already.

I stood and positioned my cock at her entrance, sliding into her in one glorious thrust. She was so wet I felt it squash onto my balls. The curve of her spine deepened into the backward arch of a woman who's instinctively giving the man better access. I plowed leisurely into her, letting my own pleasure ascend in a measured way. From her squeals, sometimes I was hitting her G-spot, or close to it.

I withdrew, stepped over the log, and walked around to her front. The air cooled on my erection. I pulled up her head by bunching my fist on dress and hair with my other hand under her shoulder. Then I shifted her back across the log until she was mostly kneeling. Due to the dress tying them together, her arms were above her.

I had her at groin level. "Open your mouth."

She only blinked.

"Open or I *will* try fisting you." I said it matter-of-factly because I meant it. I was more than happy to attempt fisting. I was sure I wouldn't get far; it was the sort of thing that needed preparation. But the appeal of that had sunk in. Another day, maybe…my balls scrunched up.

Her mouth opened.

"Nice." I played with her teeth with my fingers, poked the flimsy dress material so it popped into her mouth a little ways. "I like making you do things you don't want to, Kat," I murmured. "Like fucking your hot little mouth when you're all covered up like a present no one has bothered to unwrap." I tore a hole in the material as I spoke, then I fed the head of my cock in an inch, two. The moist warmth in there made me hum. "That's good. Suck it in. Go on…" I thrust in a small distance. "…all the way."

As I fucked her there, with the cloth getting wet with her drool, I told her what I would do if she didn't get me off in her mouth. "I'm going to fuck your ass with just your own wetness if you don't girl." I thrust in again, to the very back. She gagged like always but kept me there, swallowing, trying to do it. Hot pulsations thrummed through me, accelerating, gathering steam. If she'd just…keep…doing that. But a last thrust made her gag severely and choke, so I pulled out.

I retrieved a condom from my shorts.

"Nice try. Don't get anxious. I can do this real slow and still get off. Your ass is damn tight."

Though she whimpered and whined the whole time, I got the tip of my dick into her ass after slicking up and down between her lips and wetting it in her juices. Inching in, and in, and out to give her rest – the squeeze on me was tremendous. She gave a hot, appreciative gasp each time I pushed myself in farther.

"Like that?" I pressed with my cock again, drew a finger down her sweaty back, a wavery line on the bumps of her spine. "Hmm?" She shivered.

With some dexterous moves, I found her clit and toyed with it, revolving it with the very tip of my finger. Her moan was quiet but I was listening real hard. Besides, her ass had squeezed in on me more than once. I kissed her shoulder.

"No rush. I got all day in your ass. Let's make you enjoy this even more."

Feather-light, I played some more.

Slow and steady wins the sexy ass. I almost laughed at that thought. Then my balls bumped into her bottom. I looked down to see my shaft was finally all the way, totally inside her. The sight alone made me groan. I was surely only a few excruciating heartbeats away from coming. I gritted my teeth.

Thump thump, thump thump.

I was never, ever going to get tired of doing this to our little Kat. While I stared at nothing, I took some tight breaths and wound my excitement down a notch.

After a few more minutes of manipulating her clit, I had Kat back into ecstasy territory – gasping, moaning, and writhing on the end of my cock. Her shudders and the contractions of her ass – exquisite.

At the last orgasmic second, I remembered to grunt out, "Come for me." Then I gave one last high and deep thrust that might've shoved her over the log if I hadn't held her.

In the midst of the chaos of orgasm, I wasn't sure who came first.

I bit her nape then breathed in her scent, registering how she'd slumped into a limp, tussled mess. I whispered roughly. "I hope you like ass fucking, Kat. Because I'm in love with it."

I should get the dress off her soon. Untie her. I sat up a little to check her out, and to caress her, my sexy sweaty captive. *Note to self: next time, take pictures.*

Once I'd had my fill of looking at her lying there all delicious and disheveled, I helped her up and settled her clothing in place then I cuddled her, still sitting on the log.

With my arm around her shoulders and my mouth on her hair, I struggled with an urge to ask her if she was happy. I wanted to but her answer – I knew it would not be everything I wanted to hear. No matter how many orgasms we gave her, how thorough our love making was, or in Chris's case, the pain sessions…no matter that, she wasn't ours yet inside her head. That counted to me. Still. I wanted *something.*

I ran my finger down the chain on my neck and toyed with the shark tooth, watching it spin in the light. I dug my big toe in the sandy soil, stirred the cool sand, and made my decision.

When I unwrapped my arm from Kat's shoulders, she peeked at me. Funny how meek she sometimes was afterward, after we'd fucked her silly. I swallowed. Dominated her. That odd thrill took me when I recalled what that really meant. But that was the right word. Dominate.

Kat sighed in a contented way.

"I never told you…" she began hesitantly.

"Hmm?"

"Remember when you asked me what I didn't do anymore? After that Dom abused me?"

"Yes."

"One of the things I wasn't doing anymore was sex. I hadn't for years, until now."

Was she joking? No. This was her being honest.

"I'm glad you told me. Honored."

Her smile had turned a little wary. As if even now she worried she'd said too much.

We'd made her do it after years of no one inside her. That she trusted me enough to tell me was amazing.

"Lower your head, Kat." I shifted back a little on the log, and turned so I could see her better.

She looked up at me. I only saw trust in her eyes. "Yes, Sir."

I pulled off the pendant, then carefully draped the chain over her neck and let it fall. I arranged her hair down her back and on her shoulders. Now the tooth spun before her.

I nudged her chin so she raised her head.

"That's yours," I said quietly. "It's been mine for many years. I used it to remind me of how to conquer my fears, my doubts. Maybe it will help you."

"Thank you." She cupped the tooth in her palm and examined it.

"It means more than that now. To me, it says you're mine. One day, you'll admit that too. Won't you, Kat?"

Her throat moved in a swallow and she shrugged. "I don't know. Sir."

The subtle shake in her words – that alone buoyed me. That was a maybe in my book. Maybe would turn into *yes*.

"You will." I wrapped my hand around her fingers where she cradled the tooth. Not quite victory. But I'd won a small battle.

That was when I noticed the smoke drifting across the sky and the odd sweetness mixed with the scent of the smoke.

Chapter 24

Chris

The smoke hinted something was wrong even before I opened the front door. The engine noises had drawn me to the front of the house. I descended and watched as Scrim's range rover and a Toyota 4WD drove in. The smoke was barely there as a haze across the blueness of the sky where it showed between the trees. The smell was more noticeable. Pot? Had to be a biggish fire to be coming in like this.

After they'd parked and a man hopped out to close the gates, four men unloaded the vehicles. I'd pretty much guessed what the cargo would be, but seeing them hauling out blindfolded, bound and gagged women then carrying them into Scrim's house was…disturbing.

I was odd. I must be. Yet this was different. It *had* to be different to what we did to Kat. I had a line in the sand. Though I'd ignored this business of Vetrov's as a distant thing that didn't concern me because I couldn't do anything about it, having it here made me ill.

Scrim sauntered over, hands lazily at his sides – jeans, black work boots and that wry, nasty expression that was all his. "The boss said you knew the girls were coming, right?"

I nodded. "Yes."

"Okay. So now you double know."

One of the women, a dark-haired beauty, wriggled and squealed. To my surprise, the heavily built T-rex of a man carrying her didn't slap her. He halted to say something. His mass of black hair concealed them both as he talked. She stopped her craziness and he walked on. Goth biker look to him. Leather, black jeans, muscular.

"Pieter has a way with the girls. His first trip but he makes them behave."

I glanced at Scrim. He was angling to get me to ask what this Pieter did.

"You keep out of my way. Andreas doesn't know about what this is. I want it to stay that way." I wasn't really sure what they were up to here. A waypoint before they moved them on? Though all the kink gear made me think training. Eventually these women would be sold.

"Sure." Then he nodded like it was something he'd keep in mind as a king would to a subject's request. Man needed taking down a notch.

The smoke smell thickened.

"What's the smoke? Bushfire somewhere?" With the Daintree so wet, it seemed unlikely a fire would spread. I'd check online if he didn't know.

"Some weed growers found out the hard way that they should've gone elsewhere."

Ominous. Scrim had mentioned something about this when we'd first met. He had a hint of smugness about him.

"Someone you knew?"

"Not anymore."

I thought that through. "Your boss won't like attention being attracted to this area."

"Attention? The crocs are hungry buggers. Nothing left for the cops to find. The wind just sent some smoke our way. Nothing will happen. You'll see." He rubbed the scar on his face, gave me a last, black look then walked away.

What the hell? He'd killed someone? Everything around me seemed to give a little quiver. My world adjusted to the idea of casual killing.

I walked back up the stairs slowly and went out to the deck. I leaned on the railing, letting the sea calm me, and was still thinking when Andreas and Kat came back through the beach gate.

What had I brought down on us? Keeping separate from what they did was becoming ever more difficult. I never wanted to hurt Andreas...or Kat for that matter. These were fucking dangerous waters in which Scrim and Vetrov swam.

With his hand on her back, Andreas guided Kat up the stairs. Her clothes and her hair, face, and body, were so disheveled. He'd been doing stuff to her. Obviously. I smiled to myself. Both envy and pride were in my head. I liked them together yet I wanted some of what Andreas was nurturing between them. I just didn't know if it something I could do or if she'd accept a relationship closer than what we had.

I stayed leaning on the railing, chin on hand, as they reached the top steps. "Have fun?" The shark tooth swinging from the chain on her neck glinted.

Shit. Andreas, you bastard.

"Yeah, we did." He smiled down at her, his hand caressing her back and Kat peeked at him. There were twigs and sand in her hair, a few tears in the see-through dress.

He'd made a little claim on her. I knew how much that tooth meant to him. That was okay though, surely? We were sharing.

Get a grip. She's mine too. I crammed my instinctive jealous response down a notch or three.

Kat looked submissive through and through.

I'd never seen her like that without being roped and forced with pain. Or even so...happy, not since we'd abducted her. What did he have that I didn't? Shit. The instructor needed to learn from the pupil. Though when I looked closer, harder, her coy expression faltered and turned blank.

"Happy, Kat?"

"Yes, Sir."

Such a quick reply. I never knew the truth with her. Walls within walls.

At lunchtime we supervised from the living room couches as she made sandwiches. Seeing as I didn't have tacks or arsenic in the kitchen cupboards, I was fairly safe.

"You put the knives elsewhere this time?" Andreas murmured.

"You know I did. Asshole."

"Just checking." He leaned back and crossed his legs. "I like you better without holes in you."

"Huh."

Kat looked up from putting the chicken and salad on the bread. That contemplative expression made me wonder if she'd heard us. For a woman with so much venom, she had the most innocent face.

One eyebrow went up. "What? Sir."

The Sir never quite made the grade when she said it to me – like it was a fraction of a millisecond too late.

I shook my head and waited for her to bring the sandwiches over then kneel beside us. I put my hand on her head, enjoying the feel. I didn't know sometimes what I wanted from her, but it was more than I had. Maybe Andreas was right? Maybe a bit of gentle now and then would work?

"Go outside and clip yourself to the chair, Kat. I'll call you when I want you to return."

I waited until she'd done that then turned to Andreas. He'd already stuffed one sandwich in his mouth and had picked up another.

"Eat slower. I need some too. It's like living with a piranha."

He smiled but kept hold of the sandwich. "Spit. What did you want to say?"

"The future." I rested elbows on knees then rested my mouth on my clasped hands.

"And? Actually I was wondering…"

"What?" I glanced up from my study of the rug.

"What happens in a week or so? We're leaving but what did you have planned? How are you going to keep her…safely? And you know I want to be there too."

"My friend, Klaus, is letting me buy his house. It's good for what we need. Trust me, it is."

"Okay." He swallowed some more sandwich, and I took one up a second before he reached down again.

Three left. "Leave some for Kat, you hungry bastard."

"I will! She wore me out. I need the energy."

I snorted and sat back, ate some sandwich. It might've been good but I was too worried to taste it. "You know you're welcome to move in with us." Us, funny, first time I'd thought of Kat as part of my *us*. Maybe Andreas was influencing me? I'd never be soft like him though. "If it fits in with what you want to do. You can't be planning to rely on the stock market? That's dicey stuff even for the pros. You need big money, patience, big balls."

"Maybe. To both."

"Big balls?"

He smiled. "I want to get a solid engineering job too. I can do it locally. Oil rigs just pay better."

"I bet they do." I looked out at Kat. From the way she stared she was attempting lip reading. "It'll be a lot safer for everyone if you're with us."

"Good. It's settled then. One day, maybe, we might be able to trust her enough to let her out in public."

"I don't know." I collapsed back into the couch. "Scrim brought in a group of kinksters. I told him to stay away from us, and he wants us to do the same. Deep role play, Master and slave stuff, so don't be surprised if you see or hear anything unusual over there."

His eyebrows rose and disappeared under his hair. "Sure. We need to be super careful then."

"We do." I sat up and signaled to Kat. She'd stayed where she'd been told to. She was learning – it just took time. Someday I'd get her to truly submit to me.

"Beautiful," Andreas said quietly as she walked toward us, hips undulating like a harem dancer.

"Yes." My gut ached for a second as I recalled the other women and I flashed to an imagined scene of her being taken away by them. "Never," I whispered.

"What?" He turned back.

"Nothing. Just nothing…"

Late that afternoon I checked my emails. Vetrov had sent one.

Scrim will visit you tonight. You're to allow him in. He is bringing you a gift. Accept it for your services over the years. Do not refuse.

There was only one thing I could imagine the gift could be. No. Couldn't be.

Yet when I opened the door that night, there was Scrim accompanied by his hulking partner, Pieter, and a girl kneeled at their feet.

All that ran through my mind was, *oh shit, oh shit, oh shit.*

"Here she is." Scrim jerked his head toward her. Prim, cute, smaller in build than Kat with curly brown hair like one of those women from the 1920s who did the crazy dances. Flappers?

I crouched to look in her eyes but catching her gaze was harder than trapping a butterfly. She looked everywhere but at me. They had her in a little red dress with bright red lipstick on a mouth as rich as cherries.

"Where'd the lipstick come from?"

Pieter only glowered. Scrim shrugged. "There's heaps of makeup and girly crap. Boss said to make her look sexy so we told her to put it on."

"Right." Trying to tempt us? "Name?"

"Uhh." He scratched his head then threw a questioning glance at Pieter.

"Zoe," the big man grunted out. The piranha tattoos leaping along his arm looked ready to bite.

Zoe. "What do I do with her? And…" I listened and was sure Andreas was deep inside the house. "Where'd she come from?"

The grin on Scrim's face was positively voracious. "Do whatever you like to with her hot little bod. S'long as you don't damage her. Or get her pregnant. She came from nowhere. Not your business. Be careful what you ask."

I ignored the skulking threat in his words. "It's not me that's the problem. My partner might ask her questions."

And what the hell would I do if she begged for help?

"She won't talk. If she says a single word to any of you she knows I'll cut out her little tongue and feed it to a croc. You hear that...Zoe?" He bent and eyed her with her chin in his tight grip.

Zoe checked me out then Scrim then made an *mmm* sound. I guess her silence started early.

"Good girl. We'll be back in two days to get you. Be good. Be very, very good." From the back of his jeans the metal butt of a pistol showed. He straightened. "No more questions, Chris?" The leer was so insubordinate I wanted to smear it across his teeth.

I hated that he knew my name. "No. None."

So. She wouldn't talk. If she did, though... How was I going to explain it to Andreas?

Ice ran with my blood. Why? Why was Vetrov doing this? He'd have his reasons and I couldn't see them. I was already in so deep he didn't need anything on me. I gathered my wits before they ran off down some mouse hole. People thought I looked too tough to get scared but this, yeah, it scared me. Big unknowns did. I hated being out of my depth.

I hated the possibility I could destroy my friendship with Andreas. This was the biggest failure of trust ever.

I was so wrecked I couldn't take that next step. But I couldn't leave her out here forever.

While I was still standing there paralyzed, with her waiting for me to command her to go through the door, Pieter came back up the stairs, taking three at a time. He raised his hand and offered me a key on a chain.

Ah. She had a chain locking her wrist cuffs together as well as a stainless steel collar.

The man leaned in, scowling. "Like he said, don't damage the merchandise."

What the... Was that a warning? I followed his retreat back down the stairs with my eyebrows still raised. His last subtle gesture had been a pat on Zoe's head as he went by, so secretive I nearly missed the significance.

"Come on in, Zoe." I held the door open as she crawled past. That I hadn't told her to crawl, but she'd done it anyway, said they'd had her for more than a few days. Cowed, already.

Did it matter to me, when she was going back in a couple of days? "Look up at me, Zoe." Green eyes. What a sweet face. Was she a tourist caught while backpacking? A girl who had her drink spiked on a night out clubbing? I'd never know. But, no, this wasn't my problem.

What was my problem was the mess Vetrov had created. Why? If Andreas found out, surely his whole operation was at greater risk? If Zoe talked, though I guess that was unlikely. Scrim had scared the crap out of her. But...she might.

"Come. You can stand up." I led her into the study and had her wait on the spare chair. I fired up the laptop.

No new emails had come from Vetrov. How did I say this?

I had nothing.

I have your gift. Why are you doing this? If A finds out, your risk is increased.

He started a chat. I sat back. Thank god. Maybe I could get rid of her?

V: No. I need your friend to get dirty. Dirty hands, I have less risk.

He didn't know Andreas. The man might, just might, get the urge to save the woman from slavery. I wasn't sure anymore. I massaged my fingers into my eyes. I didn't want to find out. I may as well dump a load of rocks on our friendship.

C: If he gets dirty, did you mean to tell him the truth?

V: Perhaps. Up to you for now. Do to her whatever sexy things you like. I know you like the girls.

Shit. But, I imagined letting Andreas fuck her under the pretense that she was kinky and wanted it, then him finding out the truth. The fallout of that lie would be a monster compared to what I already had to deal with.

Then and there I decided I wasn't going to do this. But sending her back to Scrim untouched was dicey. I didn't know for sure how far Vetrov would go to ensure Andreas's silence.

"Shit!"

Zoe looked up, startled, frightened.

"It's fine." I put my hand out. "Don't worry."

She just blinked at me and trembled.

I stared back. I did not want this on my conscience. "You're not going to talk about anything here, okay?"

She nodded.

"I'm not going to touch you, neither is the other man, or…"

If Kat did things to her, that would be Vetrov's dirty hands effect again. A small hold on Kat if ever I needed that sort of thing. And we could tell Zoe this was what we perverted men wanted. It might be enough for Vetrov. Voyeurism. It had to be. I wasn't going anywhere near this poor woman with my cock.

I chained her to a wall anchor point, went into the living room and explained to Andreas the whitest version of this deception that I could. Zoe was kinky and bi and role playing the silent captive. I hadn't been able to say no to her so we'd play along with her depraved desires and pretend, pretend hard, because we couldn't afford to let slip that Kat was a real prisoner.

Then I fetched her and turned her over to Kat. If I didn't tell Kat otherwise, she'd think this was just another abducted girl, which she was. Win, win, surely? Only I had a feeling I'd missed something important. What the crap was it?

Chapter 25

Kat

Who was this?

Chris brought her over to where I sat on the floor before the couch. Slowly she lowered herself.

"Meet Zoe."

Frightened eyes.

Pretty thing with all the kink paraphernalia – collar, cuffs, and the silver chain that Chris removed. Little red flouncy dress that came to her upper thighs and clung to her curves. Red lips, tousled brown hair just long enough to grab if someone wanted to kiss her. She was the sort of girl I'd have eaten up if she'd delivered herself on a platter...back then, when I had my own life.

I sighed and whispered to her, "My name's Kat. Who are you really? I'm a prisoner. You?"

She stayed mute, maybe a little worried, mostly I couldn't figure her out. A glance at Andreas and Chris where they stood either side of the couch gave me alarm bells in the head. Mixed signals. My heart went into tango time and I could feel it thump. I looked from her to them again.

What was going on?

"Kiss her, Kat. She wants you to. If you don't Scrim will punish her." Chris looked amused.

When I'd asked that first question of Zoe, he'd actually looked smug for a second. Why?

I half-opened my mouth again. If she wasn't a captive like me, they'd made a big mistake. But – Chris, still smug.

To him, me talking meant nothing. He wouldn't let me near a free woman. I was so sure of that.

Andreas spoke up, his hand gripping the couch and squashing in the upholstery. "Maybe we should put a gag on Kat?"

"No, it's okay."

What…

If she was a captive, telling her anything went nowhere, and what Chris said – fuck, I felt sorry for her. But Andreas seemed worried. Too many things were going around in my head – not least that the longer I delayed the more agitated Zoe seemed to get.

"You okay if I kiss you?"

She nodded slightly, though the shine in her eyes had me wanting to hug her. The perverts watched us like hawks. I frowned. Least they could give us the couch.

"Come here." I offered her my hand, and when she took it, I drew her to the couch.

The guys seemed unperturbed by my change of venue. Chris perched on the armrest while Andreas hesitated but went and sat on the other couch off to the side. Not exactly intimidating but not far off – especially considering Chris worked out most days at his martial arts. Even hating him, when he started those, I couldn't stop watching him, his sweat-shiny muscles – his moves. All that karate kata shit. Drool material.

Damn. I was getting horny just remembering.

I gave him a raised eyebrow hint but he stayed at his armrest perch. Of course. What else would the man do? I refocused on Zoe.

"Will Scrim really hurt you?" I kept my voice low and unchallenging seeing she looked ready to burst into tears at any second.

Another nod. Still no words.

"Can you talk?"

Nod.

"But someone told you not to?"

Nod.

"Okay." I traced a little line up her forearm. I guess she was genuine. A real captive. "Kissing you won't be a hardship for me." I smiled. "You're just my type. But I won't do it unless you say it's okay." She nodded. "So…do you want me to kiss you?"

After a second, she did. Her nod pleased me. Funny. But in a way, despite the perverted reasons and the men watching us, I knew I was helping her. Scrim was the sort of man who hurt women casually, without worrying. Which meant something… I was on the edge of understanding.

Then it skipped away again.

"How long is she staying?" I asked Chris.

"Two days." His eyes bored into mine, like he too knew there was something rattling around in my head. "Plenty of time. Kiss her. She really truly needs you to. Scrim expects her to have sex."

For a few seconds he stared down at Zoe's head. Maybe he too was sorry for her?

"So you will do that. That's a command."

"Yes… Sir." Fuck his commands.

My forehead tensed. At this rate I'd have new wrinkles there in a few days. Fine. I'd kiss her. But I'd ignore the creeps and do it at our pace. At least I could make her happy for a while. Maybe the two of us could even figure a way to escape. I just had to get her to talk. And I had to chase down that stupid thought that lurked at the back of my head.

Chris stood and stepped in closer. I lost track of Zoe as I found myself flinching back into the couch, the cushions only let me go so far before I hit the solid frame within. My throat tightened at the intensity I saw in him. He leaned in, hand planting on the couch between me and the girl, arm making a barrier. I didn't dare look away.

Then, *pain.* He'd grabbed my hair. Fuck. Feeling like a bird knocked from the sky, I dropped my gaze to my lap.

"Up. Here, Kat. My eyes are here." His face was menacing, dark. "Don't think I can't read you. Don't think I can't see the disrespect, or the *fuck yous* in your face. Want to try me with some real pain? I can string you up now, here. Apologize."

My pussy clenched in for all the wrong reasons. "Sorry, Sir." I swallowed, waited to be forgiven.

"Thank you. You are obstinate but I have infinite patience and time. I *will* get through to you." He gave my head a shake and I held my breath. "No matter how much you infuriate me." He brushed my forehead with his palm then went back to his perch. The amusement lines around his eyes had vanished.

My theories about Chris ran around like insane moths in a candle flame. Burnt, scorched, my wings were on fire.

I shut my eyes for a second, opened them to see the look of horror on Zoe.

Shut him out. I sniffed. I found a smile.

"Come here." I pulled her down so we both rested against the back of the couch, our faces only inches apart. Cozy. I gave us a minute or so of just calming down while I had my hand casually resting from my knee to her thigh. Pretending no one else was here.

Deep breath, let it out.

"Zoe, I don't kiss any girl I haven't gotten to know, so I'll just play with you a while. Then we can make out. Okay?"

Her nod was cuter when up close. "Good." I stroked a finger down her nose. "Tell me if I go too fast."

I wasn't even sure she liked women, considering. But the more I touched her the more she responded.

"We're going to forget anything except us, Zoe. That's a beautiful name." I ran my palm down her arm and smiled back when her lips curved up a little. "I like your smile. Any girl with a smile like that has a good chance of winning my heart."

Liar, liar, pants on fire. Well, sort of, a bit of an extreme statement, but it was worth it to lift her spirits. I didn't have much reason to exist right now. This made me feel like I was doing something.

I put my hand on her neck and toyed with the hair at her nape, unwinding curls as far as they'd go to her collarbone then watching them spring back into a shiny auburn coil. How old could she be? I could ask?

"Let me guess your age? Are you twenty-seven? No?"

By way of multiple guesses I found out she was twenty-nine.

"Thank you." As a reward, I brushed my lips on hers.

Her sigh was soft. Despite the wetness in her eyes, she was enjoying my attention. I pressed in a little more, soft on her mouth. We kissed until I ventured my tongue between her lips, just the tip, and she answered with her own. Sweet little thing. Zoe seemed like the most placid submissive, but perhaps it was the circumstances. Never mind. I was over-thinking this.

I pushed open her lips with mine and turned my head at an angle to deepen the kiss. Her tremors turned into mild shudders and she shifted her thighs apart. Slowly I parted them more with my own. More kissing and her head went back as she let me kiss her how I wanted.

No hurry.

I rested my hand at the top of her thigh then murmured in the little world space we'd made between us on the couch, where the guys didn't exist.

"I'm a switch in real life, Zoe. Do you know what that is?" I brushed my fingers up her thigh, then beneath the hem of the dress. No panties. Oh myyy. I swallowed. When she squirmed, I flicked my gaze down to her legs.

I lightly rested my fingertips just below the *V* of her mons, despite my sudden need to venture into that tempting valley. Another shudder took her. My mouth quirked upward. The girl was melting before my eyes. The warmth tingling between my legs was enough to make me uncomfortable, to make me ache to kiss her harder, and other things. But, but… This was so strange.

Finally, she shook her head.

She didn't know kinky terms. Bugger.

"It means, for me anyway, that unlike with men, with girls I like to be the dominant one when I make love to them. I like to make them do things…sometimes, if they enjoy it."

She blinked and licked her lips.

I narrowed my gaze, taking in the swell of her breasts and the curve of her throat where her pulse beat. Because of everything else, I couldn't make this safe or sane, but I could make sure what happened between us two was consensual.

"Would you like to be my girl for these two days?" I made my voice mellow even if every little move she did was firing me up inside. "I promise I'll make you happy."

Such big eyes. After a long moment, she nodded.

"Good girl, Zoe. Very good." Then I sneaked my finger higher and nudged my way between her thighs and into the groove of her sex. Moistness slicked my finger. She gasped. I whispered into her neck as I tasted her skin. "For two days you can be mine."

I prayed the men kept their distance.

I took her lip in my teeth and pulled it out a little ways before I released it. It would be interesting to see how far I could go with her. I kissed her some more as I stirred her down below. My hand was under the edge of her dress. Discreet.

"I'll make you come without the guys seeing much." I cocked an eyebrow while I slipped a finger along then inside her ever so quietly. The effect on her wasn't so quiet. She gave a half-squeak as I pushed ever deeper. Her walls pulsed hot on that finger. "They don't need to see, much. Just this."

Using kisses as a guide, I made my way down to her jaw then played biting games with her throat, listening to her sighs, feeling the delightful way her body writhed and wriggled.

Her first moan vibrated from deep in her throat beside my ear. I kissed her cleavage, inhaled her scent. "You're beautiful when you do that."

She was letting me take charge. I still didn't know if that was her natural way.

"Tell me if I do anything you hate, won't you Zoe?"

"Mm-hm." She was panting now but I guess that might've been my thumb doing its thing on top of her clit.

"Almost a word. Wow," I whispered, grinning. "Do you like how this feels? Like a woman kissing you?"

She nodded, her eyes closing in appreciation, her hips squirming toward my thumb. I wiggled a second finger in, and kept thumbing in little circles.

With my left hand, I'd already found her breast. Despite not wanting the men to see…I needed to. Using my teeth, I pulled down her dress on one side, exposing her. Then I bent my head and found her nipple and gave it one lick and a suck. The pink circle crinkled and rose under my tongue. Another suck had her arching and her thighs crushing in on my hand.

"Don't squash my hand, Zoe. I can't make you come if you do that."

When she managed to lessen the force, I grinned. "Thank you. Think you can come for me with the guys watching? Do you want to?"

I pumped my fingers in and out. She looked ready to pop. Felt it too. I played with her swollen little clit.

She took a long quivery breath and nodded.

"I'm going to suck on you here and use my fingers on your clit. Okay?"

She nodded again.

Then I lowered my head and applied myself. Though I ended up baring her other breast and sucking and licking both nipples, she quickly went into that staccato breathing mode of a woman about to come. Her moisture had spread and made all of her slippery. I never stopped my thumb rubbing in those persuasive circles. Slip, slide, bump, and the quiver of her muscles began.

As the first shudders hit and she stiffened, I lifted my head so I could watch her face as she climaxed – the parted lips, the little involuntary noises. So worth it. The best part of making a girl come was watching. When, at the end, she lay panting and quiet, I kissed her swollen lips. Then I curled up with her and patted her, murmuring small, reassuring words.

To my surprise the guys respected our time and had migrated out onto the deck.

I looked at her closed eyes and the peacefulness on her damp and pinkened face and couldn't understand the tears wetting my eyes. Sniffing, I wiped them away with the back of my hand then I nestled her into the angle of my neck and shoulder.

"What are we going to do, Zoe?" I stared across the living room and out the window to where the palms swayed on the horizon. "What can we do to get out of this mess?"

That night, Chris first tried keeping Zoe on the bed with him. I guess he'd chained her up somehow. But even I could hear her tremulous sobs at midnight. He rose and put her in the cage with me, locking it and growling a *behave* at us before slumping back into bed.

I spent ten or twenty minutes comforting her, hugging her, and kissing her head while whispering things that seemed to make sense at the time. Mostly I told her I'd keep her safe. Such a lie. Didn't help when I had to wipe away my own tears. Didn't help that I knew, I fucking *knew*, that I couldn't keep her safe.

I wasn't sure why she affected me so. Our ages weren't that far apart but she seemed more innocent and vulnerable. Plus she had Scrim and an unknown future, while I had Andreas and Chris. I knew them, even if Chris had an unpredictable, sometimes intimidating, approach.

I started thinking along the lines of the thought that had eluded me earlier. Of course that was when the little minx started kissing me back. I answered her lips with mine. We kissed for ages it seemed, both of us growing hotter, groping the other more, until my assertiveness took over and I grabbed her hair so I could bite her throat.

I halted, stared at her eyes where she lay under me. I almost said sorry and let her go. The moonlight was enough to see her in art deco detail. Shadow on curve, light on angle.

"Precious, beautiful girl." I almost growled that out.

Zoe whimpered and licked her lips. Well, well. Tentatively, I kissed her throat and heard the moan of a very aroused woman. So I continued. I bit her and meandered my way down her body until my licking and nipping found her belly button. Then I spread her legs.

She groaned softly and I looked up at her. The bars of the cage stood behind her head, reminding me of where I was. I caressed her thigh, feeling the shiver of her flesh. I kissed her there too, inches from where I wanted to put my tongue.

"Are you okay, Zoe?" My voice rasped with passion. I wanted to do this to her so much. For a second I pressed my fingers to myself to still the throbbing heat. It only made it worse, of course.

"Yes."

So quiet, but this first word of hers shocked me.

"I'll keep going then?" I made circles on her skin with my fingers on one thigh and my tongue on the other. I could scent her arousal but I didn't go further. I wanted another precious word.

"Yes. Please. Please, Kat." She sat up a little, her voice trembling as much as she was.

"Okay. Lie back." I pushed on her belly.

With no one watching, I could take my time. I wrapped my hands around her thighs and put my head down and proceeded to kiss and tongue my way over the parts of her I could reach with my mouth, everywhere except her pussy. Sometimes I pulled skin with my teeth. Sometimes I'd deviate and lick across her clit. As she became more desperate, she tried to drag me down onto her cunt.

I smiled in the darkness. "Don't do that Zoe. Let me do this at my own speed." But when I pressed my lips to her clit, she groaned and wriggled her ass, lifting it upward.

"No." I released her thighs and pushed her body to the mattress. After one pitiful whine, she settled. Then I used my hands and fingers to pin her down and to spread open her pussy and expose her. "Staying still?" I breathed softly over her clit.

She shuddered once, sighed. "Mmm."

"Good." I spent an eternity dabbing my tongue on her clit, circumnavigating it like I'd found something new and delicious and was putting off actually going there and tasting. I teased her, nibbling on her sensitive inner thighs, making her *want*.

"Fuck," she said when, yet again, I traced my tongue a whisper away from her clit.

"Such a naughty girl. You've been mostly good though." So I sucked her thoroughly swollen little clit fully into my mouth and tongued her.

The suppressed squeal and then hiss of her startled breath was the best reward.

I chuckled against her. "Play with your nipples, Zoe."

Though she raised her head to look down at me, I didn't move. Her hands moved to her breasts and she started tugging at them and circling them with her fingers.

I resumed licking. The tiny arch of her pelvis upward was instantaneous. Zoe moaned and gasped, her thighs quivering. My fingers found her entrance and I coaxed her open, slid a finger into her. I fucked her, feeling her copious wetness, tasting her arousal, riding high on the power of making her crazy with lust.

Watching her writhe, knowing she couldn't stop me now unless the world fell in, it was the best.

Her wriggles and noises of passion intensified. She was ripe for an orgasm and I dedicated myself to using my tongue and mouth like the conductor of the most beautiful girl music ever. Harder sucking, firmer tongue, wetter tongue, plus deeper, wilder fucking.

Her thighs quivered in, muscles rigid, she thrust herself at my mouth. I drank in her last cries. Screw nectar of the gods. Nectar of girl was better.

As she subsided, I crawled up to kiss her, absorbing her final gasps in my mouth – her breath, her passion.

I didn't expect anything from her but she whispered, "Let me," in my ear before sliding down my body. Her tongue playing down there had me hitching my breath in seconds. I'd forgotten the feel of a woman's tongue – smaller, gentler, more able to find exactly the right spot.

I guided her only a little with my hands in her hair. By the time I was in the throes of a climax, I was gripping her with both thighs and hands and gasping out my joy. Orgasms tended to be loud and messy.

When the light clicked on, it was a few seconds before I opened my eyes. Chris looked down on us – Zoe still quietly licking around my clit and me breathing like I'd run a race. I glared at him in an exhausted way. Zoe froze.

After a while, he smiled then went and turned out the light and I heard him climb back into bed.

"Come here, Zoe. Come up here so I can cuddle you."

"Soon." She exhaled and put her cheek to my thigh, resting there. "Soon."

For a tired moment I wished I could spank her for disobedience. Time flowed past. I wandered into sleep still half aware of something I was missing.

I awoke panicking. One more day. Only one more day. Then she would be going back to him.

The next night, the last night, I realized what it was that bothered me. I sat up and stared down at Zoe, sleeping. I had to talk to her. Apart from those few previous words, she'd refused.

But I poked until she awoke and drew her up into my arms where we could whisper without, hopefully, being overheard.

I ran through things in my head. It was obvious to me that Zoe was a woman who'd been taken by a human trafficking ring…business, whatever. I'd listened to Chris talk. This house was owned by a friend of his. It must be used for trafficking in some way. Scrim was the caretaker, so he was involved. Simple. Only I'd heard Chris tell Andreas several times that Scrim was just kinky. That this place was used by people into BDSM.

That was the mismatch. That was why Andreas had been so uncharacteristically quiet. He must not know Zoe was like me, caught by men. He thought she was pretending. I think that was it.

I still wasn't sure. The logic frustrated me. So how did it help me? Or us?

Oh fuck. Of course. Chris was lying to his best friend. All I had to do was convince Andreas of that then I could step back and watch the feathers fly. Andreas wasn't the sort of man who'd stand by and let this happen to Zoe. I just had to get him to talk to her, really talk to her.

Maybe with her help I could sway Andreas? He'd think I was making it up if I didn't have some other evidence.

But despite all my urging, she wouldn't talk to me. Though frustrated, I let her lie in my arms until dawn. I had a dead arm when I awoke but it was worth it to be able to peek down and watch her slumbering. Her tangled hair stirred under my nose.

That morning, before I could talk to Andreas by myself, Scrim arrived and took Zoe back. What could I do? They'd let Scrim into the house, into the bedroom, to get her. For once in my life, I chickened out. I watched him take her even when she pleaded with her eyes. From the cage, I had to listen to her loud sobs as he towed her away down the front steps.

Someone loomed in the bedroom door, shadowing me. Not Scrim, thank god. Chris and Andreas.

I'd been surprised the men had been so distant while she was with me. I'd expected them to fuck us both. Maybe Andreas would be too moralistic but Chris – I'd thought he would fuck anything. The more I thought about how they'd restrained themselves, the more they rose in my estimation. I would've hated them if they'd touched her. Truly I would. They would have been no better than animals.

But in an odd reversal I didn't understand in myself, I also didn't want her being had by them. Being considered theirs for so many weeks had seeped into my very essence and in some twisted, depraved and horribly wrong way, I'd come to think of them as mine. This wasn't healthy.

Chris came forward and crouched before the cage door.

"Hello, Sir." I'd be good. I wasn't sure any more of his tolerance for my anger.

"You've been bad haven't you, Kat."

"Me?" Alarmed I sat up straighter. "How? I never –"

"You've been teasing us for two days with Zoe. I haven't been able to touch you. Neither has Andreas. Now we're going to punish you for it."

What was this? Appalled, I looked from one to the other, then to Chris when I heard the rustle of his clothes. He'd dragged his shorts down and had his hand around his erection. He fed it into the cage.

"First you're going to suck me off for a while. Then I think I will get you to put your ass up here against the bars so I can fuck you. Maybe then we'll let you out so we can take you together – mouth and ass."

"I..."

"Now do you see how bad you've been? You two getting each other off has got us both horny and ready to fuck you sideways for a week."

Past him I saw Andreas sitting on the bed with his cock out and his fist running up and down its length.

"Come here. Now." Chris had a gleam in his eye that said I'd pay even more if I wasn't fast.

Stunned and already so turned on I'd squeezed my thighs together over my clit, I crawled forward and gave his cock a single long lick, then I swirled my tongue around it. He was rock hard and it made me wonder how they'd lasted the two days. Zoe must really have been out of bounds for them.

I took half his length into my mouth so I could toy with it with my tongue.

"That's it." He groaned and clutched the bars so he could push up close to the cage. The feral noises coming from him aroused me even more as he sank his cock into my mouth.

A minute later he remembered to instruct me to turn and back up to the bars. He pulled my lower legs through and roped my thighs to the bars so my ass was up tight against the steel. I'd never had a Dom make me do this before. I never would have for *anyone*. Being fucked through a cage? But this whole situation made me a little crazy. The plunge of his cock into me had me lowering my head until my hair was grabbed through the upper bars.

"No way, little Kat," Andreas said. "Stay right there. I'm going to fuck you too in a few seconds."

I gasped a little. Outrageous, what they were doing. My gasp turned into a low moan as Chris slid into me again. He went in far, hitting somewhere deep that ached as his cock repeatedly thumped into the same spot. I stopped breathing, my eyes rolling back. Had his dick grown longer? I wriggled my ass higher, groaning. Fuck. I sure hoped so.

"Mmm."

I was making those small weird sexual noises that betrayed my willingness but I couldn't help myself. Already my entire body throbbed with the need to come. I wanted them to touch me properly but they alternated, fucking me in turns while holding me in place. I never knew I had a cage fetish but whenever they switched places and took me again without asking, I groaned a little louder, my heart thudded faster, and I got wetter and hungrier for more of what they did.

"Fuck, fuck fuck," I grunted in time with the thrusts of whoever had me.

I hazed out, eyes seeing nothing, rocked, shuddering, choking almost as I forgot to breathe.

"Good girl." One of them rammed into me. I was so lost I didn't register who. Someone managed to reach in and finger my clit.

"More," I begged. Someone laughed.

More. Mouth open, straining in every muscle, I shoved back at the cock tunneling into me, squirmed on the fingers, and exploded into an orgasm.

While I was panting, half-collapsed on my knees, with my forehead on the floor, they undid the ropes and opened the cage to drag me out.

"You're ours." Chris crushed my lips under his. "Never ever forget your pussy, and you, all of you, is ours." With Andreas clutching my arms at my back, I could only whimper and take the pain of his kiss and feel myself falling further and further under his dominance.

I'm me, my small voice was trying to tell me. *I'm still me.* For once I didn't care. I wanted this.

A few moments later, I was spread-eagled on the bed taking one in my mouth with the other pounding into my pussy. This wasn't just sex, it was also their way of making me theirs again. I was being repossessed.

Even though I knew what they were doing, insanely, I loved that they wanted to. *Fuck me harder*, ran through my head in a constant stream.

Then I heard the screams.

Zoe. I froze. Locked into a world of fear.

There'd been tiny cuts on her back made by a blade. I knew why. I knew her voice, her screams. My tears were dry but they made my heart ache so much. I don't think either man knew when the dry tears turned into real ones.

Chapter 26

Andreas

It wasn't until we were done with Kat, had cleaned up, and climbed back into bed with her between us that I realized she was crying. And then it was only because Chris had seen it. He had her facing him with her head tucked into his chest. The man was being far more...intimate, in a way, than he usually was.

"What is it Kat?" He cradled her head and made her look at him. "Why are you crying? We were rough, but not that rough."

I put my hand on her shoulder and gently mussed up her already messy hair.

"It's Zoe. Didn't you hear her screaming?" she whispered. She put her hand up near mine and I stroked her skin with a finger.

Not cuffed and not growling at us or trying to kill us? This seemed a pivotal moment.

"How do you know it's Zoe?" Chris asked, frowning a little.

"She'll be fine. She's only pretending." But a worm of doubt stirred.

"No, she's not." The certainty in her voice was overlaid by a tremor. I could tell she was scared. "She's not at all. Scrim is selling people, women. She was being hurt by him and I couldn't do anything. But you two can!" She sounded choked up, like she was again holding back tears. "Please. Do something."

When Chris didn't reply, I stared. If he'd said anything, almost, I would have brushed this off. But he didn't. His face was impassive but his actions said more to me.

"Chris? Tell her Zoe was pretending."

He took a long deep breath. Such a long breath, I knew without him saying anything that he was struggling. Which meant Kat was right.

"Shit. No. No." I shook my head, squeezing Kat's shoulder. "Chris?"

What the hell? This had to be false.

Pivotal moment? Bullshit. Kat was like this because she wanted something from us. She was worried about Zoe because Zoe was in the hands of human traffickers. And that meant they might do...

Hell. I propped myself up on my elbow. Chris knew about this for how long? Since we arrived? This house belonged to a friend who'd loaned it to him. "How long have you known?"

"A long time." His mouth tweaked at one corner. "So simple wasn't it. You found the flaw, Kat. I forgot that I can't lie to Andreas."

"Jeez." I massaged either side of my nose, silencing the headache that threatened. "Sex slaves? Scrim's involved?"

He nodded. Kat stayed quiet. I guess she was hoping we'd settle this in her favor. Right now I couldn't figure out which end of the world we were on, let alone how to sort this out. "What a fucking mess," I muttered. "Why didn't you tell me?"

"Because...it's been forever. Years ago I got into this, doing accounting for this man, through my family. I found out accidentally. I wasn't involved, couldn't see how I could fix it without maybe getting a hit put on me. Or going to prison myself. I forgot about it mostly. I knew, but I pushed it to the back of my mind."

"Until now."

"Yes. Until now. I didn't know they'd bring a shipment through while we were here. Didn't know you'd be here full stop."

"Uh-huh."

"If you hate me, think I'm a bottom feeder of the worst kind, I understand."

I threw back the sheet, spun off the bed, and stood. "I have to get some air. Come outside. Both of you. We can lock Kat's leash onto the chair." Like always. I hesitated a second. Even now, I wasn't forgetting what we had with her. Ingrained. A part of me, of us, whatever.

I ended up leaning over the back railing with Chris at my shoulder. The cool night air, the background insect sounds of the forest, and the wash of the sea, had calmed me a bit. Not enough though. Chris hadn't said anything for a while.

The tension built up in my head. I blamed him. I didn't blame him. I understood and some of it I didn't. Not quite. I wanted to scream, *why*. I strangled the railing under my hand, like if I gripped it tightly enough I could make all this shit go away.

I gave in, shaking my head and muttering them all out in a row. "What the fuck, Chris? Fuck! Just...motherfucking...fuck."

Silence again for a minute. "I'm sorry. I wish this hadn't happened the way it has."

"Me too." I sighed. "Would you ever have told me?"

"No. I would've kept you out of it. Unless you asked me directly."

"Yeah. Like I just did." I bowed my head and stared at my toes, what I could see of them in the part darkness. "That you couldn't lie to me...that part is what says the most to me."

"Okay."

Just like Chris. Letting me find my own way. Not trying to whitewash this.

"Fuck. Okay. Yeah. I'm done going nuts. I'm not going to throw you away as a friend. This hurt, but I can see how it crept up on you. Why you couldn't say anything."

He nodded, kept looking out across the wall to the beach. "I don't deserve you."

"Yeah, you do. You fucking do. I'd be shark food years ago if you hadn't come out to me. You'd have to be Idi Amin and Hitler combined for me to tell you to piss off. Let's just be...honest with each other from now on though? Yeah?"

"Yeah," he said quietly. "Sure. I can do that."

"This boss of yours told you that Zoe was a present or something?"

"Yes. He wanted you to get your hands dirty, so he had a hold on you."

"Shit. Really? And you wouldn't have let me touch her would you?"

"No. I guess I did that part right at least."

I thought some more, tapping my fingers on the railing. "You've had longer to think. What are we going to do?"

He inhaled loudly, exhaled. "I don't know. They're a big organization doing something illegal, something I consider far worse than what we're doing with Kat, but I've never wanted to be Superman and somehow destroy them. Because we can't. Scrim and those men are armed. We can't report them to the cops because we're in almost as deep. I don't want to go to jail. Okay?"

While I was opening my mouth to reply, he raised a hand.

"Wait. I lied. I did want to be Superman. Lots of times. I just convinced myself it was stupid. I was right. But I still felt bad for a long time." Chris shrugged. "I got desensitized, like someone watching people die in a war overseas on the TV. It became not real."

"I understand. Now we're both here, same situation. I don't know what we can do either, except go with the flow for now." I shrugged. "It's not good."

"No. If we reported this we'd go to jail for at least a year. Probably much longer. We'd be dead in six months in jail. Vetrov would see to it. We wouldn't take him down anyway. I've never met him. I don't even know where he lives for chrissakes."

"Right. That does make it fucked up. Okay." I guess we couldn't save the world no matter how much this disturbed me. However, we could do something. I turned to him. "What about Zoe? Kat likes her a lot. I like her too. Can we at least get her away from them? How many women have they got here right now?"

He was silent a while. "What, you mean buy her, or them? I guess we could... Damn. No we can't do that. You know why?"

I shook my head.

"Because Vetrov would never agree to us freeing them. They've seen too much."

"Please!" For the first time since we came out onto the deck, Kat spoke. "You have to. Please?"

"Shush." I waved my hand at her, ignoring the couple of quiet swear words she uttered. "We're going to do what we can. Chris? What if we just ask about Zoe?"

"I suppose... I can ask. We can ask if we can buy her. But Andreas, again, we could never let her go. You understand that?"

"Shit." Two women. I leaned on the balcony a bit more. "I don't know."

Kat was enough. I'd never planned to own anyone.

"He might say no." Chris added quietly. "Sometimes he does things I don't understand."

I saw nothing for ages while I thought this through. "Let's try, mate. Let's try. Between us we should be able to rake up the cash. Whatever it takes."

"Okay. I'll ask tomorrow."

I stayed out there long after Chris went back to bed with Kat. I needed some time alone to process this and Chris, to his credit, saw that and left me.

Most of my life I'd drifted from job to job. Engineers had a lot of scope with job opportunities if they chose a good pathway. With this, with Kat even, by herself, I was pinning myself down to wherever Chris was. You couldn't get much closer a friendship than owning a woman...women maybe, together. I shut my eyes and breathed in and out with the sea. The salt-laden breeze sent cool tendrils across my face.

I could do this, whether we acquired Zoe or not. Besides, I didn't think I wanted to be without Kat in my life anymore. She'd kind of sneaked up on me. I wasn't sure it was love, how could it be? But it was some sort of symbiotic relationship like that seaweed stuff and the Nemo fish. Anyone who tried to separate us from each other, and that *us* included Chris, was going to feel the hurt.

Chapter 27

Chris

With morning came the realization that life was about to get way more complex than I'd ever planned. And I *had* planned with Kat. I'd thought about it for a while before doing it. I'd had Steph in my care for days and once I saw how hers and Klaus's and Jodie's situation could sort itself out I'd begun to wonder about the *what if* factor. What if I did it for real?

We were eating at the breakfast bar with Kat sitting at our feet on a footstool. Bacon and eggs and fried tomatoes and toast. Andreas had made it. Kat wasn't the best cook and Andreas had felt the urge to make breakfast anyway. Using my fork, I toyed with the last of the bacon on my plate.

Now, in one swoop, without barely thinking at all, Andreas wanted to add another woman to our household. Difficult enough keeping Kat in line. I still didn't completely understand her. Zoe was an unknown. We didn't know her past, or who she truly was, or how she'd react to us.

I only knew how she'd been with Kat and her behavior for those one and a half days – like a mouse cowering in a corner with the shadow of a predator fallen on it, waiting to get eaten. Except when Kat calmed her down enough. Then…the two of them together, kissing, licking, wriggling, and coming. Fuck, they'd made me wonder if my balls could explode into flame.

Her and Zoe. Her and Andreas. Anger simmered at the edges of my brain. Andreas I'd learned to handle. Her and another woman was setting me off again.

"Fuck." I scraped back the stool and stooped to grab Kat's hand. "Come with me. I'm going out to have a talk. You good with this?" I jerked my head toward the mess in the kitchen.

"Sure." Andreas raised his eyebrows. He looked like I'd announced I was launching a moon rocket or something.

"Really sure?"

He only nodded and said, "Go."

I don't know what he thought I meant to say to her. Hell, I didn't know. I just knew I wanted to. This was strange territory for me.

Out on the deck, the big round chair beckoned me. We'd both fit in there. I wanted this up close and personal. But not equal. I made her stop before it and I sat. "Take off all your clothes, Kat."

She blinked at me and licked her lips. Nervous?

I nearly laughed. Even she saw that this was odd behavior for me. But she pulled her dress off over her head then went to undo the clasp on her red bra top.

Be gentler. Andreas had advised that when I'd mentioned my curiosity about how he handled her. I wasn't sure, but...

"Wait. Let me." With my hands at her hips, I turned her then I unclipped the top, slipping the straps down her arms. I made her pirouette again and admired her breasts with her standing there waiting. I never got tired of this, and I let myself smile as I caressed her.

Her breathing grew heavier, her nipples perked up. I hooked my fingers in the sides of her matching panties and shuffled them down her legs while I kissed the top of her slit.

"Mmm." She swayed.

It would've been nice to be skin to skin but I'd kept my shorts and T-shirt on. I wanted to emphasize how *mine* she was, how vulnerable too. I liked having her naked while I was dressed.

I licked her once, tasting her, and when I looked at her, the warmth in my eyes was for more than just the sex. I wanted more. I'd seen it for days in myself, but sometimes it seemed like I was blind while her and Andreas had perfect vision.

I pulled her onto my lap and arranged her until we were both comfy with her head on my shoulder. Weeks ago she would've been spitting and scratching. Not that I was telling her that.

The shape of the chair made her cuddle in.

"Pretty woman." I let my gaze travel down her curves, lingering on the best bits, which was most of her.

She opened her mouth to reply and I put my finger across her lips, pleased with how she halted and waited for me, even if she also made a small strangling noise.

"Don't talk yet." I nodded as I went on, thinking out what I meant. "I'm not a touchy-feely sort of guy. Though I always thought I communicated well with women."

Her eyes grew big, disbelief evident in every line of her face. I frowned.

"Watching you and Andreas made me want to punch him at first, until I figured out I needed to do something." I pulled her ankle in closer, arranged a strand of her hair on her cheek. "Then I saw you with Zoe."

Damn, why was this so difficult? Pressure pumped up in me, squeezing higher. I was going to crack any moment.

And she waited. I hefted her a little higher on my lap. Procrastinating. Shit.

"You want to know why I took you, Kat? Because you've been an obsession for me since I first saw you getting spanked. Yeah, what a lie that was – you an easy pushover submissive." I smiled at the way her eyes had fired up and tapped her nose. "I can read you. I know you haven't given in."

That pressure was still there. I watched her breathing, stroking her throat with my fingers and marveling that even if she didn't realize it, she was close to submitting to me. I just needed some key.

Blind man. Blind man in the land of the seeing. I still couldn't put my finger on it.

"When you were with Zoe I was almost as angry as I was when I saw you with Andreas. I wanted to take you away. Except she made you happy. You made her happy too, I guess." It was true. Their happiness was like a bubble with me on the outside. "If we get Zoe, you have to let me in. Hear me? You have to submit. Fully."

She shut down. One instant all open and accepting. Next, simmering resentment. I'd been so close.

"Not going to say it yet? I'm not ever freeing you, little Kat. You're mine and Andreas's. Once you admit that to yourself your life will be much better. Happier." A thought surfaced and I grabbed for it, committed myself. "I do want to make you happy. If you need Zoe or whatever to be that, it's done."

Fuck. Wasn't that easy. But though she didn't exactly look one hundred percent in my court, she reached up and touched my chin.

I quirked up an eyebrow.

"Thank you. Though I know it's selfish of me to want her safe when there are other women here too."

It seemed I'd said something right.

"Don't feel guilty. You can't save the world. One thing at a time." Her and Andreas were the same – wanting to be do-gooders. "I didn't hear a Sir. Bend over my lap."

"What? Oh. Bugger. I was distracted."

"By?"

"Your sexy muscles?"

Tsking, I drew a fingernail down her neck, scoring it lightly, reminding her. I added more than a touch of threat to my tone. "Kat…"

We had a battle of wills until at last she wavered and dropped her gaze. Her reply was a whispered, "Sorry, Sir," then she squirmed off me and lay down across my knees on her belly.

I decided to take it a step further. "Kiss the hand I'm going to spank you with." I offered the back of it to her. She looked up at me.

Her pupils reflected the liquid darkness that signaled a submissive giving in. She kissed my hand. Her lips were so soft. With the palm of that same hand, I brushed down over her hair, to her back, to the swell of her bottom.

I circled the sweet spot on her ass with my palm. Her eyes closed and, as I watched, her lips parted – the sweet power rush of a victory.

I wanted to fuck her so hard right then. Nail her. Make her know who was the master. I reined it in.

"Extra swats for the swearing, Kat."

Some things needed to stay the same.

I took my time and made it hurt.

A half hour later when I judged it likely Vetrov would be available, I took Andreas into the study and sent off the email.

I want to buy Z. The gift. What is the price?

We waited for a reply. Andreas on the upholstered chair while I stayed on the hard metal one. Kat was inside the cage in the bedroom. One day I prayed I could allow her out without one of us watching her.

"Going to say what you talked about?" His ankle was on his knee and he jiggled his foot as if nervous. I understood that. Vetrov made me nervous too.

"Should I?"

"Your call. If I can help?" He shrugged.

"Smug bastard."

"Heyyy! I was only guessing. You seemed like you were going where no man had gone before. Or no Chris. Though the spanking looked fun."

I glanced at the screen. Still nothing.

"I was trying to get to know her a little more."

"Hmm." He waggled his head. "Did it work?"

I thought back. "I don't know. I told her I wanted to make her happy."

"And then you spanked her so hard she cried?" Silent laughter made him shake. He put his head in his hands. "Oh shit."

"Fuck you." The laptop dinged. Email.

You want to buy? You can try gift one more time. This time do as I ask. Then we see about price.

I sat back. What was he on about?

"Bad news?" Andreas was at my shoulder, reading the screen. "What is this guy? Foreign?"

"I don't know. I always assumed he was Russian."

"Uh-huh. What does he want? Us to fuck Zoe? Why?"

Good question. It bothered me. Why not just sell her to us if he was willing to?

"This is a mindfuck," I muttered. "He's making us wonder if he'll refuse to sell her after we do what he asks. Then he has your hands dirtier. Mine too, I guess, though that's hardly needed."

"How does he know we didn't do as he asked last time?"

"Scrim. If he asked her, she'd have told him. I doubt that girl would hold anything back if asked directly."

Andreas drew in a big breath. "Yeah. True. And you know what…"

"What?"

"Zoe is scared shitless of men. I saw how she reacted around us. Doing this to her on command from your boss, I don't know if I could stomach it."

I twisted my mouth. "Me neither."

We were slightly fucked. Par for the course with Vetrov.

"Say yes. We have to try."

I nodded. "Okay. I was going to anyway."

Telling Kat we hadn't even tried to buy the girl – that scenario had left me feeling empty.

What I'd found yesterday while jogging in the forest came back to me. After tripping over a tree root and sliding into some dirt with my knee, I'd levered myself up only to spot a bone sticking out of the earth. I'd found a couple more. Nothing conclusive but they were from something large, maybe a human. It had sent a chill through me. I wasn't a forensic pathologist and there was no way in hell I was going to phone the cops and ask them to come look.

Whether human or not though, the find had reminded me of how potentially nasty Scrim and his colleagues were. I didn't know how far they'd go but I was pretty sure it was a long way past anything I'd done. Kicking someone's ass in an MMA bout wasn't the same as killing and martial arts expertise sure didn't stop bullets. I knew I was bad, different from the average man, but I didn't kill. I'd sanitized the human trafficking in my mind for so many years, and these men were far closer to evil than I ever wanted to go, if they'd killed. Deep down, lurked a certainty that they had.

Wrong, I must be wrong. Had to be. But maybe I was right? I couldn't decide and it was fucking with my head.

"So was Kat right? Had that been Zoe screaming?"

"Huh." I stared at him uncomprehending for a second, jarred by the jump from my horrible memory to what Zoe might be suffering. "I don't know. It's possible."

"I figured that."

"Bear in mind that she's stock to them. Money. As long as they can sell her they won't hurt her too much." If they thought they couldn't sell her, though?

"She's so scared of men." Andreas scrunched up his brow.

"Seemed so, but I think some men would pay for that. There's a market for most things." I hoped there was for her anyway. Her fear might make her easier to sell, or harder.

"Now I'm feeling really dirty. And that's saying something, considering."

"Yes." I leaned back into the chair, resting on my shoulders. "I'm hoping her fear will make it easier for us to buy her."

"If Scrim comes near me parading any of the other women, I may not be able to stop myself punching his teeth in."

That made me sit up. "No. Don't even think about it. The man is armed. So are his friends. It's not worth it. Stay the fuck away."

He pulled a disgusted face. "Shit. Okay. I won't touch him, but I'm still thinking it."

Chapter 28

Kat

They allowed me to wait, kneeling, by the door when Zoe was brought back. I could see her past Chris and Scrim, like a frightened animal caged in by men's legs. This time, she only wore a blue bra and panties. Her brown hair stood up in little wild curls but her lipstick was bright and fresh. I wondered, sickly, if Scrim had a lipstick fetish. I had a disgusting moment where I imagined him forcing her mouth onto his cock.

Then they let her through and the new small cuts on her body became obvious. Fresh blood leaked in tiny spots. So small they'd not be dreadful wounds but seeing them, knowing they came from the time of those screams, I wanted to get the nearest lethal instrument and hack Scrim to death.

I seethed, hatred leeching into my bones, my fingernails, but I held it in, only clawing crescents into my thighs with my nails, and I smiled at her. She crawled toward me, peeked around at the men, and when no one gave her instructions, she lay on me, with her head and the top half of her torso on my lap.

"Shh." I stroked her trembling body while I tried to hear what the men were arguing over.

"We're not fucking her," Chris was saying again.

They seemed to be going round and round arguing.

"Hang on." As if he were finding out about something trivial, like a pizza delivery, Scrim punched a text into his mobile.

While we waited, Andreas came over and squatted nearby, studying Zoe. When she didn't look up at him, he rose again and backed away to lean on the wall. Good man. Again I was slightly stunned at how nice they were being to her. Where the fuck had all the caveman attitudes gone?

"Okay." Scrim tucked the phone in his pocket. "Here's the deal. You fuck her one way or the other or you don't get her. He says fucking in his definition incudes this slave of yours fucking her with a strap-on. But he wants a pic as proof. Email it. Faces are to be on the thing. You're all to be in the picture."

Chris stared at him, rock still.

"That's it, gentlemen…ladies." Scrim mocked me, inclining his head and grinning. "So what's it to be. Yes? No? And it's one hour only, then she comes back to me while the boss decides about the purchase. Take it or leave it. No further discussion will be entered into, the man said. Got that?"

Shit. This was asking Chris and Andreas to hand over proof of a crime to whoever this boss was. My heart rebelled, aching and pounding away. They'd refuse. They would. And even if they agreed to this…me, use a strap-on with Zoe?

She was pretending none of this was happening and had her arms loosely around my waist, her face up close to my stomach while I patted her hair. I bit my lip, thinking. If it was the price of keeping her safe, I'd do it, as long as she wasn't traumatized. It wouldn't have to be more than a second for a photo anyway.

No one had spoken. When I checked, Chris was turning back after having looked to Andreas. He nodded. "Deal."

I bowed my head and whispered to Zoe, sure she had been listening. "Don't you worry about this, okay? Do you know what a strap-on is?" I hoped she wasn't as innocent as she appeared to be.

She nodded. With her face on my leg, one eye was hidden but she was sneaking a look at me.

"I'll make it like it's nothing more than…" What? Trying on a dress? It was sex for god sakes.

"It's fine," she whispered. Her hand at my back poked my waist lightly, tapping with her fingertips, like she was checking I was still me. "If it's you, I'm good with it. I trust you."

"Okay." I frowned down at her, trying not to tear up.

If this happened, we then had to give her back to Scrim for a while. I prayed the men could buy her afterward. If not, there was nothing I could do. Absolutely fucking nothing. Be positive, at the least that will make her happier. She'd heard what was happening, the agreement. There was hope.

"Thank you." I kissed above her ear. "You're brave."

They hadn't even asked my opinion of all this. I wasn't that surprised – for Chris it would be something I was told to do. With Andreas I wasn't sure. Disappointment niggled at me. I think I wanted more from him. Maybe I'd imagined him as something he wasn't?

But I considered what this meant. The picture they had to take directly involved them in this slavery operation. This wasn't just money they had to spend. It was far more dangerous.

When the door closed, Chris approached and crouched beside us. "You heard what you have to do?"

"Yes, Sir." I kept patting Zoe.

"Sit up, Zoe. I want to hear you say that too."

The girl climbed to her knees and managed to meet his gaze.

"You know we're aiming to buy you." He glanced at me. "And that Kat has to use a strap-on with you while we take a picture?"

"Yes, Sir." No hesitation there. If only she knew what Chris could be like. So far though, he'd treated her gently, like she'd disintegrate if pushed.

"Okay. Let's do this then. You're in charge of her, Kat. I'll be watching you both. Come." He clipped a leash to Zoe's collar and climbed to his feet.

Ugh. Thanks, Chris.

Then, almost as an afterthought, he reached around her and caressed my cheek. For a second I connected with him, paralyzed by…an awareness of *Him* as my master, wanting more of his touch, but he turned away.

I shook myself and followed them. *Slipping, Kat.*

One hour, we had only one hour. This was insane. Who was this person Scrim was arranging this through? The boss would be the man deciding if Zoe could be sold to us…to Andreas and Chris. I searched inside myself, wondering at the joy I'd felt thinking that. I'd have someone to share this existence with, someone to talk to. Maybe to play with.

Someone who should be free. Was I that bad a person that I wished her here with me rather than free?

I didn't know anymore. The chance of Zoe ever being free again was remote. This was a good outcome for her. It was. If this went wrong, she was going away somewhere unknown to be sold to god knows who, probably someone who liked making innocent little girls scream.

I squeezed my eyes closed. Shut that out, damn you. Shut it out. This is what's happening now. You will have a pretty girl in your arms soon and you're going to make her enjoy what happens next. That's the responsible *nice* thing to do. Because then, maybe, she gets not to be fucked by some depraved man who wants to feed off her terror.

My men treated this like some sort of mechanical thing they had to accomplish – getting us out onto the deck where, apparently, the lighting was better, setting up the camera on the phone for a delayed shot after taking a few pictures to check the area was covered by the lens. Though they discussed nothing within my hearing, Andreas's strained expression told me that at least he was shocked and unhappy.

I whispered thank you to him, as he chained us both to the big couch. He smiled quickly, nothing more. While they went to search for the strap-on in the supply cupboard of kinky toys, I lay with Zoe, just cuddling. Though I desperately wanted to know about her new wounds, I wasn't going to question her and remind her of what Scrim or some other man might have done.

The beauty of our surroundings made this seem even more perverted. Above us, splashes of reflected sunlight flickered across the cream canvas of the roof. Every few minutes, one or two orange butterflies flitted past looking for pollen or for a mate in that never-ending dance of life.

I breathed, absorbing some measure of calmness.

I had Zoe against the back cushions and I moved atop and propped myself on my arms so as to kiss her gently. My hair fell about us, framing her as I played with her lips. I murmured onto them, unable to resist punctuating my words with more kisses. "Let's get you undressed..." *Kiss.* "...before they come back, Zoe."

The more I said her name the sweeter it seemed.

"Okay." Her reply was so quiet, but she managed to smile as she said it. So I kissed her again.

"Good."

I kissed her throat, reveling in the taste of her skin and how it recalled to me the taste of her pussy. The straps of her bra slipped easily off her shoulders and I left them halfway down her arms with her breasts bulging out the top of the low-cut cups. I pursed my lips, amused and aroused. They made her look trapped. Carefully, like they were precious objects, I scooped each breast from the bra and tucked the cloth beneath.

"I could look at you all day, Zoe."

For the first time I saw fire in her eyes. Wickedness even. "Whenever I see you, I want to gobble you up."

"Oh?" I raised an eyebrow, wondering if I should lick across the top of her succulent nipples.

My clit throbbed at this naughty image of captured innocence. I wriggled until my legs were between hers and pressed myself onto her pussy.

My most desperate wish right then was to tangle and tie her arms up in those bra straps. But it was too soon, too nasty, with Scrim arranging this, too everything.

I curled my tongue up onto my lip and smiled, exulting in her in lying under me. A little growl of appreciation sneaked out.

Her eyes shone and she ground up against me.

Fuck. The little devil.

"You like this?"

I cupped her throat, wrapping my fingers around into her nape hair, wanting to see whether she still liked being controlled. My thumb probed her larynx. She whimpered. Fuck again. Hot. This was getting a little out of hand.

"I just need to get you wet..." Swallow. "So you can take the strap-on without pain. Tell me if you don't want anything."

"I won't say no to you," she whispered. "I want you to do sexy things to me. Please? I want to forget...the other things that happened." She put her arm up and brushed her hand across my lips. I licked her. "I like you. Please, Kat?"

Oh crap. What a thing to tell me. But I couldn't say no to that, could I?

"We'll see. I'm not going too far with the guys watching."

If I made her stand it would be simpler to take off her panties but I had a flashback to Chris doing the same thing to me. Instead I slipped down her body, taking unexpected nips of bits of her that tempted me too much. Her cries enticed me to nibble on her even more.

I kneeled between her legs, enjoying the view.

Her mons and the beginning of her cleft could be seen through the blue of her panties. Darker blue where her juices had dampened them. I traced Zoe's contours with my finger, bumping over her mound and dipping into the territory of her clit. I grabbed her with my teeth there, inhaling her scent, and then I licked slowly over the cloth where her clit would be, and sucked on her, once.

She squealed and clutched at my hair which only made me chuckle. At last I gave in, found the sides of her panties and wiggled them past her butt and legs. The crotch was thoroughly soaked with her moisture.

"I think you're wet enough." I smiled.

She blushed. "Shh! You shouldn't look there."

"No?" I dropped the panties to the floor and put my mouth to her to wriggle my tongue along her cleft. "My second test says you're wet enough too." With my shoulders under her thighs, I parted her legs.

A noise made me turn and lower her legs. Zoe whimpered but I ignored her.

Chris walked out carrying something. He came to the couch and tossed it down next to Zoe's head.

"Here it is. Good to see you're warming up, both of you. Keep going. We'll take a picture when you're in position." His smirk was kind though, for him. I resisted flipping him the bird, considering it would earn me a quick yet severe beating in front of Zoe.

The strap-on, I was glad to see, came from an unopened package. White silicon with ribs snaking down it, and yes, straps that went around and between my legs. I stood to remove my panties then puzzled out the strap arrangement with Zoe unexpectedly helping me.

With the rubber dick stuck out in front of me, it struck me as being both ridiculous and potentially interesting to use.

"What do you think, Zoe?" I grabbed the tip, pulled the whole dick to the right and let go, chuckling at how it wobbled wildly from side to side. Then I poked her in the ribs with the thing.

She snorted and covered her face, holding in laughter. My heart jumped a beat. I'd never heard her laugh like this.

"You look really stupid."

"Oh?" Waggling my eyebrows, I grabbed her wrists and mounted her with my legs either side of hers, pinning her down. I growled, struck by an insane desire to Domme her.

Gentle, must be gentle.

I sucked in my bottom lip then caught it in my teeth. Though I still held her wrists to the couch, she was giggling like mad. The little pushes against my hands, now and then, meant she was trying my hold but not too much. Crap.

I bowed my head and murmured. "Do you like being held down by me, Zoe?"

After a quiet moment, she shivered. "Yes. By you. No one else."

"That's good to know." I smiled. "Now let's see whether you like being fucked by a strap-on."

"Okay." A little fear there, but not much.

I reached down and found the dick then introduced the tip to her slit, sliding it up and down in her moisture until the smallest push made it sink into her. Her whimper grabbed me and sent an electrical thrill down my spine. Slowly, ever so slowly, while watching her face, I slid in further.

Her mouth opened to an *O* and she groaned.

"Oh god. That's nice, so nice. I never knew –"

I thrust in a bit more and out again, though still slow, aware of the sexy squish through her well-creamed tunnel. I smirked as shock flashed onto her face. The dildo was soft silicone. If I was careful this was going to be way fun.

"Oh fuck, fuck, fuck. Deeper please." She grabbed my butt and pulled. I resisted. "Please!"

The click of the camera made me realize they'd taken a picture. I glanced up to see no one near us. I guessed that meant they intended the first as a test, or for their own enjoyment. Bastards.

Right then I didn't care too much though. I was getting the hang of this. With Zoe squirming and moaning under me, and the rhythm of the strap-on settling into my pelvis so it seemed almost a natural movement, I was in dommy heaven. There was something intrinsically powerful about giving her pleasure with this strap-on dick. Total mental rush.

Andreas and Chris had arrived at the couch and I heard a row of faint clicks as the mobile phone took more pictures. I'd frozen at that first click.

"Keep going," Andreas growled.

Shit. I looked at Zoe and terror had replaced ecstasy. I grimaced at the men and mouthed, *please.*

They walked away though only as far as the dining table chairs, where they sat and observed us.

The moment seemed gone, wasted, but…no. I'd give her some pleasure. I wasn't going to leave her fearful. I pulled out the dick and leaned in. "Turn onto your stomach."

"Why?" she ventured timidly.

"Do it." If she protested enough, I'd stop. But she turned over. "I'm putting it in you again."

"Kat! I don't know…"

"That wasn't a no, was it?"

"Umm." She only waited, waited for me to do something.

Game on. I settled on her, sliding the silicone cock into her by guiding it with my hand. I'd decided not to move much this time. I'd make it less overtly kinky that way, maybe, less a stage show. Knowing the men were watching would make her feel odd so I only moved it in and out by an inch or so each time. But it was inside her a long way, and she started to moan with each deeper stroke.

"Push your ass up so I can reach under you." When she did, I wormed my hand beneath and found her clit. Slowly, with my hand there working in slow circles and the dick thrusting equally slowly, I brought her toward climax.

Zoe buried her face in the couch, moaning, her ass rising as she searched for that last thrust to take her over.

I put my head down and bit her back. When she moaned even louder, I shifted and bit again, feeling her little clit tight and swollen under my fingers. My fingers slipped in her juices as I bit her some more.

"Oh fuck." She breathed out once more then shuddered, locked up her muscles, and came.

I used my teeth on her before kissing the same spot then I withdrew the cock. I gathered her into my arms and rolled us so we both faced the back of the couch. The guys could stare at our butts and wank if they wanted. What I needed right then was to snuggle with her and pat her until her gasping breathing came back to earth.

"You good?" I asked softly, as I brushed my hand down her trembling side.

"Mm-hm." Zoe nodded. Her hair tickled my nose.

I lay there comforting her while the fear of letting her go crept back into me. This was going to hurt. Because I might not get her back, might not be able to save her. Christ. I didn't know her well, but there was no doubt in my mind that this was not going to feel any better than having a spear extracted from my guts.

She squirmed around so she was facing me.

"Hi." I smiled and rearranged my arm across her back to a cozier spot.

"I have something important to tell you, Kat."

"Mm? What is it, beautiful?"

"You have to be quiet. Okay?"

What? But I nodded.

"There's a gun, a pistol, in a safe in the floor of the main bedroom. Bottom drawer in the bedside drawers. Pull out the drawer and you'll see it."

What the fuck. "A gun?" I whispered. "How do you know this?"

"Don't ask, please. Just listen." Tears filled her eyes. "I want you to use it if you need to. This is the combination."

Then she told me the numbers and I repeated them back to her in a haze. What did she want me to do with this gun? More importantly, what *could* I do with one? I hated the fear and uncertainty welling up in me. Did she expect me to shoot Chris and Andreas? Or Scrim?

So many questions screamed to be answered. Least of all, *who are you?* Was she more than I thought her to be? Then I felt her trembling, saw the twitch of her mouth. Just a scared woman who'd somehow found a secret. Not even a startling secret. A gun in a safe here was like finding an apple in a bowl of fruit. More intriguing was, where did she get this secret – was it written in a book, handed over by an admirer, or was there a detailed house plan with symbols marking plumbing and bedrooms and hidden guns?

"And Kat, Scrim said they're shipping us out tomorrow." Her eyes were so sad I could've drowned in them. "And...he said I was going with them." This time the tears brimmed over.

"No. That's wrong!"

Someone was knocking on the front door. I knew who but pushed the knowledge away.

"Zoe, Zoe, Zoe." I drew her in close and said my next words with more conviction than I felt. "He's wrong. Hear me. He's damn wrong. You're coming with us. Okay?"

After a long, agonizing pause, she added a quiet, "Okay."

My anger at the world was so intense and all mixed up with an equally intense sadness.

Footsteps, the hard ones of boots.

"Woo-hoo. Got some action going there, boys." Scrim.

There wasn't time to ask her questions. Or a way to keep her. Knowing how scared she must be of what might happen tomorrow, I couldn't turn over and face them. Scrim would mock us even more if I did. Though I clung to her as long as possible, trying to give her some last shred of kindness to remember, they took her away. She was brave this time. Not me.

All I managed was a choked *goodbye* as her hand left mine, her fingers slipping across my palm. I was a devastated wreck, my heart and mind in a place where my thoughts weren't making any sense at all.

Late night, past midnight, and I was curled on the mattress, still thinking, thoughts going round and round in a circle of what ifs. What if I got the gun tomorrow, somehow before they left? I could shoot everyone, rescue me and Zoe. I imagined that very thing in my head, seeing them all at my feet, blood pooling under their heads – Scrim, his helpers… I couldn't imagine further than that, screeching to a halt when I thought of Chris or Andreas dead.

And what if Scrim had been teasing her about being shipped away and she came back to me anyway?

Chapter 29

Chris

I'd been listening to her crying quietly for ages. I hadn't planned this at all, but I rolled out of bed and went to her. When I turned on the light, she stopped. Walling herself off from me, yet again. I squinted down at her, feeling angry, tired, and determined to find a way into her head at...I tried to focus on the clock while yawning – 1 am. Bad plan.

I opened the cage and beckoned for Kat to come out.

When she emerged, I carried her to my bed and laid her on her back on the sheets, then stripped off her underwear. I could just fuck her. That would make me happy. I lay down with her, appreciating her femaleness as always – smell, looks, feel. I stroked my hand down the muscular slope of her thigh.

"You're worried about Zoe?"

The puzzled tweak of her mouth and brow said none of your business and why are you bothering asking.

I dug my fingers into her and she relented.

"Yes."

Red eyes, still wet from tears. And she wouldn't let me in, wanted me to leave her alone.

The shark tooth pendant mocked me. It was the one thing she was wearing. I never imagined I'd be the outsider in this but she connected more to Andreas and Zoe than to me. Somehow, she almost loved this other woman. They'd clicked, grown close, in just a few encounters. It was a softer relationship, quieter, without screams. That wasn't me.

The outsider...huh. Shit. Breaking her was more difficult than I'd imagined. So far she'd given way rather than broken. Some days I wanted to hear the crack when she succumbed to me. Other days, I just wanted in any way I could.

Tonight, I didn't want her sad.

I leaned on my elbow, tracing and exploring all the wonderful places on her body – hips, belly, the underside of her breasts, her shoulders. I never grew tired of just touching her. For a while I did nothing but that. It seemed to soothe her and Kat's eyes half-closed.

"I'm not a soft, gentle man, Kat."

She gave a small noise like an abbreviated laugh and her lips curved up.

"Stating the obvious, I suppose. I can't give you softness. Not most of the time. But, I am a man who doesn't give up on anyone easily. I don't like seeing you crying. I don't like why you're crying especially."

An idea came to me. Pain had a deep effect on her, as did dominance, when she let it.

She searched my face. "You don't like Zoe?"

"I don't like losing a part of you to her."

"You're not... Not really. What's going to happen to her –"

"Shh. Forget her for a while. Just me, just you." I cupped her face and toyed with her mouth with my thumb. She lay there and let me. "If I put you back in the cage, I think you're going to go back to crying. I could distract you. I've been meaning to do something to claim you for days." That made her swallow. Fear? Good. That would make the act more potent. I stroked her throat. "I want to put a clit hood piercing on you. I have a clit ring with my initial."

She gnawed on her lower lip – body language that said nervous in neon.

"Don't look so worried. I don't think I'll do it tonight, but it's in the top drawer." I pointed at the bedside drawers. "When you're ready and ask me, I'll do it." She sucked in a breath as if to speak. I pinched her lips together. "No. Don't say anything."

Likely, knowing her, she'd blurt out some words aimed at shocking me.

"When I do it, I will expect you to sit still, without being tied up."

More lip gnawing.

"You'll wear that mouth of yours out."

"Can I say no in advance? Sir."

Brat. I tweaked her hair. "In a minute you can scream no, though it may wake Andreas and if he comes in here, we might get real carried away. I'm going to use my belt on you. I suggest you stay quiet, and practice being still without being tied."

"Now?" Her forehead creased.

"Pain centers you, in case you'd not noticed. This will help you sleep."

"You just want to beat me," Kat muttered.

"Perceptive little bitch." I slid off the bed. "Lie on your stomach, bent over the side of the bed, stretch out your arms and clasp your hands above your head." Then I pretended I was confident she'd obey. I rummaged in the drawers and rescued my leather belt from the heap of underwear, wallet and coins. Out the corner of my eye, I watched her do exactly what I'd told her to.

Obedience. A groundbreaking day in history. My heart rate picked up at the prospect of beating her fine ass. My cock was already halfway there.

"Every time I see this backside, I have to roll my tongue back in." I smoothed my hand over the sumptuous curve and couldn't resist pinching her at the crease of her thigh then sliding my hand between her legs. "Nice. Hot."

"Flatterer."

Her cheekiness said she'd forgotten Zoe, but I couldn't let that past me.

Her squeak when I pinched her clit in finger and thumb was gorgeous.

I doubled up the belt, slapped it on my leg, testing the weight, anticipating, relishing, how I would soon make her hurt. "Did you speak? No more talking."

"Sorry, Sir." She shook her head, her forehead rustling against the sheets. "I…please don't make me come."

I didn't answer and only thwacked the belt on one cheek, hard enough to extract a yelp. The jiggle of flesh drew my eye. "Just count."

Silence, then came a quiet, resigned, "One."

So different. So damn different from when she arrived here. "Whatever I do, it's my decision." I cracked leather on her ass again, pleased at her jump and hiss, and the glorious red line already rising.

"Two." She wriggled.

I could smell the leather. It would forever be associated with this, making women's asses red, hearing their plaintive screams, and getting an instant hard-on when I really made them hurt.

I delivered more blows, created more lines of pink – more red wheals; some went straight to purple. I watched for those hands moving but she kept them above her head, gripping each other tight. A time or two, her fists opened and closed when I'd drawn my hand back high and made that meaty crack at the intersection of leather and female skin.

"Oh fuck. Fuck, yes." Her whimper sounded choked, like inside her mind was unravelling.

Now we were getting somewhere.

I guess she liked this idea of mine. Pain had its uses.

My headspace surged higher and higher. At times like this I was as triumphant as a climber reaching the top of Everest. I was steeped in adrenalin, my blood heated, my pulse fast, my breathing calculated.

Kat's back ran with sweat. Runnels of it trailed down her sides and into the cleft of her bottom. Her skin shone.

I paused to trace some of the marks, feasting on them like a vulture with a ready meal – absorbing the shudders and little whimpers she gave out when I squeezed and played with my crisscross red and blue artwork. Her knees shifted on the rug but her hands stayed where I wanted them, and clenched. Waiting for more, waiting. She lay with her face to one side, her eyes shut tight.

"Where are you Kat? Hurting good? Ten more?" This time when I sneaked my hand between her legs and found her wetness she only huffed out a shaky moan. "That's what I like to hear – those sexy sounds."

I played some more, alternating dishing out pain, by squeezing and pinching, with touching her pussy.

"What do you want, Kat?"

Rhetorical question. I didn't wait. I slipped a digit in and out her entrance. Her ass tilted, seeking my fingers. I thrust deeper, wriggled two into her entrance and used my thumb on her proud little clit. I toggled it slowly, moving her clit in circles, making it swell until it was even harder. "This is begging me. Say it. Beg me to make you come."

But she only circled her toes on the floor. Holding back? Not allowed.

I nipped her shoulder, pinched her, and slapped her butt a few times.

"Please." She shook her head, her voice muffled by sheet. "Just beat me."

"You little liar. You know I can do this to you. I will do it, when I want to."

"Please don't."

Embarrassed I could make her come? Still?

I chuckled and stood, shook the belt out and whopped three on her ass fast and hard. Her squeals put the finishing touch on my erection and I stroked my cock as I waited. I let her wonder when the hit would come.

I hadn't marked the back of her thighs much, so the next six went there, then I switched up and did more on her butt. Red, blue, and hot pink. My mind buzzed. Her breathing had gone crazy staccato and she was rubbing her groin on the bed.

After what she'd just said, this was hilarious.

"Stop." I squashed her onto the mattress, making the bed dip. "My job. Be still."

Kat sobbed and stopped writhing.

"Good girl." I rested my cheek on her ass, so I had a view down into the valley of her cunt, and recommenced finger fucking and pinching and slapping. On the out thrust stroke, my fingers gleamed with her arousal. I bit her ass, smiled at her muted squeal. "I can smell you."

Her following muttered but undecipherable words sounded dangerous.

I kneeled behind her and parted her legs, opened her up. "Fuck your little hot cunt on me."

I slid two fingers in, amused at how her walls immediately clamped onto them. Such seductive heat and wetness. "Do it, Kat."

After burying her head in the quilt, she gingerly backed her ass onto my fingers. Shameless and in-fucking-credible – the shove of her pussy onto me, the sticky slide. Her cunt fucking grew bolder, harder, and she groaned and wriggled, squirming like a woman impaled on a spear.

"Good girl. Now you get your reward." I fucked her some more, rougher, deep as I could go, then switched to a thumb in her pussy and wormed a finger into her asshole in spite of her protests.

Then I leaned in and burrowed my head between her legs, bit her thighs and lips, and used my tongue on her deeply red clit. Moaning, she stuck her ass higher, straining to get more of my mouth.

Curving my tongue over her clit and sucking brought her swiftly to the brink. When she stiffened and the sheets shifted as if she'd wrenched a handful in close, I sucked harder, ever harder. Squealing, squirming, her thighs squashing in on my head, she came, gasping and making cute little grunts.

When she grew quiet, I wiped her wetness from my face, flipped her onto her back and nestled up on the bed with her. Her chest heaving, Kat put her arm across her face.

I surveyed her body, struck by the paleness on this unwritten canvas. Her little clit stood out, all pink, all tempting me. I could. *I could.* This was mine. I'd marked her, made her cry, made her come, but she never ever admitted I was her master. The need fired up. I rolled off the bed and went to the drawer, gathered equipment – antiseptic swab, needle receiving tube, needle, pliers, ring, and brought them to the bed.

"You are going to stay still for me, sweet thing." I parted her legs and put my knee up on the bed to steady myself.

She peeked with one eye, past her arm. "Wait! I thought…"

"Changed my mind. Doing it now. You need a reminder as to who owns you."

Methodically, I swabbed her clit, moving it to and fro to get into all the fleshy nooks and crannies.

"No. Please." Her whisper carried urgency and I could see the tension in her thighs, but…she didn't move away.

I took a moment to examine her, to communicate both determination and calmness. "Yes. Be still."

She might be super sensitive after coming, but I liked that. That evil thought sustained me for a few cock-throbbing moments. The power. The pain. The mind fuck. I had a good excuse. The more I fucked around with her the more I'd exhaust her…surely?

The needle receiving tube looked far more fearsome then the needle itself. I held it up and let the light caress the silky smooth straight steel. Glint, baby, glint.

Nothing held her attention more than that tube. She was rigid, scared, but not moving.

"Twitch a fraction of an inch and this might go through your clit instead of the hood. Move and this will be far more painful than anything I have ever done to you. The clit has more nerves than the penis. Understand? *Do not move.*"

Kat took a death grip on the sheet to either side. "Yes." Her voice wobbled. "Be careful. Please, Sir."

I nodded and leaned in. I'd watched many videos on how to do this and she had what seemed normal average clit anatomy. I could do this. I hoped. Haha. That part I wasn't saying. My cruelty had limits, apparently.

I slid the tube under her hood and pushed up until it stretched the tissue thin where the tip met hood at the top. I ignored her whimpers and tiny flinch. *Concentrate.* The needle tip I poised above, on the other side of the stretched flesh. As I'd worked, her clit had shrunken a little. From fear, I supposed.

"Going in now." Firm and steadily, I pushed the needle through the hood and into the tube.

"Ow, ow, ow!" Her voice hitched as I swiftly attached the ring then fed the lot through so it curved into her clit hood. I removed all the bits and used the little pliers to attach the bead. The engraved C on the ring stood out well though I supposed she'd never read it without a mirror.

Pretty. Cute. Sexy.

"There. Done." I stood and stretched.

Her hands covered her face and she looked out warily. "It is?"

"Yes."

"It didn't hurt as much as my tattoo." She shuffled up, propping herself on her forearms, and peering down. "It's a little ring?"

"Yes." I plonked myself down on the bed and splayed my palm on her stomach. "My initial is on there." I tapped her nose then kissed her softly. Strange, the glow that now spread through me. "Mine." My eyes felt overly wide. My self seemed so in tune with her. Like this meant more than mere jewelry. "Say, 'I'm yours', Kat."

She twisted her mouth and slowly repeated my words. "I'm yours?" There was a lilt at the end. A question mark.

I didn't care, because this had cemented my ownership. I'd made her part of me with this simple gesture. "Yes, you are."

I lay there a while, thinking, recalling a hint Andreas had dropped. About something she'd told him but not me. Now seemed a good time to ask, when she was vulnerable. It bugged me that she was holding back.

"Andreas said there's some secret you haven't told me." I shuffled up onto my elbow. "About why you were so tight when I first had sex with you."

"Oh. That." She caught her lip in her teeth and I reached and took hold of that naughty sexy lip.

"Tell. You're not allowed to keep secrets from me. Not important ones like this. It is important, isn't it?"

"Umm." Kat gulped. "Yes." She closed her eyes. The buzz from the orgasm still softened her face.

"Tell." I inserted my finger into her mouth, pleased at how she automatically licked me and sucked until I pulled it out. "Tell now. Before I decide to pound you because you sucking me like that is fucking hot."

"Oops." She looked at me, searching. "Okay. Okay. I...hadn't had sex for years, not actually getting..."

"Seriously? No penetration?"

"No," she said quietly. "That's why I was so tight. You freaked me out. Erik did my head in. I couldn't."

"Hmm. You should have said. You should have told me before you told Andreas. Do not keep secrets." So this was why she'd always refused to have sex. Why she never kept a Dom or any long-term relationship. Everything made sense.

"I'm sorry." Her brow corrugated and I smoothed her frown with my wet finger.

"Good. I would have been more careful if I'd known, but..." I surveyed the wonderful hills and hollows of her body and was struck again by that need to own. My cock pulsed. "Yeah. I would've still fucked you, but I'd have been careful."

She snorted but I saw a smile there still. Small but real.

I'd give her time. Maybe that's all we needed... *We.*

When I finally picked her up and took her to the cage again, she crawled in, collapsed on her side on the sheets, and shut her eyes. Sleep seemed to come within a minute or two.

Her peaceful, if exhausted, expression warmed me. I'd never given her pain to assuage distress. Always it had fed my sadistic streak. I felt good. Blissfully good. I gave so much to my friends like Andreas, why not her, my little slave? Light bulb moment. I did need to care for her more. Andreas had known this, days ago.

I'd been so wrong. No matter what I'd thought and said before, I hadn't really seen her as a person.

I switched off the light, lay back on my bed, and stared at the moon-splashed ceiling. Dom philosophy 101. I'd better be careful. Next I'd be knitting beanies and sending them to African orphans.

Chapter 30

Kat

My dreamless sleep was shattered. Bangs somewhere…on a door, sent my heart accelerating. Head up off the pillow, I listened to Chris slide from the bed and go down the hallway, and then to voices. My ass and legs hurt so much. My clit ached, reminding me his ring was there. I'd slept despite the throbbing. He'd been right. The pain had helped. It was novel to think of Chris helping me like he had.

And strange having the clit ring – a constant memento of him. I didn't, for once, hate him for appropriating my body. I liked it in a scary kind of way. I turned that over in my head. *His?*

At that thought, a sexual thrill trickled through me from my clit and that definitely scared me. I squirmed, squeezed my thighs together, feeling the hardness of the ring near my pussy.

Shouldn't be thinking that. I needed to get away from him not nearer. *Away.* This was like a propaganda exercise. This was a trick. Only I felt ill and sad and ever so tired when I contemplated continuing this struggle against what he wanted.

He wants me but what about what I want? I had a life, didn't I?

Andreas came to the bedroom doorway and seemed to listen before he unlocked my cage and ushered me toward the front door. My nakedness registered but I had no choice. I'd grown used to being exposed around the men, but he grabbed my dress from the chair and clothed me, adjusting the fall of the lace at my hips. He bestowed a kiss on my forehead.

As we entered the small foyer, he murmured, "Sounds like you need to hear this." He gave the hand signal and I kneeled.

I'd never seen Scrim look flustered but now he had the crazy-eyed jittery mannerisms of someone on the edge.

"Come on, fuckit, I need another man I can trust and you're it."

He trusted Chris? Since when?

Chris seemed unruffled, only shaking his head. "Give me a minute."

"We haven't got time. Decide. With me or not. But if it's not, you need to pack your bags and head to Brazil or somewhere fucking far away because not only will the boss not be happy, neither will the cops if these women talk to them."

What? I couldn't blink. Had someone escaped? Was Zoe among them?

"Wait. Rush me and you get nothing." Chris turned away leaving Scrim all but grinding his teeth. He walked to us.

"What is it?" Andreas moved so their conversation was a little private.

"Someone may have helped the women escape. Scrim thinks so. Though they didn't get a car, their cage got unlocked and they went over the wall. Looks like someone also put up a ladder for them. Zoe has gone too." He glanced at me.

Oh god. I didn't say anything. Joy blossomed. The girl was away!

Funny though, a second later, regret sneaked in. She was gone from my life. I even felt sadness that I'd lost a friend. How fucked up was I?

Andreas reached down and patted my head. "Maybe they managed all that themselves?"

"Don't know. Scrim's sure he has a traitor. He wants me with him."

"He trusts you more?"

Chris made a doubtful face. "If I go…Scrim's men are armed and they have some way of tracking the girls' collars so they have a chance of catching them. He figures they have half an hour head start, at most. One other thing – he's guaranteed me Zoe when, if, we catch her, and he seems damned certain they will."

"Wow. He must need you then."

"I guess we have a lot at stake and he figures that makes me on his side."

I couldn't stop myself though my hands shook and I bunched them in my dress. "Sir. Please. Let them go."

He frowned and, apart from a glance, ignored me. "If they get away, we're stuffed Andreas. The cops would track us down. This place would be found."

"Yeah." Andreas scraped his hand down his face. "Shit. We might have some time but we'd be found eventually. Trails like phone texts, DNA, I'm sure there's witnesses to our road trip too. Things would add up."

"I'm sorry, mate. Never meant this to happen."

Scrim interjected. "Let's stop pussying around, hey? Get your ass downstairs in five minutes. I've got to grab stuff and people." He turned to go but halted and added, "This is no Disney thing. If you come, just remember these women are like bottles on a shelf. Sometimes I have to eliminate stock." He jogged off down the stairs.

Dread sent sharp tendrils into my blood. He'd kill the women? I half swallowed, my throat seizing up.

Andreas slapped the wall beside his head. "Okay, he's gone. Chris, fucking bottom line. If they start shooting at people at night, you could get injured, killed, doing this."

Gun. I had a gun. Despite a lack of logic, that seemed like it could lead to a solution. I backed away on my knees. "I'm feeling sick…"

They dismissed me with hand signals. I'd never been allowed alone in the house. Ever. I fled barefoot back to the bedroom, hauled out the drawer Zoe had told me to move, and there was the steel lid set in the floor. Number pad. Handle.

Frantic, with my stomach contents trying to arrive in my mouth, I punched in the combination to the number pad. Locked still.

"Shit, shit, shit." Again.

Slow down. I swallowed bile.

Get it right this time. *Punch. Punch, punch.*

The little handle turned and the lid opened. There lay a gleaming pistol and a magazine of bullets. I took a deep breath and picked them up, slid the magazine in. Everything clicked together so easily. I'd never fired a gun but there were a shitload of bullets. Maybe I should've counted them, but I wasn't game to try removing the magazine, sure that something would fall apart.

This must be the safety. I flicked the switch on then off again. Point and pull the trigger. Easy. And who was I going to shoot?

I ran back to the foyer, halting the other side of the wall from where Chris and Andreas were. They were silent.

Then Andreas spoke. "On the other hand, I'd rather leave Australia than see you killed trying to get women back for a slave trafficker."

I peeked around the corner and saw Chris nodding, stern look to his face like Andreas had just delivered the commandments in stone.

What did I want? With one hand hanging at my side and the heaviness of the gun dragging it down, I rubbed the heel of my other hand into my forehead. Think.

Run while they're distracted? See if I can get out via the deck, if they left it unlocked? Unlikely but possible.

Only Scrim said he was tracking the women. *If* he caught them, and it seemed possible…he might kill them? Maybe if they struggled? Maybe if they ran when told to stop? I could see Zoe doing just that. I wasn't sure of the reasons that might make him do it, but he might.

Fuck. I banged my hand into my forehead.

I didn't want her to die. I wanted…I wanted to send Chris to go fetch her back. If he was there, he could help her.

"I am so fucked," I whispered.

What if she might have truly gotten away? What if I was the cause of her being caught again? What if she got herself killed? I couldn't see Zoe giving up again easily. If Scrim caught her, she might be a mouse, or she might be a screaming person he'd have to drag back here. Kicking and screaming and spitting.

I could see it, and the bullet in her head. The blood. Or maybe he'd just strangle her, that'd be quieter.

"He doesn't want me to come, does he?" Andreas again.

"No. And how the fuck would that help us anyway? You need to stay here with Kat."

Shit. I leaned on the wall, feeling like I needed an extra brain to sort this out. My head ached. What if I just went and shot everybody? Like in *Resident Evil*, I could be the badass chick who mows down her enemies with dead-accurate shots.

Fuck yeah.

I hefted the gun, reading the etched writing but not really seeing past the blur in my eyes.

I'd rather toss away the slim chance of her freedom and beg Chris to get her back. Though I knew, and couldn't deny, that I also wanted her in my arms, because, just plain because, I did.

"Decided?" Andreas murmured.

But I didn't want Chris to die either, and I trusted Scrim as far as I could toss a feather.

With the gun behind my back, I squeezed around the corner, pivoting slowly around the door frame on my shoulders.

"You okay, Kat?" Andreas swung as if to see me better.

"I –"

In one stride, Chris had me against the wall. Arm like steel across my neck, his body pinning me, the gun and my hand holding it fastened to the wall as if stapled there by his grip. I was forced up on tippy toes, feeling the sting where the ring pierced me.

His face was an inch away and his eyes dissected me, separating thought and mind so the words on my tongue vanished and my will fell away to nothing.

I blinked, breath caught in my throat.

"What are you doing, little Kat?"

That I could answer. "Giving you something, Sir. To help you." I gulped.

"The pistol?"

"Yes, Sir."

"You want me to go search for Zoe?"

Did I? Wrong or right, I did. "Yes, Sir."

Then he stepped away and with relief I could reassemble some of my mind, though most of me was in tatters. I'd never seen him as my Sir. No one had been since *him*. Yet then, for that moment, he had been. I swayed a little, needing time, space, so I could rescue myself, let alone Zoe. If anyone deserved my submission it was Andreas. I didn't need Chris.

But, he'd stepped away? When I had a gun? I'd been looking at his chest and I marshaled the courage to stare at him.

"Then do it, now. Give me the gun." He surveyed my face, concentrating, as if seeing me for the first time.

What big blue eyes you have, Sir.

I'd always been able to force myself to meet his eyes in any emergency. Not now. My gaze slid away like glass slipping on ice.

I was on the edge of a precipice, teetering, with the clouds blowing past. If he blew on me, I'd fall. I shuddered. *Fuck.*

I cleared my throat and went to hand him the gun.

"No." His hand was on me again, slowly he raked his fingers upward through the nape of my hair and he tilted my head back, tightening the grip as he twisted his fingers. Delicious force. I groaned. My eyelids fluttered. My clit throbbed, in time with my heartbeat, reminding me I had a part of him in me, always.

"Look at me, Kat."

I did, for all of two seconds, before the glass on ice effect hit me again. I wavered.

"No. Look at me. You could have tried to use this to shoot us, couldn't you? To get free. But you didn't."

"Yes," I whispered, squirming my already sore butt against the wall. I was ashamed that he'd figured that out. Obvious though. Looking at him staring back at me was so uncomfortable, and yet, he was so *there*, so determined to make me see *him*. Nervous, I swallowed.

Away. Need to get away, remember?

His hand moved a little more. Pain twisted in. "Yes, I see you too, Kat."

Then he released my hair, and slipped his hand a little lower, to my neck, and he stroked me there for a moment before he drew me to him and wrapped his arms about me, surrounding me with him.

I...let myself go. For the first time ever, I sank into him, his scent, the feel of his muscles moving against me, the sound of his voice at my ear and of his heart thudding.

"Andreas told me I should be gentler with you. But you only need a little of that, don't you, Kat? What you really need is me, as I am – a big bad sadist.

"On a day when you're sad, and a man who loved you would bring you flowers, I'll give you pain if that's what you need. Fuck flowers. But if instead of pain you need the head of the person who caused your sadness, I'll do that for you too. I'll bring you their fucking head."

I couldn't stop listening as his words rumbled out.

"They say if you love someone, you let them go free. Understand this. I'm not letting you go, Kat, not in a million, million years, because what I have for you isn't love, it's obsession.

"Now I want you to tell me. What are you?"

His murmur had stolen in and invested some part of me. My heart it seemed, from the warmth there. And yes, I knew this wasn't exactly love from me either. I had simply done what he'd said – I'd finally comprehended what I was.

Getting away meant leaving him behind, and if what I needed was him?

The price for having *him* was terrifying. For it was me.

But nothing held me back anymore. I was prepared to pay.

My pulse beat so loud it filled my head; my fingers trembled against his shirt feeling his body beneath. How solid he was when I was fragile. I was warm, safe. I buried my nose in his shoulder, inhaled. The world disassociated and floated.

He released me, and I slipped away and went to my knees. "I am yours, Sir." Then I put the gun down and my palms to the floor and I bowed my head, amazed at the liberating feeling that flooded me, washing away my resentment and anger. "I am yours," I repeated softly, because the words seemed to work magic.

He went to one knee before me. "I know. You are mine."

I understood. I'd lost a part of myself yet I'd gained something also. *Him.*

From below rumbled the sound of vehicles starting.

I raised my head, surprised at the tears in my eyes. "Zoe?"

He smiled. "You want her? I'll get her for you."

My world had turned upside down. Now, I was scared that *he* wouldn't come back. I closed my eyes trying to sort this out. I was right though. *This* was right. I needed him. I was like a jigsaw that had found the last piece.

I sighed and resurrected my tougher self, sat back on my heels. I nodded. "Thank you, Sir." I couldn't stop saying what came next. "Please, come back."

I was such a wuss.

"I will."

Chapter 31

Chris

Please come back.

That she cared enough to say that...I was still in shock.

I readjusted my hands where they rested on my knee, wishing I could instruct her to do something deeply kinky just so I could see her finally obey me without question.

There was triumph for me in what she'd done as well as a very simple and pure pleasure. I'd wanted her submission for so long. I'd had subs spout versions of the same words many times but hearing it from Kat, who'd fought so hard against it – the ultimate thrill and power rush and satisfaction.

I couldn't resist cupping her face in my palm. When she leaned her cheek into my hand, an unfamiliar ache spread in my chest.

What a time for this to happen. I needed to move my ass or Scrim would leave without me.

"May I give you the gun, Sir?"

It lay next to her hand on the timber floor. Innocuous metal. Potential violence. I wasn't a weapons man unless it had a sharp edge or was my own body.

"Yes."

She took it up in both hands and offered it to me with the pistol laid across them. An unusual way to do it, as if this meant more to her than merely a weapon. As if this were her submission made solid.

"Thank you." Keeping hold of one of her hands, I checked the safety was on then tucked it into the back of my jeans. I looked up and found Andreas where he was propping up a wall. "Grab me a T-shirt?"

"Sure."

Once he was gone, I could pay attention to Kat again.

Her mouth pursed and she wriggled and tried to disengage her hand from mine.

"No. Do not." I hung on to her fingers, pleased when she instantly relaxed.

"Sorry, Sir. Umm." Kat ducked her head, then peered up at me, blinking. She wiped her eyes.

The ache in my chest intensified. This had struck her as deeply as it had me.

Formal words seemed *right*. "I accept your submission, Kat, and I thank you. But there's something I need to know. Where did this weapon come from?" There so many possibilities that could be disasters in the waiting.

The wavering in the line of her mouth said she was worried.

"Kat ?"

"Zoe. I don't know how she found out but she told me it was in a safe in your bedside drawers, and she gave me the combination. She seemed to be frightened that she even knew about it."

"I understand how difficult that must have been to say. Thank you for telling me."

Then I kissed her hard, only pulling away when Andreas jogged back into the room.

He threw me the shirt and I stood to yank it on.

The fast stomp of boots on the steps forewarned us. One of Scrim's men poked his head in the door and grinned. "Scrim says to get your ass in gear! You're got one minute." He chuckled. "Last guy who fucked up a shipment is six feet under, and his girlfriend paid too. She was fucking hot."

"I'll be there." *Asswipe.* I stared him down until he left, then I turned back to Andreas. "Right. Gotta go. Be careful. Keep our girl safe." I flashed Kat a dark smile.

"You too!" Andreas shouted as I hit the stairs, going down them three, four at a time. "Don't come back with any fucking holes in you!"

The first 4WD was edging through the gate already. I jogged up to the second. When the rear side door opened and Scrim hollered, I climbed in the back.

Once inside, the driver gunned the engine and we surged forward.

"Made it, did ya." It wasn't a question. Scrim leaned in and put a pistol on my lap. "Beretta. Silenced so it won't be as accurate at a distance, but beggars aren't choosers. It'll do the job. Like I said to the rest of these shit kickers, don't shoot any of these girls lest you have to. They're valuable."

"Right." Nice to know. Any man who tried shooting Zoe was going to need to duck fucking fast.

"And here's the piece de resistance. Night vision glasses."

He set to pointing out all the features. The man was efficient. Knew his job. Once he'd helped me get them on my forehead, Scrim fell silent.

Half crescent of a moon up there. Not a lot of light but some. Moonlight bathed the interior of the vehicle in light silvery greys whenever the tree cover overhead broke. Scrim's hard-edged face turned even uglier, and the glimpses I had of the men in the front looked just as mean. This could've easily been a platoon of soldiers going out on night patrol.

This was where my obsession had brought me – out at night hunting women. It wasn't something I'd ever brag to Mum about. She'd slap me into next week if she knew.

Where were we going? I needed more info and so far Scrim hadn't coughed up much. Most importantly, who did he think was the traitor?

The man in the passenger seat up front held a smartphone with a beeping app. "Lost them somehow," he grumbled.

"Give it here, Pieter." Scrim leaned forward and put his hand between the seats. "You South Africans probably only just got your spears upgraded to muskets."

"*Kak.*" Pieter smacked the phone into Scrim's palm. Was that a South African swear word?

"Ahh. Yeah, you got the brightness turned up too fuckin high. Easily fixed." He nudged me. "You'd think a guy who's killed a few hundred terror-bloody-ists could use a phone."

Was he trying to taunt Pieter?

"Look at that. It's got satellite GPS positioning on their collars." Obviously bragging, Scrim showed off the screen. It was multicolored and had flashing red dots alongside what seemed a river. "All four of them are showing. They're going between the river and the road. Sensible way to find your way to the bridge. Mating season's gone so the crocs will be slow. What they don't know is…" He tapped the map. "There's a new little branch of the river that they're running toward. We can trap them in there. No fucking worries."

Pieter spoke without turning. "Won't the ladies just go across the little bit of water?"

His South African accent was close to a Kiwi one but different enough to sound odd. Pieter looked bigger in here than I remembered. Incredible Hulk territory. The big ones tended to go down hard when you kicked them but this guy was ex-military from what Scrim hinted. Maybe I should've brought some kryptonite?

"Ladies. Fuck. Don't think I'd call them that anymore, dude. Yeah, they might if we don't get there in time. But there's a couple more creeks that don't show on the map. Last wet season ripped some new holes in the riverbank. All the maps are out of date. This'll be like catching fish in a barrel."

"Isn't that shooting fish in a barrel?" piped up the guy driving. He had long blond hair that whipped back in the breeze from his open window – like some misplaced hippie.

"Whatever," Scrim chuckled. He typed into the smartphone. "Okay, I got Matt and Red to stop at the right place and we'll catch up and follow them into the bush. If you bag yourself a girl, use your duct tape and zip ties. Here, Chris." He dumped a bag on the seat between us. "Take some. No bagging only this Zoe, though. You got to help us with them all."

"Sure." I nodded, easier to agree than argue. "Understood."

The euphoria from Kat's submission had drained away and been replaced by stomach-tightening apprehension. I needed to be focused anyway. Anything could happen. I fingered the click-on key chain light attached to the set of keys in my jeans pocket. Anyone wearing night vision goggles could be incapacitated by a bright flash…unless they had a cut-out filter. Worth keeping in mind.

Less than a minute later we pulled up behind the first car. No one was left inside but Scrim had been getting updates via text. When we entered the scrub off to the side, Scrim stuck with me and waved Pieter and the blond driver off to the right.

This situation was surreal. Zoe would be scared into next week. Where she found the courage to do this I couldn't imagine. The woman had been barely able to function around Scrim as it was. She must know he might do something terrible to her if he caught her. I vowed then and there to keep her safe. I already had vowed that to Kat, in a way, but now, yeah, it was way more personal. Kat was a tough lady. I knew she could take me kidnapping her. Zoe looked as fragile as a lacewing bug.

Pieter and the driver had a second smartphone that Scrim had downloaded the app onto.

"Keep an eye out and text me if you need to," he instructed them. After waiting for the distance between us and them to lengthen, he started talking. "Keep up with me. I want you covering my back. Pieter got into Australia illegally because of his dear little criminal past barring him from entering the country. He's ex-military from the South African armed forces and he's my best candidate for the man who helped them escape."

With night vision, navigating under the trees was simple. These things weren't some cereal packet variety – they distinguished between leaves and earth and whatever else was around extremely well. Scrim and my own body stood out like a green Christmas tree with lights. A few times I glimpsed the other men off to the right, slinking through the forest.

"What if you're wrong? Maybe the women managed this all on their own?"

"Maybe."

The crunch of leaves underfoot seemed loud compared to the smaller noises of the night animals and the clicking and chirruping of insects. I could almost smell the river nearby, the air was that thick with moisture.

"But I don't think so, and Pieter is sweet on one of the girls. Jazmine. Could be one of the others but my gut says it's him."

"And you trust him not to do something to your driver?"

"Blondie? Hah. The man's tougher than he looks. He's ex-mil infantry too. Almost made it into the SAS. 'Sides, I told him to be careful around Pieter."

The men off to the right started jogging but Scrim tagged me and pulled me to a halt.

"Quick rundown of a few things. Something as a gift first. To show you I'm on your side, okay? The lodge is wired with hidden webcams. Anything you've done in the living room or the bedrooms, Vetrov has recorded. I wasn't exactly supposed to say this. It's how I knew your girl was escaping. Vetrov messaged me. It's also how I know your friend let the woman go."

For a second, I forgot to inhale or exhale. Everything? Then a half second after…why did he want the photo of us with Zoe. Just another mindfuck? He knew about Andreas too?

"Shocker, hey?"

The goggles showed me his usual devious leer. The man was enjoying this. He was on my side? What crap. "Yes. Shocker. Thanks for saying."

"My pleasure. It also means the boss is very suspicious of your friend's involvement in this escape."

Shit. Bad. Real Bad.

"So, you better perform unless you want to have a fatal wildlife interactive experience, as the boss likes to put it. Bottom line?" He pointed at my chest, still casual like as if he was reading a kid's story. "You dead. Your friend dead after being mangled with something like a wood chipper. Nasty fuckin' things. Your lady, probably shipped off after being fucked a few dozen times. Got that? I'm just being practical. Okay?"

I struggled not to punch a hole clear through his throat and kept my voice steady. "Got it." Inside, I was wrestling my screaming and my rage down to acceptable levels.

Fuck him. How dare he threaten Andreas and Kat? But, I was outnumbered. Compared to Vetrov, I was a little man. I couldn't stop him if he decided to have me killed and do worse to Andreas and to Kat.

"Good. I'm not your enemy. Really, I'm not. Second thing. I'm gonna test Pieter when we catch the girls. I'm going to threaten to shoot that girl he has the hots for. You keep watch. Shoot him if he tries anything."

Scrim was asking me to commit murder. Out of the question. But the gruesome reality twisted my gut. I couldn't say no.

"That sounds very dicey. Dangerous. Especially as my aim is better with a rock than a bullet."

"Now you tell me? Yeah, you might be right. I'll have another think. Come on."

I had an urge to ask him if his boss knew he cut the girls, or Zoe at least. Maybe she'd been the only one, but I didn't think Vetrov would like merchandise being damaged. Bad timing. I needed Scrim on my side. Later. An email would do it.

This time we set off running.

He was so sure this was Pieter that he was planning to test him. If it came down to shooting or killing Pieter, could I do it? Scrim was my channel to Vetrov, my way to get Zoe. I'd become his little helper, not a role I liked. Whoever had helped free the women was crazy about one of them, surely? I loved that sort of crazy. It was me. If Scrim told me to kill and I refused, I was probably fucked, we all were, and Zoe, my present for Kat, would be off the menu.

I kept running. A short while later, someone shouted up ahead and there was a feminine scream that cut off and merged into a low babble of voices.

"They got someone." Scrim veered off toward them and we soon came upon the two from the first 4WD. They'd found two of the women and had them down on the ground, already zip tied.

Scrim nodded. "Good going. Get 'em back to the car then one of you catch up to us."

We set off again. The driver and Pieter weren't far ahead. Maybe one of them was going deliberately slow?

We loped up to a small creek and then turned to follow it toward the main river.

"Fuck. They're just up ahead. Haven't moved much. I wonder if they think they can hide and we'll go past?" Scrim managed to chuckle even though we were both panting lightly from the run. The man kept fit.

Had the night grown darker and had that given them false hope? They wouldn't know about the goggles. The screams would've carried to them. Maybe Zoe and Jazmine had simply been so worried that they'd made a mistake?

"Just here," Scrim whispered as he slowed then stopped, planting his feet wide.

They were hiding. The goggles showed them crouching low. Pieter and the blond guy arrived off to our left. Somehow they'd crossed over our path. Now the women were boxed in. Us on two sides, the river and creek on the other sides.

I said a mantra to get my heart rate down and my mind functioning clearly. Now was when it could all go to crap. We advanced, slow, purposeful, no talking. They'd be hoping we'd walk straight past them. I aimed for the smaller silhouette. Had to be Zoe.

Two yards, one, Blondie was on her other side. I lunged down and grabbed her, hearing the squeak then a scream that blasted my ears. Her legs flailed until I sat on her.

It was her – I was certain. Zoe's soft body struggled against my muscles and found no give. She sagged to the ground, sobbing in agonizing jerks that broke me a little. Poor thing.

I had to get her quiet. There could be campers, people somewhere nearby. Nothing was certain. Blondie was taking care of her legs and wrists.

I'd grabbed a ball gag from Scrim's bag instead of duct tape. Swiftly, I fitted it to her mouth and strapped it on while I talked. "Shh. Shh. It's fine. It's Chris, Kat's friend. You're not going to be hurt, Zoe. I'll look after you. You're coming with me back to Kat."

I kept up my flow of words and slowly her sobs turned to quiet crying. I stroked her hair for a few seconds then I stood.

More movement, the thrashing of leaves, and gasps that went nowhere, said they'd caught Jazmine somewhere ahead. I hoisted Zoe onto my shoulder and carried her to where they'd taken down Jazmine. If Pieter had ideas about this woman escaping and him meeting up with her, he must've decided to play the innocent tonight. Try again another day maybe. If I were him I'd not bother.

Wait, no, if it were Kat…yeah if Scrim tried to take Kat, I'd have no hesitation in putting him into an early grave. But Pieter didn't seem that committed to this woman. Maybe Scrim had it all wrong too.

At least Scrim hadn't tried to shoot her. I dragged off the goggles and wiped my forehead. Fucking muggy, once you went running. Sweat ran down my face.

As they worked on Jazmine a few yards away, I lowered Zoe to the ground. This woman was putting up more of a fight than Zoe. My eyes adjusted fast to the lack of goggles. The tree canopy was sparse here. The moonlight filtering down through the gap gave the scene a fairytale quality, if it weren't for the muffled noises of a woman being hogtied. Somewhere high above, an owl launched, hooting softly as it glided off in search of prey.

From below in the creek bed came a splashing noise as if someone had dumped a big log in the water.

"Crap." Scrim rose. I heard him snort back some phlegm before he spit. "Damn it woman, you gave me an appetite for lurv with all your wriggling, but that splash just took it away. That's gotta be an old croc. We woke the bugger up. Let's get going. You finally got her legs tied, Pieter?"

"I have." The big man climbed to his feet.

Success. Thank god. My muscle tension cranked down a notch. My heart beat a little slower.

"Good." Scrim stepped back in my direction. Metal gleamed in his fist. "Now you shoot her, Pieter. Blondie? Chris?"

Calling us for support?

Shoot her?

Fuck. Plan number two, Scrim? Wish you'd warned me. A yard from Scrim. Four from Pieter. More from Blondie who was on the other side of all of this. Blondie already had his hand swinging up with his weapon in it. This was a better plan than Scrim's first one. Scrim already had the man in his sights. And if Pieter refused, I suppose that proved who the traitor was. Cause the man had to be in love to do what he did. Didn't he?

Could I kill him? I had to or risk losing everything if Vetrov decided I'd been bad. Even losing Zoe wasn't an option. She wasn't just Kat's girlfriend but a way to wash away some of my dirty past. Save her. Kill Pieter. Simple, as long as I shot straight. Three against one.

But Pieter was in love.

Love. Weird. I admired a man who went there. Who could feel like that, who could dedicate himself to a woman. It was one step from obsession...

I expected the man to say *what* and look baffled while he weighed up his options. Unless he was truly uninterested in the woman...and callous, had to add in callous if you could shoot a bound and helpless women for no particular reason. My heart and mind, by now, had caught up, wound up, to fighting speed. Waiting, waiting, for something to happen. I was rising from my crouch and calibrating distances.

Thinking this didn't take long.

By the time I was standing, Blondie was down with a knife in his throat. One choked cry from him – then down, falling on his back, writhing. Hard to breathe with a knife in your windpipe.

Scrim had missed two important points. Pieter thought and moved like lightning.

But so did I.

Life is full of choices. Which? The side of shooting helpless women, or the side of an almost obsessive love?

I brought Scrim down with a kidney punch to his back and a chokehold as he fired skyward. The silenced gun made a small *phut* noise. Then I smashed the side of his head with one blow and kept him as a shield. I'd never killed anyone before. I had today. Knew it. It drove an ice spike directly to my soul. But I was glad. One cockroach less in the world.

Now I had Pieter breathing hard over there with a gun almost up, from the way the light flickered along its length. I shone my little flashlight in his eyes and heard the *phut* of his weapon.

Behind me, Zoe shrieked then cut off.

Shit oh shit. Had she been hit? For a few seconds, I fought the screaming need to turn and check she was breathing. *First. Stay alive.*

Pieter had dived earthward and was no doubt aiming where he thought I was. I bet he'd ripped off his goggles.

"Stop," I grated out but I kept my volume low. "I can see you. I can shoot you, before you get past Scrim's body. I've killed him."

Scrim gave one last gurgle and stopped breathing as if to put a neat full stop on my statement. Fuck, I was a murderer – another notch on my belt of evil fucking deeds. Pieter hadn't shifted. "I'm letting you go, man! I'm on your fucking side. I could've shot you already. Now go!"

All the while I was aware of that other man Scrim had ordered to return. If he came now…

"Go! Just make sure she doesn't go to the fucking cops. Okay?"

I probed backward with my foot and was sure I heard a gasp from Zoe. Didn't mean she wasn't hit though, or bleeding.

Finally, I saw him rise. Slow. Careful.

He tucked away his pistol, strode to Jazmine and stripped away her bonds with a quick flick of a second knife.

Must remember to invite him over if I ever needed something sliced and diced.

"Thanks. Got your back, man, if you ever need it. Zoe said you weren't a *doos*. That counts with me."

I nodded even if he couldn't see it. And made a note to find out what a *doos* was.

Then the two of them jogged away.

When I was game to turn, I found Zoe breathing. Now what? I had her, but maybe I'd crapped all over my chances of keeping her? Vetrov…if he found out what happened, I'd be duck slash croc food at the bottom of a river. Two of his men were dead. One gone missing with one of his women.

How could elation feel so bad? I may have signed the death sentences of everyone. Me, Andreas, Kat, Zoe. The women would be made to wish they were dead.

I shook away my dread of the future. Clear head. Think your way out. There *must* be a way. Only my stomach kept rolling like it was filled with something rotten that wanted out.

"Zoe, are you hit anywhere? Tell the truth." I crouched beside her and tried to check her.

She shook her head then waited, rigid.

I squeezed her arm. "You'll be fine. I'm taking you to Kat."

Christ. Close call. No holes in either of us. No knives even. All I had to do was find that perfect excuse for Scrim's men, and for Vetrov.

Think, fuckit, think. There had to be an answer that would convince Vetrov.

I rolled Scrim's body down into the darkly shadowed creek bed for the croc to snack on when he felt like it. A long, gray lump surged forward and lumbered for the body.

Croc. Huge one.

I did what every man does after he escapes almost certain death. Hands on knees, I puked. Then I wiped my mouth, and decided to buy a lottery ticket next time I had the chance to.

I rescued the goggles, found car keys in Blondie's pocket, then walked out with Zoe on my shoulder. Met the other guy before he even made ten yards from his vehicle. After I put Zoe in my 4WD, we returned to the creek. He believed me when he saw the knife in his man's neck. Guess he never figured me for a knife man. I told him I'd run away when the gunplay started as I couldn't hit the side of a barn. The mean and doubtful look in his eyes dissipated when I stood there and stared back. I guess Pieter had a bad rep.

"You better have a bloody good way of explaining that to Vetrov."

Yeah, good point. It was one I was working on.

We looked down at the massive croc doing its death roll with Scrim and decided, wisely, to leave it to eat.

"Vetrov can figure this." On the way to the 4WDs he sent off a text or two. "Okay. I'm volunteered to clean up this mess. And you, you poor bastard, Vetrov says explain."

"I will. When I get back to the lodge."

My heart beat so forcefully it hurt my chest.

"You can get the fuck out of here. Me and Red will get Blondie. There aren't too many roads out of the Daintree. The changeover men were coming in from up north tonight to take the girls to the airfield. Pieter picked a bad place to start a run from."

After that, he seemed more concerned with getting a blanket to carry Blondie's body and leaving ASAP. I drove back with Zoe on the passenger seat next to me. Though her eyes were dark and she still had the gag in, I'd put her head in my lap. That might, possibly, be reassuring. Plus I told her a few more times that she was now mine, and Andreas's, and…Kat's.

But there was still Vetrov. Fucking Vetrov. The man who could have us all killed on a whim. How did I explain this in an email and sound utterly convincing?

I had a thought. One possibility. It might work. Fucking had to.

We'd been a five-minute drive from the house at most. And a world away. Two people had died since I'd left them. By the time I walked in the door, with Zoe over my shoulder, my shaking hands were still again. The triumphant scaredy cat Dom returneth.

I had a sudden vision of me chucking a match on this place and letting it burn. Of walking away with the lodge afire, and flames lighting up the sky behind me.

If only.

I kept going down the hallway with Zoe and met up with Andreas and Kat.

"Scoot." I ushered them both ahead of me. Andreas took the girl. Once I had Kat curled up with an untied and ungagged Zoe on the couch, I bear hugged Andreas for a second. My throat closed in.

"You okay, mate?" he asked.

Hated weakness. I shut it down. I'd tell him about the exact details of the killing later, if he wanted me to. I said everything all nice and loud despite Andreas raising an eyebrow. Zoe knew it all and Kat was tough.

"Bad things went down. We caught two of the women but two people got killed – Scrim and another man. Pieter, one of Scrim's

men did it. Tough bastard. He wanted to get away with one of the women. Once the shooting started, I ran." I screwed up my face and shook my head as if disgusted at myself.

Andreas looked taken aback. His eyebrows went up so high they disappeared under his hair. "You ran?"

"Yep. I can't hit the side of a barn with a pistol. Scrim never asked me but it's true. Give me a down-and-dirty hand to hand and I can do it, not guns." I dragged the two pistols from my belt and handed them to Andreas. "Store them somewhere secure while I go email Vetrov."

"Wait." He put up a hand. "Are we safe? I mean there are people on the loose who might give us, as well as this whole operation, to the cops."

"I don't know." I looked over at the couch where Kat seemed to have a handle on comforting the girl, whispering sweet nothings in her ear. "Pieter was here illegally. I guess that makes it unlikely. I think he was in love with this woman. I'll be back in a minute. Take them all out to the deck and wait for me on the sofa there."

He raised his eyebrows. "You want me to move them?"

"Yes."

I left Andreas to think and walked to the study, praying I'd found the right answer to my puzzle.

Vetrov was online and waiting, from the speed of his response.

I gave him the same spiel I had Andreas. That I'd run when the gunfight started.

V: I never took you for a cowardly man.

C: I'm sensible, is all.

Then I went for the one thing I needed from him, apart from absolution for not stopping Pieter.

C: S promised Z to me if I helped him. And I did, best I could.

I had to wait a while.

V: Is not a gift. I will send you bill. Maybe you owe me another time. Rain check, yes?

Shit. I grinned. Yes! Either he'd watched the living room webcam, or he simply believed me. The webcam seemed likely. It was why I'd spoken loudly. Thank you, Scrim. You did one good thing in your life.

C: Sure. Rain check.

This was way better than being dead. If I could just forget that Vetrov probably had a whole library of BDSM porno recorded with us featuring. I sank back in my chair.

V: You are a lucky man.

C: Why?

V: Pieter did not shoot you. I have decided not to shoot you because I just got word that we caught him and her. You need to go kiss the ground and say thank you to whatever gods you believe in.

My mind went dead silent. Then my heart started up again. I didn't know why, but Pieter's fate made me feel dreadfully sad. I didn't know him at all except that he'd been willing to sacrifice a lot to get his woman safe. Nothing I could do. That made me feel like shit. The man was good as dead. Maybe her, Jazmine, too.

I needed to go see and touch some good people. I levered myself out of the chair.

Out on the deck, Andreas had managed to sit at one end of the big sofa, then there were the two women with Kat resting her head on his lap and Zoe snuggled into her. I eyed them.

Andreas cocked an eyebrow. "Daddy want to come join in?" His look was questioning though.

I nodded to him in a *yeah things are good* kind of way.

"Move your fat ass, you bastard." Then I got Kat to sit up on her elbow while I squeezed in next to him. "Put your head back down." Gently I encouraged her to rest her head. Getting comfortable, she wriggled a bit down the sofa, taking Zoe with her. "My lap this time. He's had his turn."

My elbow in his side made Andreas cough.

"Ow." He rubbed his ribs and leaned on the armrest. "Asshole, you've got a hard elbow. So everything is sorted out?"

Ugh. There was so much I couldn't say to him right then and there. So much.

If it hadn't been for the killing and the fact that I knew the human traffickers were at this moment dragging Pieter and his woman away to be tortured, or that the other women were once more slaves, I could have been content. But Scrim was dead. I had Kat. I'd found Zoe. We were alive and staying that way. Big pluses.

I pushed away my sadness, the pain I still had eating at me from the deaths and everything. I closed my eyes a second, stroking Kat's hair. I summed up. "Yes. It's sorted. I'll fill you in later."

"Okay. Great to have you back in one piece."

"Me too." Kat squirmed her head around. "I'm so glad to have you back too, Sir." Then a cheeky look came over her. She sneaked her tongue onto her lip, and her eyes took on a defiant gleam as she grinned one-sided. "Can I call you asshole too?"

"Fuck no." I grabbed her throat and growled. "If there was a wall handy I'd shove you up against it and fuck you just to show you how wrong you are for saying that…after I birched your ass with a raw stick from a tree."

This woman was never going to stop testing me now and then. I think I liked that. The challenge. Yeah, I did.

Her reply was demure. "Sorry, Sir."

Now that response had been beautiful. I stroked her skin, loving the smile that danced on her lips.

"Pretty girl, this is a good time to show off what I've given you. Kneel in front of us."

"I'll be back." She patted Zoe then wriggled out from under her to kneel where I pointed. From the way she grimaced the bruises on her ass were hurting.

"Thank you." I nodded, pleased. There was nothing wrong with thanks, as long as she obeyed quickly. The novelty of her doing that would take months, maybe years, to wear off. "Lift your dress and show Andreas."

"What's this?" He sat forward and studied her as she raised the white lace. The edge skimmed her thighs, revealed her pussy, and reached her waist.

"Stop there." I gestured. "Open your legs." The little ring glinted gold on her clit and I couldn't help grinning.

"Wow. When the hell did you do that, Chris? It's beautiful."

Kat blushed deep red.

"Last night. Notice it has a *C* on it."

"Uh, no. I'd have to get closer to do that." He guffawed. "Like have my nose in her pussy just about. I can do that if you want?"

"You can check it later, you pervert. I thought however…" I bent forward and carefully tucked the material of her bodice under her breasts, baring them both. "I thought I could also pierce her nipples." As I squeezed first one nipple then the other, I watched her trace her lips with her tongue tip. "I'm right, you can be left."

"Generous of you. I like that idea. Let's do it. Or rather you can. I'll watch."

Kat had said nothing during our discussion. The serenity on her face intrigued me. "Do you like that idea?"

Delicately, her eyelids lowered and stayed there as she answered. Her breathing was so slow as to be almost trancelike. "I do, Sirs. I love that you both want to."

I ran my fingers down the side of her face. "You know this will hurt far more than the clit ring?"

"Yes, Sir. I want to be yours. I understand." She opened her eyes, and I'm sure mine widened. In that crystalline moment we seemed as one in mind as we had ever been.

"Finally," I murmured.

Her melting look of absolute adoration was enough to send a world of peace to my heart. "Come back up here."

Zoe shifted out of her way and Kat wormed back onto the sofa to where she'd been and laid her head down in precisely the same place on my lap.

A completeness settled in, with all of us together – Andreas and her and me. Then Kat's fingers stirred in Zoe's curls and the girl slowly turned her head to peek up at me.

"Hi there." I smiled at her. Tear tracks on Kat's face might make me want to give her more pain, if she wanted it, or needed it, or simply if I wanted to do it on that particular day. But on Zoe...

"Hey. You're safe now. You can talk. You're allowed to. Really."

Slowly, she nodded to me. Her brunette locks stirred against Kat's chin.

"Zoe, this is how it will be. You are Kat's, but Kat obeys me and Andreas. We're not going to touch you sexually. But you are now ours. I'm sure that given enough time you will come to be happy with us."

Quiet as a mouse all right. All she did was stare, nod once then hide under Kat again.

At least she accepted my statement without screaming. She wasn't another Kat, and I was so glad of that. She'd fit in, eventually.

"Yeah, you're safe." Kat kissed her head. Then she wriggled her index finger under the side of Zoe's panties – there was barely a thread holding them together and her thigh was grimy with smears of dirt. A second later, at the urging of that finger, the last thread snapped.

My Kat was a bit of a Domme with the girls. I gave her the *look*. "No getting your Domme on unless I give the word, Miss Kat."

She bit her lip.

"Say the magic words."

"Yes, Sir," she whispered.

"Good. There's a question I need Zoe to answer. Zoe, how did you find out about the gun that was in the safe?"

She half-turned her head. "Pieter told me." Her voice wobbled. "He wanted me to tell Kat in case she wanted to try getting away. I'm sorry. I didn't know you."

It made sense for Scrim's men to have the details about any weapons stored here. That Zoe had told Kat wasn't amazing either. If

Zoe knew of any other stashes, I didn't care. We were leaving soon and in the meantime I would keep her caged or under control.

"Thank you for saying. And, I nearly forgot, do you know what a *doos* is? Pieter said you told him I wasn't one."

She snorted. "I think it's a cunt in South African."

"Ah. Lucky you didn't say I was one." When she gave a small smile, I found myself smiling too. "What a relief." Then I heaved in a huge sigh and relaxed into this multi-cuddle of men and girls.

Truth be told, I hadn't been so hopeful, so lacking in anger for weeks. Maybe it was the numbing effect of having seen and taken part in two killings?

I hoped not.

I didn't ever want to feel numb about that sort of death. I toyed with Kat's ear, running my finger up and down the curves, thinking, feeling my way past all the crazy stuff I'd experienced with her these past few weeks. She'd stopped being angry at me. A big smile spread and pushed out my cheek. I'd have looked a real doofus if she'd bothered to check but she was busy playing with Zoe.

That was it. Without her anger and hate, mine had drained away. Hate begets hate. Anger begets anger. Did love beget love? Whatever. Sometimes you had to be grateful for what you had. Things were looking up.

Chapter 32

Zoe

How had I gotten from being a gamer girl hairdresser attending a LAN gaming convention in Brisbane to this? Comprehending was never going to happen. From getting totally sloshed after the *Call of Duty* game to having a man cut me with a knife for his own fucking joy?

Scrim was dead though, wasn't he?

Another tear or two dribbled down my cheek onto the couch cushion. I couldn't quite believe he was dead. Sometimes I'd run away from the pain, gone into my head, and he'd been a character from a game doing things to me, another role player. I hadn't felt it much then, only when I returned.

The horror when I'd counted the new holes leaking blood.

Scrim dead... It was as if Santa Claus or Satan or the Terminator had been declared dead. He was bigger than real. The man had ten new lives or something and would respawn when I wasn't ready for it from some dark corner of the house. Scrim had seared a hole in my brain I'd never lose.

The other women they'd recaptured, what had happened to them? Lysa and Effy? I was so lucky. By now they could be anywhere.

I sniffled quietly but Kat seemed to notice it and she patted me more firmly, and let her other hand fiddle with my hair.

I reached up to touch her fingers.

If only I could leave, but I couldn't. These men didn't seem as bad as Scrim but they weren't normal either. No one should own a person. I didn't want to be owned. If they tried to force me into their bed, I'd… Shit, I didn't know what I'd do. But maybe they wouldn't. I could be happy for a while with Kat, if they'd just let us be, if I didn't have to watch this Chris do what he'd said – punish her with pain, birch her ass raw. Ugh. I shuddered.

Except Kat seemed to cherish me like no one else ever had – girlfriend or boyfriend.

Getting your Domme on. Chris's words. I shivered. I knew what a Domme was. She gave off such a delicious menace, sometimes, when she looked at me, or made love to me. It intrigued me as well as made me want to hide in a corner…and wait for her to find me.

I sighed. The evilness of the day was still there, in my heart, but lying here with her was slowly washing some of that darkness away. I breathed in her scent, soaking up her pervading warmth that said I could trust her to pick me up and save me from nearly anything.

But one day, I'd have to leave. I could find someone else who'd love me. Just maybe not the same.

One day, I'd grow a backbone, find an escape method, like finding an Easter egg in a game, and I'd go home.

Epilogue

Pieter

The taser hit me in the ribs again. I seized up, back arching so sharply my spine creaked and my mind went la la for a few seconds, or maybe it was an hour. I had no idea really. I came to with my lungs burning and my head thumping with pain at every pulse beat.

Jazmine.

I raised my head from the floor. Car of some sort...tried to recall what they'd thrown me into, and couldn't. Dark. Nighttime still. We went over some bumps and the car rattled, my already pounding head bounced. My hands were tied behind me by something like a bunch of zip ties. Ankles too, and they'd linked them to my hands.

She wasn't here. We were so screwed.

"Awake are ya?" Someone kicked me in the stomach. "Be good or I'll zap you again and get Red to fuck your ass for good measure. Not that you aren't up shit creek anyway. Damn I'd love to be there when Vetrov takes care of you two."

Two? I clung to that. She was still alive. So there was hope.

I'd never give that up. Not until we were dead.

The End

Glossary of US and Australian terms

In my last book, Book 2 of the Pierced Hearts series, Bind and Keep Me, in the interests of not jerking most of my readers out of the story with some unfamiliar word usages, I opted to sometimes use the US word instead of the Aussie one.

However, since then I've been told by many American readers that they'd rather I use the Aussie words. I've mostly done that with this book and below is a glossary to help you figure out words that may puzzle you. I've kept some words that weren't used in this one just for fun, and to educate my overseas readers on our Aussie-isms.

If you want to tell me of any other words that tripped you up, feel free to pop a comment on my facebook wall.

Cari Silverwood on Facebook
https://www.facebook.com/cari.silverwood

US word vs Aussie

Cell phone = mobile

College = University or Uni

Cooler = esky

Dishcloth = tea towel

Dob = snitch on ie tell tales

Flip flops = thongs

Popsicle = ice block

Shrimp = prawn

Spatula = egg flip

SUV = Four wheel drive

There may be others I missed seeing. I have also used US spelling throughout. Though this book is self-published both of my earlier publishers, Loose Id and Lyrical Press, used US spelling.

To join my mailing list and receive notice of future releases, go here:
http://www.carisilverwood.net/about-me.html

Books by Cari Silverwood

http://www.carisilverwood.net/books.html

Connect with Cari Silverwood on Facebook

https://www.facebook.com/cari.silverwood

Cari Silverwood on Goodreads

http://www.goodreads.com/author/show/4912047.Cari_Silverwood

Books by Cari Silverwood

Pierced Hearts Series

Take Me, Break Me

Bind and Keep Me

The Badass Brats Series

The Dom with a Safeword

The Dom on the Naughty List

The Dom with the Perfect Brats

The Dom with the Clever Tongue

Cataclysm Blues Series

Cataclysm Blues

Rough Surrender Series

Rough Surrender

The Steamwork Chronicles Series

Iron Dominance

Lust Plague

Steel Dominance

Others

31 Flavors of Kink

Three Days of Dominance

The Dom with the Clever Tongue

Book 4 in the Badass Brats series

Reece and Scarlet have everything a loving couple could want, except a hot kinky sex life. Malachi, an experienced Dom, steps in to help them sort that out. Not only is he a terrible memory from Reece's past, he's a smartass and damaged goods too.

As they all learn to trust each other, Malachi becomes more than just their kink coach. It's a full-on brat smackdown, and no heart gets out unscathed.

Warning: Contains unrepentant brats, surprise orgasms, a Domme with training wheels, and a Dom whose tongue is registered as a weapon of mass seduction

Across the room, Reece looked up from her sketch and laughed. "This is the third time this week that you two play video games for hours. Scarlet's been dragging her ass out of bed in the morning. Jude hasn't complained about her falling asleep at work yet, though, or Sabrina would have told me. I think I should pitch this as its own sitcom. You're too funny."

Malachi quirked a brow, his dark eyes serious. "I think your kitten needs petting, Scarlet. She's sounding neglected."

"What? I'm fine. You two have fun. I have work to do. I'm just glad that Scarlet has found a little friend to play with." Reece snickered and leaned over her sketchpad.

Scarlet cleared her throat. "Come here." She snapped her fingers and pointed at the spot between her and Mal on the couch. As expected, Reece's glare was tempestuous and foreboding. She didn't take shit from anyone.

"Come on," Scarlet coaxed. She patted her lap. "Come here. You know you don't want to sit all the way over there if you can be curled up over here."

"I'm not actually a cat, you know. Offering to give me catnip and pet me won't work all the time."

From the corner of her eye, Scarlet saw Malachi shake his head slightly as he frowned at Reece. She sighed and walked over. What was that about? Because it was her birthday?

Reece eased herself gently down between them as though she was afraid to touch anyone. Scarlet pulled her sideways until her head was in her lap. She ran her fingers through Reece's hair, combing out little knots and running her short nails along her scalp. Reece sighed and shivered, snuggling in.

"Put your legs up on Malachi. I'm sure he won't mind." Scarlet's gaze slid to him. He looked pained.

"But I'm wearing a dress."

"Now, Reece," Scarlet growled sternly. "Are you afraid he's going to see your sexy blue panties?"

She gasped then blushed.

Malachi smirked. "Did she tell you she showed me her panties the other day?"

"Oh, did she?" Scarlet wasn't sure how she felt about that.

"I almost fell out of the chair. It wasn't intentional," Reece grumbled. She put her legs up on his lap then shoved her skirt down tightly so he wouldn't see anything. "Leave it to the pirate captain, here, to take advantage of an innocent damsel in distress."

"If I really was a pirate captain I'd keep you tied to the mast where I could play with you for hours. Can you blame me? Have you looked in a mirror lately? Besides, I only looked. I didn't touch. That's not against the rules, is it?"

It was obvious to Scarlet, at least, that Malachi wasn't joking. He wanted Reece in a bad way, but was doing his best to be polite and hide it most of the time. His gaze strayed to the girl's bare calves, and Scarlet saw his hand twitch. The heat in his eyes should have melted off her clothes.

"No," Scarlet answered. "Especially not if she's deliberately flashing you her cute underthings. You're only human."

His big hand came down on Reece's ankle, swallowing it. How did a man with such big hands make such beautiful art? He'd shown them some of his sketches the other day and they were so colorful and expressive that Scarlet was sincerely moved.

The muscles in his arm played under his sleeve of tattoos as Reece tried to wriggle her ankle to freedom. "Let go!"

"Do you really want me to? I'm not hurting anything," he said quietly. Reece looked up at Scarlet and she smiled back reassuringly.

"It's only your ankle, beautiful. We aren't Puritans. If you don't like it tell him. I don't mind his hand being there if you don't."

Reece gave a one-shouldered shrug and relaxed back onto Scarlet's lap. She drew her fingertip from Reece's chin, down her neck then wrapped it lightly around the base of her throat. The girl shuddered and squirmed almost imperceptibly. She loved this.

What if he went further? Scarlet envisioned him sliding Reece's skirt up her thighs to run his finger along the lace border of the blue panties that Scarlet had bought her a few weeks ago. Reece loved being touched. If there were two of them touching her, instead of just one, it would blow Reece's mind. The screaming orgasm she imagined they could give her had Scarlet ready for almost anything. Being horny made her way too open-minded some days.

She stroked along Reece's throat as Malachi drew little circles along her anklebone and foot. Reece sighed contentedly and her body went limp. She looked relaxed, but Scarlet could tell otherwise. Her breathing was unsteady and the bump of her nipples stood out clearly on her shirt.

Scarlet slid her arm under Reece's shoulders and pulled her up for a kiss. Reece grabbed onto her and their tongues met. Her hand went to the hem of Reece's dress. The garment had crept partway up her thighs and Scarlet let her work-roughened fingers slide along just under the edge before snaking upwards. A moment later, Reece gasped and slapped her hand away.

"What?"

Reece's face was flushed and her eyes motioned to Malachi.

"He's seen you come before, baby. I don't think he minds."

"Not at all. Feel free to forget I'm here."

Scarlet almost snorted. As if Reece could forget. As if she could, herself.

"Malachi, this isn't what we talked about." She squirmed in their grips and Scarlet watched in fascination as Malachi's good-natured features sharpened. Something about this had just thrown his Dom switch. He looked sexy mean, not that she was into guys…much.

She didn't talk about it often, but Scarlet had gone through two crushes on guys in her entire life. One was an A-list actor who was hotter than any man had a right to be. The other was a guy she'd hung out with for years in high school. They had friend-zoned each other early on, but she'd loved his brain so much that his gender had become inconsequential. Mal actually reminded her of him, except that Mal was both funnier and had more of an edge to him – like there was something dangerous lurking behind the dazzling smiles and sexy tattoos. It was a miracle he was single.

No, it was easier to pass for a lesbian, rather than explaining she was bi but wasn't attracted to ninety-nine point nine percent of men. Her experience with guys showed her that if they thought they had even a small chance of bedding her, they'd mess up a perfectly good friendship. Except for her buddy Caleb, who'd never looked at her that way after the first week or so.

But that didn't mean she couldn't throw Reece under the bus. She knew Reece liked him, and the idea of watching Reece and Malachi together was fucking hot.

Rough Surrender

From Lyrical Press

At a time when airplanes are as new-fangled and sensational as the telephone, Faith dares to fly. The one territory she has not explored is her own sexuality. In Leonhardt she discovers the man who can teach her how a woman surrenders her body and her mind. However, Leonhardt has a shadowed past and his own learning to do. He doesn't have the right to keep Faith from flying, even if he thinks airplanes are flimsy death-traps made of canvas, timber and their inventor's prayers.

Faith has her limits, Leonhardt has his flaws, and sometimes the nicest people get murdered by unscrupulous bastards. Even if Leonhardt can save the woman he loves, the battle for Faith's heart will be the hardest one of all.

WARNING: BDSM, anal sex, orgasms galore, and a Dom who likes to claim his property with pen, ink and bondage.

One master, one woman who craves surrender, and a sky that will challenge them both

"That's better. Relax, darling. You're meant to enjoy this." His hands moved, untangling and unrolling the last lengths of her hair, drifting lower, following the contours of her upper back to her waist and circling her there, pausing for a moment before leisurely curving across the mounds of her bottom.

What she was allowing this man to do stunned her.

"You have lovely hair, Faith, a beautiful body. I could touch you like this all night." Leonhardt kissed her neck, tickling her with small nibbles. "I'm taking your dress off now. Your answer, my dear?"

An answer? He wanted speech when her throat had seized up? "Yes. Sir."

The wall behind the chaise lounge was cream…the lounge was timber and blue and her legs shook. Already.

From the sound, he'd knelt then his hands encompassed her ankles and ran a little way up beneath the dress. Cool air caressed her body as he took the garment up. "Raise your arms, Faith."

She did so. The dress pooled on the lounge where he tossed it. She'd never stood before a man in her underwear before—in corset, drawers and stockings—and this was a man who knew how to control her with mere words. The longing to know what he meant to do made her breath come harsh to her ears. Her lips parted.

"I like a woman who obeys my commands." He rested his hands on her shoulders.

Before she could stop herself a small noise escaped her lips.

"Do you have a question?" His hands moved on her muscles, massaging and spreading a delicious warmth that pooled in her breasts and groin.

"Yes. Uh, sir."

"Ask then."

"I don't obey." She let her head slowly drop forward as he continued the massage, and his body moved in to mold against her back. A hard length pressed along the crevice of her bottom. "I don't. Not normally. Just you. And here. Uh. That's all, so nice."

He laughed a little, softly, near her ear. "I could tell you liked it, sweetheart. Obeying me here and now is all I want." He stepped away, keeping a single finger in the center of her back. "I'm going to take off the rest of your clothes, Faith and bind you."

Oh my God.

"Now is when you should say, no, my dear. Then I'll go."

She licked her lips. Say, no? And miss what her body craved? He'd done what he had at the workshop—made her throb exquisitely in all her private places. She said nothing, wanting, needing, to see what else he could do.

"You want me to stay then."

"Yes, sir."

"Good." This time she heard roughness in his voice. "Good."

He drew off her shoes, her drawers, her hose and corset until she waited there naked with the air caressing her skin. The man in her room was still clothed...and she was naked. Her heart thudded, fast and anxious.

"Put your wrists together, behind your back." His voice softened as he moved away. Something knocked, then came muted noises. Mr. Meisner returned and stopped there, just behind her, within reach, where she couldn't see, waiting.

She sucked in a breath, let it out slowly, and did as he ordered—put her arms at her back. He wrapped some sort of rope around her wrists, tightened the bindings until she could do no more than twist her hands one against the other.

"The curtain cords," he murmured. "Being an engineer, I like to use chains and metal when I can, but this will do, for your first time. How does that feel, Faith?" He set his hands on her hips. His skin on her naked skin. She shuddered, feeling wetness seep between her legs. "Turn around and look at me. Now."

Of a sudden, seeing him looking at her was scarier than staring at the wall and knowing he did things to her behind her back. She bowed her head, felt her hands again—roped together. The position made her breasts jut out and as she looked, her nipples puckered and poked out like fat buttons.

"Faith. Turn and face me."

"Yes, sir." She shuffled around and his hands stayed on her, sliding at her hips, just above there, where she ached. His big brown eyes were on her and she couldn't help but look up into them and be caught, the sensation turning topsy-turvy, messing with every thought in her head. Mr. Meisner had her in his hands.

"There, love. I do believe you like this." His eyes crinkled and his mouth moved in the most heartwarming smile she'd yet observed. "You don't need to answer that. I can see. In this." He put both hands on her breasts, cupping them then brushing each thumb once across her nipples.

"Oh." She swayed and found her eyes half closing.

"And this." Deliberately, while his gaze still locked with hers, he let one hand leave her breast, trail down her stomach, across the triangle of hair...

No. He wouldn't. She tugged at the ropes around her wrists but nothing gave. Her helplessness fed into the heaviness curling tight and low in her stomach. The nub of flesh inches from his fingers peaked and hardened. She tensed then arched into his hold, and still he watched.

His hand slid between her legs and paused there. "You've no hair on your lips down here, Faith." His eyebrows rose a smidgeon.

He wanted her to speak? Just being there, still, his finger confused her, kept her thoughts centered on the minute details of what he did. "I...I remove it. A friend in Paris showed me. For cleanliness and all...um." Her explanation trailed away, swallowed by the sensations bubbling up.

"Hmm, I like the result." His gentle baritone hum...the spot his finger touched...her nakedness and the power this man had over her, and, oh, the way he watched, it all roiled deliciously around inside her.

She gulped then held her breath as...his finger followed the line of her slit, where wetness collected, and slow as a tongue licking the edge of an ice cream, nudged aside her lips, and dipped inside her. There. Oh. Yes. A coil of simmering energy seemed to squeeze down into the tightest ball, and quiver to be released. His thumb found her nub and pressed down firmly. Over and over and over.

Her heart stopped. The room shattered. Her breath came out in a choking squeak from her gaping mouth. Nothing existed except the storm of pleasure bursting upward from where he probed and pressed. Unable to stop herself, she jerked and moaned through each wave of the storm until her body was wrung dry of the very last shudder.

When the room centered and she raised her eyelids, Mr. Meisner held her in his arms, snuggled to his chest. He rubbed her back, just like he had on the boat. "There you go, sweetheart. Lord. Never seen any woman orgasm that easily. You do like this. Do you understand? You like being tied up."

www.CariSilverwood.net

www.facebook.com/cari.silverwood

Made in the USA
San Bernardino, CA
29 November 2015